PRAISE FOR GUNNAR STAALESEN

WINNER OF THE 2017 PETRONA AWARD

'Gunnar Staalesen is one of my very favourite Scandinavian authors. Operating out of Bergen in Norway, his private eye, Varg Veum, is a complex but engaging anti-hero. Varg means "wolf" in Norwegian, and this is a series with very sharp teeth' Ian Rankin

'The Norwegian Chandler' Jo Nesbø

'Razor-edged Scandinavian crime fiction at its finest' Quentin Bates

'Not many books hook you in the first chapter – this one did, and never let go!' Mari Hannah

'A fast-paced page-turner with a sharp, first-person narrative, and a shocking, troubling, existential and heart-poundingly emotional tale. *Wolves in the Dark* is a treat for fans and a great place to start if you are new to the series. A must read' Crime Fiction Lover

'With its exploration of family dynamics and the complex web of human behaviour, Staalesen's novel echoes the great California author Ross MacDonald's Lew Archer mysteries. There are some incredible set pieces, including a botched act of terrorism that has frightening consequences, but the Varg Veum series is more concerned with character and motivation than spectacle, and it's in the quieter scenes that the real drama lies' Russel McLean, *Herald Scotland*

'There is a world-weary existential sadness that hangs over his central detective. The prose is stripped-back and simple … deep emotion bubbling under the surface – the real turmoil of the characters' lives just under the surface for the reader to intuit, rather than have it spelled out for them' Doug Johnstone, *The Big Issue*

'Easily the darkest book in the Veum sequence; Staalesen continually reminds us he is one of the finest of Nordic novelists' Barry Forshaw, *Financial Times*

'The grand-daddy of Nordic Noir has had detective Varg Veum on the go since 1977. Poor old Varg has been arrested for having child porn on his computer. He scrolls back through his memory to work out who might have had the motive (and the IT smarts) to fit him up, with chilling and perilous results – all told in a pleasingly dry style' *The Sunday Times*

'This is at times an uncomfortable read, yet fascinating, thrilling, and action-packed too. Varg sits on the edge of official, and dangles his legs over lawful, yet his morality is clear to see and feel. *Wolves in the Dark* is another profound, dark, yet enjoyably readable tale from Staalesen and I can thoroughly recommend joining this series' Liz Robinson, LoveReading

'Varg Veum, and all his flaws, make for a dark, gripping thriller. The self-inflicted gaps in his memory keep the reader guessing right along with him as to what he is and isn't capable of. Dipping back into Veum's cloudy memories of the last few years throws up so many possibilities, one of which is his own guilt … by the end, all the strands twist back together to make for a satisfying ending to a compelling read' Shots Mag

'Mr Staalesen's lastest – ably translated by Don Bartlett – employs Chandleresque similes with a Nordic twist … *Wolves in the Dark* may yield a few shocking coincidences … but in this case the journey seems more important than it's direction' *Wall Street Journal*

'Veum has never before faced a case with so many loose threads, and, in untangling them, he comes to realise that neither politicians nor police officers take the plight of victimised refugee children seriously. Staalesen does a masterful job of exposing the worst of Norwegian society in this highly disturbing entry' *Publishers Weekly*

'Shocking, nail-biting and tense, this is THE thriller of the summer' Blue Book Balloon

'If you like your thrillers dark and gritty then this is definitely the book for you' The Book Review Café

'The gritty no-nonsense style stops extreme emotions from exploding. Staalesen's storytelling is at its finest, as always firmly underpinned by astute observations of changing society … Staalesen knows how to keep weaving the most intricate web of connections set in Bergen's criminal underworld, while taking on the disturbing subject of child abuse provides an opportunity for a wake-up call for his complex and unforgettable character' Crime Review

'Staalesen has created a sharp and intelligent but also vulnerable PI with whom the reader builds a strong rapport. The end of *We Shall Inherit the Wind* was a devastating blow to both parties and *Where Roses Never Die* is a shared recovery. Staalesen is an expert of his craft and once again he has delivered an absorbing mystery expertly solved by his endearing PI, Varg Veum' Live Many Lives

'Staalesen's greatest strength is the quality of his writing. The incidental asides and observations are wonderful and elevate the book from a straightforward murder investigation into something more substantial' Sarah Ward, Crime Pieces

'Gunnar Staalesen was writing suspenseful and socially conscious Nordic Noir long before any of today's Swedish crime writers had managed to put together a single book page … one of Norway's most skillful storytellers' Johan Theorin

'An upmarket Philip Marlowe' Maxim Jakubowski, *The Bookseller*

'The prose is richly detailed, the plot enthused with social and environmental commentary while never diminishing in interest or pace, the dialogue natural and convincing and the supporting characters all bristle with life. A multi-layered, engrossing and skilfully written novel; there's not an excess word' Tony Hill, Mumbling about…

'There is a strong social message within the narrative which is at times chilling, always gripping and with a few perfectly placed twists and turns that make it more addictive the further you get into it' Liz Loves Books

'Staalesen proves why he is one of the best storytellers alive with a deft touch and no wasted words; he is like a sniper who carefully chooses his target before he takes aim' Atticus Finch

'His writing is truly masterful; careful crafted and honed over forty years of writing, and Staalesen has created, for me, one of the most immediately compelling and intriguing characters I have read this year' Jen Med's Book Reviews

'An unforgettable, addictive novel that will have you waiting with bated breath for the next in the series' Ronnie Turner

'Compelling, dark and perfectly plotted with a protagonist that shines, *Wolves in the Dark* is a great read that will appeal to those who yearn for a more complex storyline than their usual crime thriller' Bloomin' Brilliant Books

'The plot is compelling, with new intrigues unfolding as each page is turned … a distinctive and welcome addition to the crime fiction genre' Never Imitate

'A well-paced, thrilling plot, with the usual topical social concerns we have come to expect from Staalesen's confident pen…' Finding Time To Write

'Amazingly descriptive and powerful writing, a revolting and riveting plot, masterfully weaved, and the ticking of the clock to save a man from his past and his present' Chocolate 'n' Waffles

'*We Shall Inherit the Wind* brings together great characterisation, a fast-paced plot and an exceptional social conscience … The beauty of Staalesen's writing and thinking is in the richness of interpretations on offer: poignant love story, murder investigation, essay on human nature and conscience, or tale of passion and revenge' Ewa Sherman, EuroCrime

'*Where Roses Never Die* is somewhat lighter in tone than previous instalments in Staalesen's series. It even hints that Varg Veum's lengthy romantic dry spell might be coming to an end. The author also does a superior job of building suspense in regards to both the kidnapping and robbery cases, stitching clues into his plot that leave one wondering about the crimes' connections. His portrayals of the players involved in these puzzles benefit from multiple, gradually unfolding dimensions' Kirkus Reviews

'Dark, melancholic and menacing, this is a book that asks us searching questions. Top notch' Café Thinking

'Staalesen is undoubtedly one of the best authors in this genre! Highly recommended!' Bibliophile Book Club

'This is really Scandinavian crime writing at its very best. There is something dark and haunting about this novel that will test every sinew of your emotions as the truth emerges' Last Word Book Review

'It isn't just (or even primarily) a case of finding out "whodunit". It's not simply a "Where's Wally" exercise in recognising the clues and putting them together with a "Hey, presto – he's the murderer" outcome. The Scandinavian approach also focuses on the aftershocks. The sundering judders, shudders, waves and even ripples that spread out into the lives of people affected by the trauma of the central event. It's at this that Staalesen really excels' The Library Door

'An intelligent and insightful novel and I'm looking forward to reading more of Gunnar Staalesen's books' Hair Past a Freckle

'Fairly short chapters and the changing back between past and present made this book move along at a great pace, and just enough crumbs of clues meant that I was reading faster and faster to reach the conclusion' Reflections of a Reader

'The ending was satisfying but still left things wide open for the next book and I can't wait to see what happens next. Fans of this series will be pleased and new readers will be fans as well by the end' Novel Gossip

'Gripping and satisfying, *Wolves in the Dark* is proof that this father of Nordic Noir has lost none of his enduring powers' Claire Thinking

'A cracking read' P Turner's Book Blog

'This is a hard-hitting novel that truly encapsulates the very essence of Scandi Noir and I can see why this series and character have been so successful' The Quiet Knitter

'There is a claustrophobic feeling to the story, a sense of unease surrounding this seemingly tranquil suburb. Whilst everything may have appeared normal on the surface, there were secrets just waiting to emerge. This is a well-paced, suspenseful book that keeps you guessing until the very end' Owl on the Bookshelf

'A powerful, engaging and compelling thriller which has lost none of its punch in translation. Would I recommend you read it – well that will be a HELL YEAH!' Chapter in My Life

'Averse as I am to gushing, with some authors it's difficult to remain completely objective when you have genuinely loved every single book that they have ever produced. Such is my problem – but a nice problem – with the venerable Mr Staalesen and *Where Roses Never Die*, which merely compounds my adoration of this series to date' Raven Crime Reads

'A brilliant crime thriller, which I absolutely loved. It reminded me slightly of an Agatha Christie novel, not with the main character but with the brilliance of how the whole plot had been written and how it had me totally clueless as to how everything fit together and who was behind the disappearance of the young girl. Can't recommend highly enough and this is one author whose books I will certainly be checking out and reading more' By the Letter Book Reviews

'There are unexpected twists throughout the story, which are cleverly placed to make sure you keep turning the pages. It's a very enjoyable read about a group of people who aren't necessarily what they seem. Would I recommend this book? Definitely!' Damp Pebbles

'An enticing, gripping read' Segnalibro

'It's cunningly plotted and kept me guessing right until the end, when I not only gasped but also shed a tear as all was revealed. A perfect choice for fans of Nordic Noir as well as intense chilling crime fiction' Off-the-Shelf Books

BIG SISTER

Big Sister

GUNNAR STAALESEN

Translated by Don Bartlett

**ORENDA
BOOKS**

Orenda Books
16 Carson Road
West Dulwich
London SE21 8HU
www.orendabooks.co.uk

First published in Norwegian as *Storesøster* by Gyldendal in 2016
First published in English by Orenda Books in 2018

A catalogue record for this book is available from the British Library.

ISBN 978-1-912374-19-9
eISBN 978-1-912374-20-5

The publication of this translation has been made possible through the
financial support of NORLA, Norwegian Literature Abroad.

Typeset in Arno by MacGuru Ltd
Printed and bound in Denmark by Nørhaven

For sales and distribution please contact *info@orendabooks.co.uk*

If you look on the map for Buvik, in the county of Ryfylke, you'll be looking in vain. The place only exists in my imagination, along with all the characters and events in this book. But Bergen, Haugesund and Skudeneshavn do exist, the last time I checked anyway.

—*Gunnar Staalesen*

Bergen, Norway

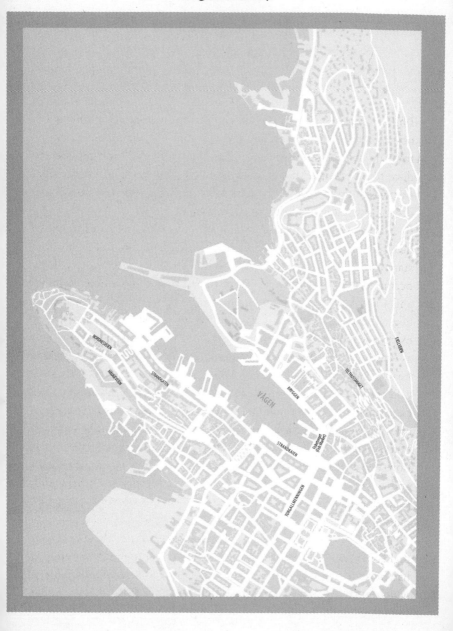

1

I have never believed in ghosts. The mature woman who came to my office on that wan November day was no ghost, either. But what she told me awakened something I had long repressed and opened the door to a darkened attic of family secrets whose existence I had never suspected. From behind my desk I sat staring at her, as I would have done if she really had been just that: a ghost.

2003 had been a volatile year in all ways. I had barely escaped the heavy hand of the law the previous September when the builders started to knock down walls around me. The hotel that had originally occupied the two top floors had now taken over the whole building, and a massive renovation programme was in full swing. With a heavy heart, the hotel director had accepted my old contract with the property owner, which stipulated my right to have an office on the premises for as long as I was running my business. But during the rebuilding phase I had to move out. Until the reopening in May I had worked from a so-called 'home office', a corner of my sitting room in Telthussmuget. I had never invited clients home. Most of them I met at various cafés and eateries in town and round about. It had given me an involuntary overview of the quality of coffee served in this region. With a few notable exceptions it was one I could have foregone. I was as black as pitch internally and as nervous as a novice priest at a Black Metal Fest in hell. And, even after several days of twitchy abstinence, this nervousness wasn't relinquishing its hold.

When I got my office back in May it was still in the same place, four flights of stairs up from the street, but I had lost my waiting room. It had become a hotel bedroom, and my office was now in a corridor in which you had to strain your eyes to find the door that led, if you came on the right day, to where I resided. The waiting room wasn't a serious loss. As the years had passed it had been of less and less use. I had never walked past without a quick look at the sofa, though, to check if there was another corpse lying there. For those wishing to see me now there were some sofas in the hotel foyer, where the changing pool of desk staff now had the additional dubious role as my receptionists.

They hadn't done anything to my office. But it still took me a week to tidy up, during which time I took the opportunity to dispose of old crime cases and sort out my filing cabinet. When I had finished this I celebrated by purchasing another bottle of Taffel aquavit, which I carefully placed in the bottom left-hand desk drawer, where the Simers family had traditionally held sway for as long as I'd had the legal right to this office.

In many ways I was content with the result. I had the same office; it was only its environment that had changed. The address was still Strandkai 2, third floor.

Everyone was welcome to bring whatever they had on their minds. It took a lot to surprise me. Unless they came from Haugesund and said they were my sister.

2

She met my gaze. 'Has this come as a surprise to you?'

'Not entirely.'

'Mum told you about me?'

'No. But after she died I found a copy of your birth certificate and adoption papers.'

She sent me a searching look. 'And it never occurred to you to make contact?'

'No, I'm afraid not. I was in the middle of a divorce at the time, and besides ... I suppose I thought that if she'd kept it a secret all her life I was showing her a kind of respect by letting bygones be bygones.'

Her eyes held mine. She had introduced herself as Norma Johanne Bakkevik. Born in 1927. Her eyes were clear, a cornflower blue, her hair was silver and, despite her age, it was easy to see she had been a beautiful woman when she was young. But she didn't remind me of my mother. Her sartorial elegance was a little passé – a dark-blue cape over a red-and-black spotted dress. She was fairly light on her feet for a woman of seventy-six, and there was something determined and focused about her that I couldn't associate with my mother either, not the way I remembered her.

'I can understand that. It was only when my adopted parents died and I went through their papers that I discovered the name of the woman who was my mother. When I reached the age of majority they told me I'd been adopted, but I was given to them when I was only a few days old and I'd grown up with them, so for me it wasn't that important then. They were my parents, and still are, in my head. Your ... our ... She became a stranger for ever.'

'Mm.'

'When I visited her in February 1975 she was surprisingly open, though, once she'd got over the shock.' She smiled wryly. 'She had the same expression as you about a quarter of an hour ago.'

'Right. Did she tell you who your father was?'

'Do *you* know?'

'No.'

'Yes, in fact she did. A peripatetic preacher who regularly came to Hjelmeland, Ryfylke, where she grew up. I've tried to find out about him as well, but it hasn't been easy. He's hidden his traces well, if I can put it like that. Peter Paul Haga.'

This went through me like an electric shock. 'Was that really his name – Peter Paul Haga?'

'Yes. Does it mean anything to you?'

'It cropped up in a case I took on several years ago.'

'Does that case have any relevance?'

'No. It might sound a bit odd, but it was, in fact, a hundred years old. And Peter Paul Haga played a minor role. As a murder victim actually.'

'A murder victim!'

'Yes.' I gave her a brief rundown of the very special crime case that had come my way right at the end of 1999. She followed attentively but after I had finished she stared into the distance, beyond the office, far back in time.

When she finally returned, she said: 'Did our mother know about this?'

'Doubt it. She'd been dead for many years when I got the case, and I didn't find anything at all about Peter Paul Haga in the papers she left.'

'What *did* you find?'

'Not a great deal. Your birth certificate and the adoption papers, as I mentioned. And some newspaper cuttings about a jazz band calling itself the Hurrycanes.'

'Really? Was she interested in jazz?'

'Not as far as I know. I remember her as a quiet soul who used to go to church on Sundays. Without my dad though. He sat at home reading about Norse mythology. I preferred to go walking in the mountains.'

'Sounds like a strange family.'

'Yes, I suppose we were.' Now it was my turn to fall into a reverie.

She broke the silence. 'Can you remember if she was ever in Haugesund?'

'Only travelling through. We often used to visit my mother's parents in Ryfylke in the summer and would take the night boat down to Stavanger. But a couple of times we went through Haugesund because she wanted to call in on a cousin and an old aunt there.'

'Yes, I asked her the same question when I visited her. All she told me was that she'd been to a cousin's wedding there in January 1942. By the way … I think she said the bridegroom came from Bergen and played in a band here.'

'Maybe the Hurrycanes. I suppose that's why the newspaper cuttings were among her papers.'

'Yes, maybe.'

'Have a look at this.' I opened a desk drawer and rummaged around until I found a yellowing envelope. I took it out, opened it and held up one of the old cuttings I still had. It was from a local paper, *Bergens Tidende* by the look of it, some time in the 1950s: a jazz quintet from the interwar years known as the Hurrycanes was going to perform at somewhere called The Golden Club. Underneath the picture were all five names of the musicians. The only one I had taken any note of was the saxophonist, Leif Pedersen, because a childhood pal of mine had mentioned him in connection with a house I had searched. In fact I had visited this house as a child with my mother – it belonged to a friend of hers who was related to this self-same Pedersen. I remembered thinking this was perhaps why she had cut this article from the newspaper, not that I had given it any further thought. But now Norma had come up with another plausible explanation.

Out of habit I scribbled down *The Hurrycanes?* in my notepad. If I had a quiet day, and experience told me there would be quite a few of them, I could always delve deeper, for no other purpose than entertainment.

'Have you got any children, Varg?'

'A son, Thomas, who lives in Oslo, and a little grandson, Jakob, who's two years old. And you?'

At once her face was sad. 'I had two. Petter and Ellen. But Petter died in 1980. He was on the Alexander Kielland oil platform that capsized. But he also left one child. Karen, who is twenty-four now. Ellen hasn't had any children.'

'So Mum has some descendants she never met.'

'Yes, she has. I met her only once. On the 5th of February 1975. That was when she told me about you, and since then I've followed your movements, at lengthy intervals, and always from a distance. But I've seen your name in the news sometimes, especially now that we can search online.'

'You're online?'

'Yes, of course. Does that surprise you? I may be well over seventy, but I'm not decrepit quite yet.'

'Of course not. I've never been the quickest at these things myself, so...' I gestured apologetically.

She smiled condescendingly. 'But ... you might be wondering why I'm visiting you today of all days?'

'Yes, now you mention it, I...'

Her shoulders seemed to slump, she was like an old doll casually tossed aside by a child suddenly too old to play with such things. 'In fact I've got a commission for you.'

'A commission?'

'Yes, a case, or whatever you call them.'

'Both are an integral part of my vocabulary.'

Again she was lost in thought. Then she visibly pulled herself together. 'This is about my god-daughter. She's gone missing.' I just looked at her, waiting for more, and she added: 'From here. From Bergen.'

3

What she told me was not so different from what I had heard many times before, but the fact that the person who was telling me was my own half-sister gave it an extra edge. I listened attentively and made some notes as and where necessary.

Emma Hagland was nineteen years old, born and raised in Karmøy, Rogaland. She had taken her final exams at Haugaland School in June and moved to Bergen in the course of the summer to start her nursing course at the university here. After some to-ing and fro-ing she had moved into a kind of collective with two other girls. They shared a flat in a block in Møhlenpris, in Konsul Børs gate.

'The problem was,' she said, 'that it was next to impossible to get in touch with her. If we rang her she never picked up. However, she did reply to texts, now and then at any rate.'

'I suppose she was busy, wasn't she? At the beginning of an academic year there's bound to be a lot to take on board.'

'Of course, but we wanted to know how she was! How she was getting on. After a while we began to get quite desperate.'

'Yes, I can imagine.'

'But then, a few weeks ago, it got even worse. We kept ringing. No answer. I sent off one text after another. No answer to them, either. We called her best friend from school, Åsa. But she's studying in Berlin and had only spoken to her on the phone in recent months. She knew nothing. We were at our wits' end.'

'But you had her address, didn't you?'

'Yes, we did,' she nodded. 'We rang her landlord, but he just said he didn't know what the problem was. People came and went. It was like that all the time, he said.'

'What did he mean by that? That she'd moved out?'

'Yes, it transpired that was what had happened. After some discussion with the landlord we got the names of the girls she shared the flat with. We managed to contact one of them on her mobile. Not that it helped much. Emma had just moved out, she said, at the end of October. She had paid her share for the month and, from what this girl had gathered, Emma had received a better offer somewhere else.'

'I see. But then…'

'Still no answer from her phone!'

'Have you got the names of these people? The landlord and Emma's room-mates?'

'Yes.' She gave them to me and I noted them down in my notepad: Knut Moberg. Kari Sandbakken. Helga Fjørtoft. 'The girl we spoke to was Helga.'

'Just explain to me … You talk about "we", but my understanding was you're only her godmother. She has a family, I take it?'

Her face clouded over. 'Yes, she has, but … it's a bit complicated. I'm in contact with her mother. She lives in Haugesund.' She appeared to hesitate before continuing. 'The father left them when Emma was two.' Another short pause, then she finished what she had to say: 'He lives in Bergen.'

'Right! So you've been in contact with him?'

'Yes, we have, but he says he had no idea she was in town. He … They've never communicated.'

'Never? Not since she was two?'

'No. As I said, it's a bit complicated.'

'Norma, I used to work in child welfare and in all the years I've run this business…' I made a sweeping gesture with both arms, as though I were showing her around the royal palace, '…I've seen and heard all manner of things. It'll take a lot to shock me.'

She nodded. 'I understand. But this is still difficult to talk about.'

'There are many reasons why people split up. The burden on young parents can simply be too much, with disturbed nights and difficult days, that kind of thing. Then, of course, the romance has gone and one of them meets someone else. And there can be other reasons. But since we're talking about a father who's had no contact at all with his daughter for seventeen years, from what you've told me, the most likely assumption is that this is linked with sexual abuse.' As she didn't answer at once, I added: 'Or substance abuse, of course. Alcohol or some other stimulant.'

She nodded thoughtfully, as though she were reflecting on what I'd said and weighing up the likelihood of what might have been the cause.

'Do you know the family well?'

'Her grandmother was a good friend of mine. I've known her mother ever since she was a little girl. That was why I was asked to carry her at the christening in May 1984, of course. In Avaldsnes Church.'

'So I assume you know why the father left them?'

Her eyes roamed around, as if to see what I had on the walls, but found nothing to detain them and came back to me. 'She's not in a very good place, Ingeborg isn't.'

'Ingeborg. That's … ?'

'Emma's mother. I do what I can to support her.'

'Has she any other children?'

'No, only Emma. That's what makes her so desperate not … to lose her.'

'Let's not cross that bridge until we come to it. I'm sure there's a natural explanation for everything. Have you contacted the police?'

She gave a slanted smile, infused with cynicism. 'They said more or less the same. There was sure to be a natural explanation.'

'The police here in town?'

She nodded.

'Do you remember who you spoke to?'

'It was a woman. Bergesen, I think she was called.'

'Annemette. I can have a word with her.'

'I don't know if that'll help. They haven't done a thing. She suggested that Emma's phone might've been stolen. That goes on all the time, she said.'

'But she would've rung her mother from a new one, wouldn't she?'

'Yes … probably.'

'Well, I'll see what I can dig up.'

'Of course you'll be paid. I haven't come here to exploit you. Because we're family, I mean.'

'That would be a first,' I said. In one of my desk drawers I found my list of fees and passed her a copy across the table. 'Here you can see what you have to agree to anyway.'

As she read, her face became tauter than a temperance preacher's as he studied the wine list in a gourmet restaurant. I hastened to add: 'But I give a discount to close family. That goes without saying.'

She nodded and smiled, and when she looked at me again her mask slipped, as though she was about to shed a tear. 'Thanks, Varg,' she said with a tiny pause before my name.

'I still haven't had an answer to my question. What was the reason the father left them?'

'It was something … sexual. Not with Emma, though.'

'OK. So?'

'It was an old business. When he was a young boy. And then it reared its ugly head again.'

'In what way?'

'I'm not quite sure, but … it was something he'd done when he was very young, and Ingeborg got to hear about it … She kicked him out.'

'I see. But he lives in Bergen, you say. Have you got his name and address by any chance?'

'I've definitely got his phone number. And his name, of course. Robert.'

'Robert Hagland?'

'No, Ingeborg reverted to her maiden name after the divorce, and Emma took it, too. Robert's surname was Høie, but he added another when he moved. Now he calls himself Robert Høie Hansen. In fact, his father's name was Hans.'

'I'll find him then.'

Her brow furrowed. 'But don't tell him it was me who sent you.'

'No, no. Discretion's my middle name. That ought to be on my business card. Varg D. Veum. One more thing, though. I hope you have a photo of Emma.'

'Yes, of course I do. How could I forget?'

She opened the robust handbag she had with her, stuck a hand inside and took out an envelope. She handed it to me and I opened it. There was a sheet of photos inside, the kind you get from a machine. One of them had been cut out. The others were almost identical. Emma Hagland stared at me with a serious expression, smooth blonde hair, thin lips and an indefinable melancholy in her eyes, like a newly fledged confirmand being confronted for the first time with the realities of life.

'Are they any good?' Norma asked.

'If that's how she looks now, yes.'

'They were taken in July, when she came to study here.'

'Well, I'll see what I can find out. But I need her phone number.'

She gave it to me. 'And here … I've got her bank card number, if you have the opportunity to check on it.'

'I'm afraid only the police can do that, but I'll see what I can do. This is my business after all.' I smiled at her encouragingly. 'It'll be fine, you'll see…'

She smiled back, if not with quite the same conviction. 'Anyway, it was nice to meet you finally.'

'It would've been even nicer if this hadn't been the reason. But we'll have to talk family next time. What are you going to do now? Go back home?'

'Yes, I came on the coastal bus this morning and I'll be going back as soon as we've finished.'

'I might have to take a trip down there in a while. If needs must, I mean.'

'In which case, you'll be more than welcome!'

I thanked her and accompanied her to the door. Before we parted she leaned forwards quickly and gave me a hug.

After she had gone I stood staring at the closed door as though she might reappear at any moment with a couple more surprises up her sleeve. My astonishment was still deep within me and it was going to take a few days before I would be able to get over it. Good job I had something to do. *Just get on with it*, I told myself.

But still I wasn't quite ready. Looking out of the window, I felt as if I was being dazzled, not by the sun but by the light from a past I never wanted to relinquish, a childhood which in some way had made me and my half-sister the people we had become. The stamp your parents imprint on your brow is there for ever, visible or not. You rarely get to know the secrets they take with them to the grave.

4

How many secrets can a person have? Why had I not heard about my half-sister before? Might my father not even have known? Was there anything else they had kept secret and I would never find out?

In my mind I returned to my childhood home on the Nordnes peninsula of Bergen. The street was Fritznersmuget, right on the very edge of the cluster of timber houses between Nordnesgaten and Nordnesveien that had survived the bombing in June 1940 and the huge harbour explosion in April 1944. When I was growing up there we were surrounded on all sides by houses. In the last year of my mother's life everything around us was demolished. Our house stood there like a last redoubt on the battlefield of what once had been a neighbourhood of small dwellings, but which in the years to follow were replaced by four- and five-storey blocks in the style the town planners of the 1940s had determined the whole of Nordnes was to adopt: from a timber-house village to a concrete townscape. Fortunately, they couldn't afford to implement everything at once. By the time they had reached Nykirkeallmenningen in 1960 they had changed their minds and the timber constructions along Lille and Ytre Markevei were spared, despite being on the original list for demolition.

From as far back as I could remember, I always had an image of my father, tram conductor Anders Veum, with his nose in a book about Norse mythology, the subject that fascinated him most, for some reason. He died in 1956, when I was fourteen, and it still hurt that I never really got to know him. For that matter, I didn't get to know my mother, either. They were both closed, private individuals who kept their secrets to themselves. One of these – perhaps the biggest – had just walked out of my office and left me wistful and melancholic, lost in memories of a time that would never return, memories that would inevitably be erased one day when we, still cherishing them, were also gone.

The little I knew about my parents' past I had from my mother's cousin, Svend Atle Moland, whom I had met on a few occasions. Best of all I remembered the journey to Hjelmeland, to my maternal grandfather's funeral in 1960. Svend Atle, my mother and I went there from Bergen. At that time Svend Atle had recently retired from the police. On the return journey by boat from Stavanger he and I stayed up in the saloon after my mother had gone to sleep in the cabin she shared with another woman. Svend Atle had treated me to a bottle of beer and as the occasion was already intimate he had begun to tell me about the time he met my mother and father, long before the war broke out.

'Ingrid came to Bergen on the Haugesund boat in 1928 and I'd been sent to the quay to welcome her. By chance we met Anders on the way up to Blekeveien, where my parents would give her lodging, and as it was the year the Great Exhibition was in town, we invited Ingrid to a beer at the exhibition pavilions that evening. And, as they say in the papers, the rest is history. They became a couple.'

'Was my father already working on the trams then?'

'Yes, he was. He came to Bergen in 1926, during the great tram strike, and committed the cardinal folly of accepting employment on the trams, unaware that it was as a strike-breaker. It took him years to shake off the taint. And I can clearly remember … there was always a kind of sadness about Anders, as though he were grieving over something he never revealed to us. He didn't smile much, your father. Ingrid is by nature much more light-hearted, but even she has moments of being pensive and distant.'

'And she worked at the United Sardine Factory in the dockyard, she said.'

'Yes, she must've been there until she had you, during the war. For the first few years she was in service, but after she and Anders got married and no children were immediately forthcoming, she was employed at USF. Canning sardines for king and country.'

He didn't have much more than that to tell me. Slowly he moved on to talk about the years when he had been in the police and some of the cases he had worked on as a detective. Later it struck me several times that it might have been in the course of this conversation that I initially got the idea of starting up in the profession myself, although my childhood friend Pelle and I had already opened our very first detective agency in the early 1950s, in one of the blocks that was being constructed in Nordnesveien. Our only big case was tailing a girl from Nordnes to Minde; she had recently moved into our street and her name was Sylvelin. All we received for our pains were the first grazes to our hearts, both of us.

Later I only met Svend Atle Moland on rare family occasions, most of them funerals. After he died himself during a walk on Mount Gulfjell in 1978 I went to his funeral in Møllendal Chapel without ever having told him that I had actually opened my own private detective agency three years before. However, he may have heard from other quarters because it wasn't exactly a secret.

My mother had died three years earlier, and now here I was, almost thirty years later, wondering if there was even more she hadn't told me, apart from the fact that I had a half-sister in Haugesund I had never met.

I was unlikely ever to find the answer. With renewed determination I shook off these gloomy thoughts, pushed the chair back from my desk, went to the clothes stand and put on the coat that hung there. Then I walked across Nygårdshøyden to start work on the job I had been given by Norma Johanne Bakkevik, which was the name on the business card she had left with me before taking her leave.

In November night falls quickly and the street lamps were lit long before I had arrived at the address in Konsul Børs gate. The front door was locked – hardly surprising in this part of town. I leaned forwards to study the names on the list beside the loudspeaker. There seemed to be a motley collection of tenants: some foreign names, some Norwegian ones. I found both Fjørtoft and Sandbakken beside one of the bells. On the same strip a third surname had been crossed out, although I was still able to read Hagland underneath. At the top of the list was Moberg, the surname of the landlord Norma had mentioned. So why not? I pressed the bell and waited for a response.

5

A woman's voice answered. 'Hello?'

'Hello. My name's Veum. Can I talk to Knut Moberg?'

A slight pause. 'I'm afraid not. He's not at home. What's it about?'

'I have a few questions regarding one of your tenants.'

'I see.'

'Emma Hagland.'

Another slight pause. 'She doesn't live here any longer.'

'No, precisely. She's gone missing.'

'Oh. Well … What did you say your name was?'

'Veum. Varg Veum.'

'You'd better come in. I'm on the third floor.'

The lock buzzed and I pushed the door open.

'Thank you,' I said, but she had already gone.

It was a classic 'chimney' house from the 1890s, properly renovated and fireproofed since then, I hoped. At any rate it seemed to be in fairly good condition. On the left, two lines of post boxes hung from the wall. On the right there was a poster with what turned out to be the house rules. Next to it hung a fire extinguisher. The house smelt fresh and clean, and the neon tubes on the ceiling emitted clear white light above me as I went towards the staircase and headed upwards. Even though I had passed sixty a year ago I was still more than fit enough to manage three flights of stairs in Møhlenpris without having to stop on every landing for breath.

On the second floor I noticed a door with a trim sign stuck to the door with no visible sign of an adhesive. My PI brain assumed the solution was double-sided tape. A white piece of cardboard had been cut into an elegant oval shape and inscribed with a felt pen. The two names on it were formed in such beautiful handwriting it bordered on calligraphy: *Helga Fjørtoft & Kari Sandbakken.*

I climbed the last flight of stairs and was met in the doorway by a woman in her early forties. 'We haven't got a lift,' she said with a little smile.

'I noticed,' I smiled back.

'Exercise is healthy, they say.'

'That's what my GP said last time I was there. Ten years ago.'

She arched her brows. 'Fit as a flea then?'

'Fitter. I'm very fussy about my hosts.' I proffered my hand. 'Veum.'

She shook hands. 'Ellisiv.' And she held my hand for longer than normal.

'Unusual name.'

'A queen's name. She was married to Harald Hardråde, if I remember correctly.'

'So that's why you're so elegantly dressed on a Monday?'

'No, it's because my husband isn't at home.' She uttered a sound that was halfway between a snigger and a hiccup, and at once I thought: *she's not sober.* In fact she could barely stand. That was why she was resting her hip against the doorframe in a pose that had initially seemed quite inviting.

Ellisiv Moberg had light streaks in her dark, dishevelled hair. She was pale, with big bags under her eyes, insufficiently camouflaged under the make-up, and her pupils were large and shiny, framed by a mixture of blue and sea-green. Her dress was elegant enough, finishing above her knees, and with big red Chinese dragons on a dark-blue background and a split so high up one side that the Promised Land couldn't have been far away. 'May I offer you something?'

'Well, actually…'

'A glass of wine?'

'It was Emma Hagland I…'

'My husband won't be coming home today.'

'No? Where is he, if I might ask?'

'On the road.'

'On the road?'

'Visiting every contact he has from Ålesund to Stavanger.'

'And by contacts you mean…?'

'He has an agency.' She ran the tip of her tongue over her full lips to one corner of her mouth, where it rested like an inquisitive little creature. 'Wine. I can offer you a superlative Saint-Émilion.'

'Strictly speaking, I'm a beer and aquavit man.'

'Who never likes a taste of something different?'

'Oh, yes. It happens.' I tried to demonstrate my utmost regret as I added: 'But right now I'm a little strapped for time, so…'

She sighed loudly and rolled her eyes. Then her gaze hardened. 'Right! I can take a hint. What are you actually after?'

'I'm here regarding an Emma Hagland.'

'Yes, I gathered that. She doesn't live here any more. I told you.'

'She didn't stay for long, I understand.'

She reached out an arm, but stopped mid-movement, as she lost her balance. Annoyed, she said: 'No. My husband takes care of the tenants. They only come to me if they have complaints.'

'And what do they complain about?'

She waggled her head. 'Well, what do they complain about? The water's not hot enough, the radiators don't work, the neighbour downstairs plays his music too loud … yada yada yada.'

She turned towards the hall and I saw her arm move to the door to close it. She failed at her first attempt.

'So why did she move out so quickly? Do you know anything about that?'

She turned her head slowly from side to side. 'No.'

'I'd better come back another day. When your husband's here maybe.'

She appeared to be considering this, then she nodded. 'Yes, you do that.' She sent me a last despairing glance before she went behind the door and pushed it until it locked in my face.

I stood there for a moment. Imagining her sinking to the floor on the other side. But that was only in my imagination. In reality she had probably staggered over to the superlative red wine and raised her glass in a sad salute to Émilion and whatever he or she was a saint of. As for me, I went down one storey and rang the bell at Helga & Kari's.

6

The young woman who had opened the door a fraction peered through the crack, keeping the security chain on as an insurance policy between her and reality. She studied me with a gaze that seemed anxious, almost jumpy. She had short, slightly messy, dark-blonde hair, a face with no make-up and a mouth that shook like a leaf in autumn, just before it falls.

I put on my very friendliest smile, introduced myself slowly and clearly, and told her the reason for my call.

'Emma? She doesn't live here any more.'

'Yes, I know. But her family's very concerned about her.'

'Family?' She shot me a sceptical look.

'Her mother anyway. I've been commissioned to find out what she's doing.'

'Commissioned?'

'I'm a private investigator.'

Her eyes widened and she immediately went to close the door. I discreetly placed my shoe in the gap, hoping she didn't have too strong an arm. 'I have to find out what you know. Are you Kari?'

'No, I'm Helga.'

'If you don't want to let me in, we can go and have a cup of coffee somewhere.'

'No, it's fine. Let me just…' She pointed to the security chain. 'You'll have to…' and nodded towards my shoe.

'Right.' I withdrew my foot, not entirely sure that was the right decision.

She closed the door completely. Then I heard her unhook the chain, and she opened up again. 'Come in.'

'Thank you.'

I followed her into the plain, featureless hallway. She hesitated for a moment then took me through the second door to the right. 'This is … our common room,' she said.

It was sparsely furnished as well. In one corner there was a television that must have been ten years old or more. At the opposite end there was the traditional coffee table, sofa and armchair arrangement. The table was scarred with rings left by glasses and bottles and not without a certain coating. I could imagine it had been surrounded by sundry intakes of students. Møhlenpris was the closest neighbour to the university in Bergen and several student collectives were taking over the old flats in the area. The pictures on the wall looked to have survived a couple of generations – 1980s' pop art, more circles than squares, as if marking the distance from the previous decade when the dream of world revolution had dominated the scene. On the only bookcase I saw the spines of some popular novels in bestseller format and a handful of paperbacks of the kind you have to be very careful not to call women's books, at least not with women present.

In the middle of the table there was an empty wine bottle with a candle forced into its neck, but the bottle looked quite new and the candle had only burned down a little. As yet there was no pattern of melted wax. I noticed the name on the label: Cheval Blanc Saint-Émilion.

She pointed gauchely to the sofa, as a sign that I could sit there. I followed her suggestion. She sat down on the chair opposite. Her choice of clothes was simple: faded jeans and a plain grey jumper, and on her feet narrow, brown slip-on shoes. After sitting down she tucked her legs underneath her bottom and placed her hands on her knees as if to have full control over all movable parts.

'I haven't a clue where she is…' she announced.

'No? But she did move out?'

'Yes.' She nodded several times as though to make sure I got the point. 'She took all her things with her, even if that didn't amount to much. She put everything in one suitcase.'

'Surely she must've said where she was going?'

She chewed her lip and eyed me nervously. 'No. Should she have done?'

'Yes. What about her post?'

'We hardly get any. I don't know if she'd even registered her move here. It wasn't that long ago she moved in anyway.'

'In the summer, I was told.'

'Yes, I suppose it was. The end of July.'

'But … she must've registered her move officially?'

'I'm sure she did.'

'Well, I can check on that. How did you get to know each other?'

'We put up notices all over the place, at the student centre and the various colleges, saying we had a room free, and she was the first person to contact us. We asked the landlord if that was OK, and he said it was. So she moved in straight afterwards.'

'She talked to the landlord as well, did she?'

She nodded. 'Yes, we have to of course. We sign a contract with him.'

'Knut Moberg?'

'Yes.' She sent me an enquiring look. 'On the third floor.'

'Yes, I was there, but only his wife was at home.'

She just nodded slowly, without making a comment.

I focused on the empty red-wine bottle with the new candle. 'Is he a nice landlord?'

Again a hunted look flitted across her face. 'Yes, I suppose he is. We don't have anything to do with him.'

'No?'

'Not unless something needs doing. We pay the rent online.'

'Nothing black in other words.'

'Black?'

'Yes, you know, under the table.'

Still she appeared not to understand what I was talking about, and I decided not to pursue the matter this time.

'Why did she move out so quickly?'

She looked down as she shrugged her shoulders. 'Dunno.'

'Did you fall out?'

Her eyes shot up. 'Fall out? No! We were the best friends in the world, Emma and I.'

'What about Kari and Emma?'

She hesitated. 'Not such good friends perhaps.'

'What do you mean?'

'Well, Kari may be a bit more direct than I am.'

'Anything particular you have in mind?'

'No, nothing more than what I said.'

'The two of them quarrelled?'

'No, no, they didn't quarrel. But … I guess they had their own opinions, both of them.'

'What about?'

'You'd better ask Kari about that.'

'OK. Where is Kari?'

'Now?'

'Yes.'

'Out. She didn't say where she was going.'

'So you don't know when she'll be home?'

'No idea.'

I sighed. 'Well … tell me … did you have any impression of Emma in the time she lived here?'

'Mm, any impression …?' She looked to the side of me, towards the window, as though the answer lay outside.

'You must've chatted?'

'Yes, we did.' Now it was her turn to focus on the wine bottle with the candle. 'We were together some nights, just her and me, when we were, erm, a little … pixilated.'

'Oh, yes?'

Now she looked straight at me. 'We talked about our fathers. How lucky she'd been to get shot of hers early on! Even though she mightn't have seen it like that. While I could've coped very well without mine!'

Two big red flushes spread across her cheeks, but I wasn't there because of her, so I made no attempt to enquire further. Instead I said: 'Her father lives in town though, doesn't he?'

'Yes, and that was why things became a little intense for a while. Why we began to talk at all.'

'What do you mean?'

'She said … She said she wanted to go and see him. She'd found his address and all that. But I said: "Are you sure you want to? You don't know who he is, why he left you and why he never maintained contact."'

'Ah, so you knew that?'

'She'd already told me: no contact.' And then came another personal outburst: 'She has no idea how lucky she was!'

'What happened then? Did she visit her father?'

She slowly inclined her head. 'Yes.'

'And … did you find out how it went?'

She shrugged. 'No, but she seemed stressed when she returned that evening. When I asked her how it had gone she didn't want to talk.'

'And that was when?'

'In September.'

'And what happened then? Did she visit her father again?'

'She never talked about him, but I felt … I don't know. I think it'd had an effect on her, somehow, whatever happened. At any rate she became even more introverted after that.'

'And when did she decide to move out?'

'At the end of October.'

'Because she'd received a better offer elsewhere?'

'Where did you get that idea from?'

'That was what one of you said when Emma's family phoned from Haugesund.'

'That must've been Kari they spoke to. I haven't spoken to anyone.'

'I'd better … I take it you have Kari's phone number, do you?'

'Yes.' She cast around. Then she got up and went towards the door. 'Just a minute.'

She came back immediately with a phone in her hand. She pressed a few keys and found the correct number. She held out her phone for me, so that I could tap the number into mine. 'Thank you. I'll ring her later. And yours?'

She gave me that, too.

'Could you tell me which day it was that Emma moved out?'

'Which day?'

'Yes, or the date.'

'It was a Wednesday.' She looked at her phone and opened the calendar. 'It must've been the 29th of October.'

'Sure?'

'Yes, because two days later she had to be out. Change of month and another month's rent to pay.'

I noted the date. Then I nodded towards the wine bottle on the table between us. 'Isn't that pretty expensive wine?'

Once again she shrugged. 'Kari got it earlier this autumn. It wasn't the kind of wine Emma and I drank … on the evenings I mentioned. Ours was a bag-in-a-box, so to speak.'

'Well,' I started, taking out my business card. 'Here you are. You've got my number, address and everything you need if you remember any more. And I'll be back later. I have to have a chat with Kari, I think.'

She nodded in acknowledgement.

'Thank you for everything you've told me.'

She accompanied me to the door and closed it firmly behind me as soon as I was outside.

When I was back on the street I dialled Kari Sandbakken's number, but all I got was a prerecorded answer: *Hi, this is Kari. I can't take your call right now, but if you leave a message, I'll call you back. Bye.*

'Hi,' I said, feeling as stupid as I always did when I was talking to a machine. 'This is Veum. I need to ask you some questions regarding Emma Hagland. Could you call me? Thank you.'

But the thanks didn't help. She didn't call back, not that night, nor later.

7

I had no problem finding Robert Høie Hansen in the telephone directory. The address gave me some bad vibes though. Sudmanns vei was where Beate moved when she left me for Lasse Wiik thirty years before, never to return. I had never got any further than the front door of the house they shared, when I was picking up or handing over Thomas before or after his weekend visit. As soon as he was big enough he came to me under his own steam. But now Lasse Wiik was dead, Beate lived in Stavanger, and I had no idea who had bought their house. I glanced up at it as I passed, but I didn't notice any great changes since the 1980s when I had last been there.

From Sudmanns vei you have Mount Sandviksfjell towering up behind you, with the steep, paved Stoltzekleiven trail like a kind of zip in the middle, and the view of Byfjord and its surrounding splendours: the islets of Svineryggen, Måseskjæret and Kristiansholm, which are all now landfast. In days gone by they used to hang thieves on Kristiansholm. Later the town had a seaplane harbour and still now the occasional seaplane takes off or lands there. Over the last decade the other two islets had acquired modern high-rise buildings.

Robert Høie Hansen lived on the slope at the lower end of the road, behind a panel fence stained the same colour as the house, which was older than the one where Beate had lived, probably built during the interwar years. In a little carport to the right of the garden gate was what looked like a sizeable motorbike, covered in a grey, tailor-made tarpaulin and secured with a chain and a padlock to a post. The garden was reasonably well kept with no eye-catching features that would stop you in your tracks.

I unlocked the garden gate and stepped inside. When I was halfway to the front door, it opened. A small, lean woman, dressed in a red-and-black tracksuit with silver reflective stripes down the arms and legs, rushed out on slim running shoes and had already closed the door before she caught sight of me and paused.

'Yes?' she said. 'Anything I can help you with?'

'Robert Høie Hansen. Does he live here?'

'Yes, that's my husband. What do you want with him?'

She was wearing a white hat pulled down well over her hair, which prevented me from seeing more than a few dark-red strands sticking out at the back. Her face was slender and dotted with pale freckles, and it looked as if she had left her eyebrows indoors. Her eyes were narrow and bluish-green and she had a slight tendency to squint. She jogged impatiently on the gravel and cast a longing glance at the mountainside behind me.

'It's a family matter.'

She eyed me sceptically. 'Oh, yes? Not that hysterical daughter of his again, I hope.'

'Are you referring to Emma?'

She rolled her eyes. 'So it is … again!' She half turned to the door. 'Well, he's at home. You just have to ring the bell. He'll explode with delight. As for me, I'm off up there.' She pointed to Stoltzekleiven and the weather vane on the mast at the top, an arrow, hard to see at this time of the day.

With that as her parting shot, she quickly walked around me, opened the garden gate and set off at a run. I watched her go. She maintained an impressive speed and I felt a stab of envy. Even in my best years I would have struggled to keep up with her. But perhaps she was just showing off. As soon as she was out of sight she probably slowed down to a more normal tempo for anyone having to climb the 313.5 metres to the top like a mountain goat.

I walked to the closed door and rang the bell.

'Yes? What is it now?' came an irritated voice from inside, then the door opened wide.

The man filling the doorway was close to the hundred-kilo mark, dark-haired and possessed of a full but trim beard. Except for the light-blue denim shirt, he was dressed entirely in black: leather waistcoat, jeans and boots. A substantial stomach hung over a leather belt and a big, shiny silver buckle with a stylised bull's head on. But he didn't seem fat. There was a lot of solid bone in his body.

When he realised it wasn't his wife who had rung the bell, he gave me a quick once-over. 'Yes?'

'Robert Høie Hansen?'

'Yes, what do you want?'

'The name's Veum. Varg Veum. I'm here about Emma.'

His eyes narrowed. 'Oh, yes? What about her?'

'She … Her family has lost contact with her.'

His eyes blinked in quick succession. 'Lost contact? What do you mean?'

'She's moved from where she lived after she came to town this summer, but didn't leave a forwarding address and isn't responding to calls. Not phone calls anyway.'

'Really?'

'That doesn't concern you?' When he didn't answer, I added: 'After all, this is your daughter we're talking about.'

'It's not quite like that … What did you say your name was?'

'Veum.'

'Veum. I don't know how well informed you are about my family situation.'

'I have the gist.'

'So you know I haven't had any contact with my daughter for a number of years, since she was two in fact?'

'I do. But I also know she visited you here earlier this autumn.'

The man seemed to grow in the doorway. He raised his voice. 'Visited? Tracked me down more like. A bit like you now.' He made a gesture in my direction, a powerful arm with big hands. It was hard to imagine a starker contrast with the little stoat who, for all I knew, was already halfway up Stoltzekleiven.

I tried to see past him. 'Have you got time for a little chat?'

'Isn't that what we're doing now?'

'Inside?'

'We can do it here.'

'Up to you. So what happened when she tracked you down?'

'Nothing. I didn't want anything to do with her.'

'With your own daughter?'

'Didn't you hear what I said? I hadn't seen her since 1986. I didn't know her and I didn't want anything to do with them – neither her nor her mother.'

'So you just sent her packing?'

'She burst into tears; it was all very awkward, as both Liv and Andreas rolled up at the same time – her from hospital and him from school.'

'Liv and Andreas are … ?'

'My wife and my son, yes. Afterwards I had a job explaining to them who this girl was.'

'OK. Do you mean to say neither of them knew about her?'

'Liv did, but she'd never met her. And Andreas … no.'

'But …' I protested, hands outstretched.

'You don't need to repeat yourself. My own daughter! If you had an inkling of a fraction of what's behind this, you wouldn't have cared. You would've just gone on your way. And that's exactly what you're going to do now.'

I watched him. He was puffing himself up even more and it was obvious he could trample over me like a prize bull over a bewildered toreador if I objected.

'All I can say is I think this is strange. Your son, for example. How did he react to hearing he had a half-sister?'

'His jaw dropped. And then he went to his bloody machine. That's what he likes most.'

'Machine?'

'Computer. He sits in front of it until his eyes go square!'

'But he must've asked you some questions. Afterwards.'

'Not a single one!'

'And your wife, how did she react?'

'That's none of your fucking business. She already knew, and she's a nurse, so she knows what's what.'

'Hm? What do you mean by that?'

'She has empathy. Empathy! Do you know what that word means?'

I grinned. 'I've heard it before, yes. But she probably had a few questions for you as well, didn't she? After the drama with Emma at the door.'

He leaned forwards, which made him seem even more menacing. 'And she got some answers. Which you won't.' He raised an arm as if to sweep me away. 'Piss off! This has got nothing to do with you or anyone else.'

Nothing was likely to make me more curious than someone saying precisely these words. I made a last attempt. 'So it doesn't bother you that she's gone missing?'

'Missing? She's found herself a guy. Or she's decided to make a break with that dreadful mother of hers. What do I know? And I don't care, either. Goodbye!'

With that, he retreated into the house and slammed the door in my face.

I stood making a few mental notes. *Liv. Andreas. Nurses. School.* I wasn't going to allow myself to be fobbed off that easily. I just had to look around for a back door into what he didn't want to talk about. There was always one. Without exception.

From my car I tried to ring Kari Sandbakken again, but I got the same voicemail, and this time I didn't leave a message.

I took the evening off. I knew who I was going to contact the following day anyway.

8

In Bergen, November is the month of the grey monk. The snow comes later. The sun makes a guest appearance or two. Most days are grey and more often than not it rains. Not summer's short bursts; not October's long downpours, which flood the streets and cellars because the relevant authorities haven't cleared the autumn leaves this year, either; nor spring's refreshing rain, which washes away the remnants of winter and makes the town clean again. In November, rain is the personification of gloom, as though really it wants to be snow, like a teenage girl with her head in the clouds, dreaming about becoming a prima ballerina one day.

This was the weather that met me on this Tuesday too – cold, dismal rain, broken only by some impatient gusts of wind coming in from the sea and the many low-pressure fronts queueing up out there, waiting to be released.

I'd had another go at ringing Kari Sandbakken and received the same voicemail message. I wondered whether that should give me cause for concern: another tenant from the same flat not answering the phone. But when I dialled Helga Fjørtoft's number and got no answer, I took that as a sign that neither of them was up yet or they were on the way to the first lecture of the day. Maybe.

Before leaving home I had searched for and found the phone numbers of mother, father and son in the Høie Hansen family as well as Knut Moberg's. I had located Moberg's agency in a company directory, under the not very original name of Bacchus Bergen and with an office address in Industrihuset in Bergen. It struck me that, before I left, I should have discovered what Robert Høie Hansen did for a living as well, but I definitely hadn't seen his name in any company directory.

All the numbers saved in my phone, I walked the ten minutes it took to the police station.

The first time I met Annemette Bergesen she was working for Kripos. She had been on the Hurtigruten boat that I had caught during one of the more curious cases of my career, one that led me from Bergen to Trondheim and ended in a dramatic meeting with the ghost of a monk in Nidaros Cathedral. The following year she moved to Bergen because she had found someone to marry, a microbiologist, unless I was mistaken. Now, ten years later, she had to be in her late forties and she had swapped her big glasses for contact lenses, which tended to make her face seem naked and vulnerable.

She met me at the top of the stairs and guided me to her office on the third floor. 'Stopped using the lift, Varg?'

'I take every available opportunity to exercise.'

'Looks like you're keeping in pretty good shape.'

'Thanks, and the same to you.'

As a detective in what those outside Police HQ still called the crime investigation department, she dressed in civilian clothing and always with discreet elegance. Her dark hair was dyed with grey streaks, no doubt to camouflage the fact that some snowflakes of the kind that never melt had fallen on her locks as well. From her office she had a view of what had been the new Workers' Assembly House for a short period. Behind it towered the fourteen-storey 1970s Town Hall. In the evening she could flash light signals to the mayor if she felt the urge. Although she was hardly likely to receive an answer.

She showed me to a free chair on the opposite side of the desk and got straight to the point, like the efficient officer she had always been. 'You said something on the phone about a missing-person case.'

'Yes. My client … she said she had spoken to the police – you, in particular. But there hadn't been much of a response to her enquiry.'

'Right.' She looked at me coolly. 'Can you give me a bit more detail?'

I did, but before I could finish she interrupted me. 'Yes, now I remember. The girl had packed her suitcase and left the flat she shared with some friends. Packing a suitcase suggests nothing criminal has happened. She's either found a more reasonable rent or she's got a boyfriend.'

'But she didn't leave an address and she's not answering her phone.'

'Yes, but is she not answering or is her phone not connected?'

'Good question.'

She arched her eyebrows and slanted her head. 'You call yourself a private investigator, don't you, Varg?'

'I do, but I was bit distracted by … well, the client.'

She smiled. 'An attractive blonde?'

'No, no, no. Close to eighty. Turned out she … we … are distant family.'

'Well, well. Let me give you a helping hand. I've already mentioned the two most common reasons for a young woman deciding to move house. And as far as not answering her mother on the phone is concerned, in many families there are conflicts that young people are only too happy to leave behind. It could be something like that, couldn't it?'

'Yes, maybe. She has a father in Bergen she hadn't met for many years.'

'Have you spoken to him?'

'Yes, but he didn't have anything to tell me, either. Nothing that led anywhere, at any rate.'

'And you're sure she's still in Bergen? She might've gone abroad. Nowadays lots of kids travel for a year without even asking for permission from those back at home.'

A sudden thought struck me.

Annemette was alert enough to notice. 'You've had an idea?'

'No, just a thought. She has a friend who lives in Berlin. I'll ring her.'

'You do that.'

For a short while we sat looking at each other expectantly. She had such beautiful, regular features, and I remembered her having made an impression on me when I first met her on the Hurtigruten boat eleven years before.

'So, in other words … the police aren't going to do anything further in this case? I mean … you're the ones who can check her phone … or any transactions on her bank card.'

She leaned forwards and took a pen and a notepad. 'I'll make a note of her name, Varg. Have you got the numbers?'

I gave her a piece of paper with all the information on, and she wrote it down.

'Great. Should I have an hour to spare, I'll check our sources. But as I've already mentioned, I doubt we'll find anything. If you run across anything that might give us greater cause for concern, I assume you'll be in touch.' She got up, a clear sign that the audience was over.

I followed suit. 'I'll find my own way out.'

'Yes, I know. The last time you were here, you did just that, didn't you.'

'I did.' But being reminded of that was no great source of pleasure.

'Good luck then,' she rounded off with a sudden warmth in her voice. 'I hope you find her.'

'Thank you.'

Down on the flagstones in front of Police HQ, I cursed myself for my lack of professionalism when Norma Johanne from Haugesund visited me. I found her number on my phone and called.

'Varg!' she answered after two rings. 'Have you got anything?'

'Not yet. But I need some more info.'

'Of course.'

'When you and her mother tried calling Emma, what response did you get on her phone?'

'Just the usual reply, not even her own voice, just the automated thing saying the subscriber can't answer now because the phone's either switched off or is in an area where there is no coverage.'

'Always the same reply?'

'The latest one was this morning.'

'This morning?'

'I call every morning after I get up, Varg. One day she has to answer, if she's …' Her voice cracked with emotion, ever so slightly. 'If she's alive, that is.'

'I met her father last night, and she'd been there, but he didn't invite her in. He just sent her packing.'

'The bastard! Oh, I'd like to … Yes, I would.'

'Bastard? Is there anything else you can tell me about him?'

She considered the possibility. 'No. Not now. Not yet.'

'It might be important.'

'It cannot possibly have anything to do with this. What's important now is to find Emma.'

'True, and speaking of that … Her friend in Berlin. Could I have her number?'

'Yes, of course. Didn't I give it to you yesterday?'

'No, I … we forgot.'

'Her name's Åsa Lavik.' Once she had found the number she read it out to me. I noted it down, and we hung up.

Another shot in the dark probably. But it had to be fired. I walked back to my office to call from there, the safest place not to be disturbed.

I nodded to the young lady at the hotel reception desk and took all the stairs up to the third floor here, too.

9

'Hello?'

With Åsa Lavik at least there was no automated voice. She answered after the first ring, so must have been sitting with the phone in her hand, which incidentally I had noticed most young people did nowadays, as though transporting their own beating hearts.

'Åsa Lavik?'

'Yes, who's that?' Her voice was high-pitched, girlish.

I said who I was, what I did and why I was calling.

'Hasn't she turned up yet?'

'No.'

'It gave me such a shock when fru Bakkevik – her godmother – rang. I hope it's nothing serious.'

'For the time being, we don't know, but we're hoping for the best of course. Have you got time for a chat?'

'Yes. I'm on the U-Bahn going to the UdK, so I've got at least ten minutes before we arrive.'

'The UdK?'

'Universität der Künste. University of the Arts.'

'I see. You and Emma were best friends, fru Bakkevik said.'

'Yes, we met when we changed schools and soon realised we had a lot in common. After that we stuck together like glue.'

'So you'd say you knew her well?'

'Yes, I would.'

'But this year you went your separate ways?'

'Yes, I wanted to train as a clothes designer and when I was accepted for this course in Berlin I couldn't say no.'

'And Emma was never tempted to join you?'

'No. I think going abroad seemed too risky – too big a jump – for her. So she went to Bergen instead,' she said with a little laugh.

'Bergen is probably abroad for some,' I said, and she laughed again. 'But perhaps she chose it because her father lives there?'

She paused. 'Well, maybe. She had definitely begun to have a very difficult relationship with her mother.'

'Why was that?'

'Mm … I don't know how much you're aware of, but she had her problems, too. The mother, that is.' She lowered her voice so as not to be overheard. 'Drugs.'

'Yes, I guessed there was something like that. Do you think Emma wanted closer contact with her father?'

'I think she hoped for that, anyway. We were actually in the same boat, Emma and I.'

'What do you mean?'

'I lost my father too, but it was for other reasons. We often talked about this – both of us being fatherless.'

'I can understand how you became such good friends then. Did you still have contact with her after your paths … took you different ways?'

'Emma and I?'

'Yes.'

'We're both on Hotmail and have often used Messenger. And then we chat on the phone sometimes.'

'Is it a long time since you've heard from her?'

'Yes, actually quite a few weeks now.'

I made some notes before continuing. 'Mm … Did she tell you she'd visited her dad and how it'd gone?'

'Yes. He still didn't want anything to do with her, she said. It must've been terrible for her. I had tears in my eyes when she told me.'

'Did you have any impression of how she'd reacted to this?'

'She was furious – when she told me about it at least. Or was she? I'm not sure. It might've been despair.'

'And later – did she say any more then?'

'No, I haven't heard that much from her over the last month, and I've been very busy here. It's the first semester, and the Germans are not slow to make demands of their students. I've already got to hand in an assignment in two weeks.' Her tone changed. 'The train's arriving now. I'll be on the platform in a minute, if you don't mind waiting.'

I sat, phone in hand, listening to the noise of people talking, maybe the doors opening, a signal and then the slightly echoey sound of a station concourse.

Then her voice was back: 'Hello. Are you there?'

'Yes.'

'In fact I have to hurry, but we can chat as I walk.'

'Thank you. Actually I have only one more question. Emma moved from where she was living at the end of October. Packed her suitcase and no one has heard from her since. Did she say anything about this?'

'No, nothing at all. That was why I was so surprised when fru Bakkevik rang trying to find her. And then I felt guilty because I hadn't contacted her myself for so long.'

'So you've no idea where she might've gone? She never talked about a boyfriend?'

'No, and she would've done, I'm sure, if she'd had one. We teased each other about this. We'd left relationships behind us in Haugesund, but now we were free and unattached, both her and me. Ready for new experiences. I'm sure, though, if she'd had someone she would've told me. The only thing she did mention was something about a touchy-feely landlord, but she'd put him in his place, and apparently there were no repercussions.'

'Mhm.' After a brief pause I said: 'And what about you?'

'Me? A boyfriend?'

'Not that it's any of my business, but...'

She laughed, it was a dry chuckle. 'I don't even have time to think about that! And it's only girls on the course. And the boys that study here, well ... ha ha ha.'

Now I could hear traffic noise in the background. 'I can hear you're in the street, so I won't hold you up any further. Thank you for all your help and, if you should hear from her, I hope you'll let me know. You can see my number on your screen.'

'OK. I have to cross the road now.'

'All the best.'

'*Auf Wiedersehen*!' she said with a slightly more cheerful laugh this time.

I hung up and underlined one of the names on my pad: Knut Moberg.

10

Since the police hadn't taken Emma's disappearance seriously and nothing, as yet, suggested there was a crime involved, I was limited in the number of ways I could tackle the case. I rang the National Register, but the only address they had for Emma Hagland was her home in Haugesund. 'But that's not unusual,' the woman there said. 'Often it takes several years before they report a move and then it's normally after pressure from the Tax Office.'

Accordingly, the next place to try was where she was registered as a student, at the nursing college. As far as I knew, it was in Haukelandsbakken, right next to Haukeland Hospital. I made several attempts to communicate by phone, but no one was willing to answer questions about students in this way. In the end, I decided it was simplest to appear in person.

It had stopped raining. The bus to Haukeland went from Strandkaien. It was quicker than walking all the way up to Øvre Blekevei to fetch my car. On Line 2 most of the buses were electric, so I could tell myself I was doing my bit for the environment at the same time.

Haukelandsbakken is a long, steep road, and the tallest of the mountains around Bergen, Mount Ulriken, towers up to the east. In the 1960s an annual skiing race was organised down the slope here under the name the 'Ulriken Downhill', but since then Haukeland Hospital had grown exponentially and the fields below the Øvre Haukelandstræet smallholding, known by many as Markusplassen, because of the previous owner, a Markus Andersen, were history. There wasn't enough snow during the winter these days to put on a skiing race, either.

Haukeland Nursing College for radiographers and nurses was right at the top of the hill, a modern concrete building with two wings clad with grey metal plates inspired by corrugated iron. From the front entrance you saw straight into an atrium with a little water feature in the middle. A sign in the covered foyer pointed me to the right and in an office I found the guardian of all requisite information. She was a woman of that indefinable age between forty and fifty, with large glasses and hair tied back in a bun. She asked for some ID and I showed her my bank card. It only documented who I was and when I told her I was a private investigator she took it as a joke, bursting into a long, trilled laugh, and said, 'Well, that's another one for the record.'

'Nice to know I can bring a little happiness into your life.'

She said, still laughing: 'Yes, but I'm afraid I can't help you. We're not allowed to release such information to outsiders, even if they're ... PIs.'

'This is about a young woman whose family can't get in contact with her.'

'Yes, I know.' Her face adopted a more serious expression. 'I'm sorry, but I have rules to follow.'

'So who should I talk to? Is there a director of studies here?'

'Yes, there is, though I doubt she's free now.'

'Do you doubt she is or do you know she isn't?'

'I know.' Now I was beginning to get on her nerves.

'Doubts and beliefs are a tricky area.'

'Tell me, did you say you were a private investigator or a preacher?'

'You're not going to let yourself be converted by either, I see.'

'Not today,' she said, and swivelled round to her desk as an indication the conversation was over.

'But tomorrow?' I replied, mostly to myself, as I retreated.

Some students passed me on their way out of the building. I walked quickly after them and caught them up in Haukelandsbakken. I asked if they were first-semester students, which they confirmed with enquiring expressions. There were two girls and a boy, dressed in striking sports gear, as though they were actually on their way down Mount Ulriken and not coming out of a lecture theatre, an auditorium or wherever they had been indoors.

When I asked if any of them knew a student from Haugesund called

Emma Hagland they shook their heads. However, after showing them a photo, one of the girls nodded. 'Yes, I might do. I think I may've seen her, but I'm not absolutely sure. There are so many of us.'

The other two leaned forwards. The young man said: 'Yes, she looks like one of those who came to the first lectures and then stopped. I remember thinking she must've dropped out. Decided the course wasn't for her.'

I looked at him. 'Did you speak to her?'

He flushed. 'No, never. I just ... noticed her.'

The two girls sent him sidelong glances, and one of them sniggered.

'What's your name?'

'Lars. Why?'

'Mm.' I shrugged. 'Matter of form.'

'Nothing has happened to her, has it? Are you ... family?'

'No, I'm a private investigator.'

That made them look at me differently, with curiosity rather than disdain. 'So something *has* happened?' said one girl, before adding: 'My name's Siri.'

'No one knows yet. She's been incommunicado for quite some time and we don't know where she lives any more. Her family's worried.'

They nodded in unison, like three synchronised swimmers at a prayer meeting in Salem.

'None of you can help me, then?'

'No,' said Siri, turning to the other two, who shook their heads, both with regret in their eyes.

I gave each of them a business card. 'If you should hear something, here are my phone number and email address.'

They took the cards and examined them eagerly. We walked together for some way down Haukelandsbakken, past the big red kindergarten that had taken its name from the mountain behind us, Ravneberget. By Ulriksbanen Station, where cable cars transport tourists and walkers up to the top of the mountain, I took out my phone and signalled that I had to make a call. They gave a friendly nod and continued on down.

It had occurred to me that while I was in this area I could dial the number of Liv Høie Hansen, who, her husband had informed me the previous evening, was a nurse at the hospital.

She answered after five or six rings. She sounded out of breath. 'Yes? Liv here.'

'Hi. This is Veum. We met briefly yesterday.'

'Uhuh.'

'I was wondering if I could have a couple of words with you. Where are you now?'

'By the Sandvik weather vane. So if you feel like a run up Stoltzekleiven, then...'

'Today, again?'

'I try to get a run in every day, and this afternoon I'm on duty, so...'

'At Haukeland?'

'Yes, but I can't stand here getting cold, so...'

'When do you clock on?'

'At three, but I'm much too busy when I'm at work. I haven't got time to talk to anyone then, so...'

'And you clock off at...?'

'I run home then, via Fjellveien.'

'I see. When?'

'At ten. But I've got nothing to say to you, so...'

'Your son...'

'Andreas.'

'He's at secondary school, isn't he?'

'Yes, at Bjørgvin, but...'

'OK, I understand. He's at school now. What does your husband do actually?'

'Robert? He's a porter.'

'At Haukeland as well?'

'Yes. I haven't got any more time for this. As I told you, I'm getting cold.'

'Yes, I'm sorry. See you this evening then.'

She didn't hang up. I could almost visualise a question mark above her head. 'What?'

'I might join you for a run.'

'Ha ha,' she said, and this time she hung up.

And I had to come clean. It was an empty threat. A woman who had run up Stoltzekleiven twice in twelve hours and maintained the pace I had seen the previous evening would leave me for dead before we were halfway to Bellevuebakken, so…

I left the rest hanging in the air, as she had done with most of her answers.

11

I caught the bus back to my office and pondered my next move. Knut Moberg – I felt I had to talk to him. I rang Bacchus Bergen, but all I got was the message: *We're away. Back in the office on Wednesday the 12th of November.*

I had made a note of his mobile as well, and when I called, I got a reply: 'Moberg.'

'Veum here. I have some questions. Have you got time to answer them?'

'Veum?'

'Varg Veum. Private investigator.'

'Oh, yes?' Suddenly he sounded considerably more measured.

'I'm ringing about an ex-tenant of yours: Emma Hagland.'

'Jesus! I've said already. I have no idea where she is.'

'And you? Where are you?'

'What business is that of yours, may I ask?'

'Well, I was thinking … we should meet face to face.'

'No need for that. I've got nothing to say. The girl moved without leaving a forwarding address.' After a little pause he added: 'And there's no point asking any of the girls she lived with. They don't know anything, either.'

'Sure about that?'

'Yes. Veum … I'm just about to drive onto a ferry. I have nothing to tell you.' Another pause. 'Good luck. I hope you find her.' With that he rang off and I was left with the feeling that I was banging my head against a brick wall whichever way I turned.

I sat looking at my notepad. I hadn't finished with Knut Moberg yet, but it looked as if I would have to wait until he was back in

Bergen. Emma's half-brother, Andreas, was someone else I wanted to talk to. I glanced at my watch. School was coming to an end, but I had no idea what he looked like. However, I did have his mobile phone number. Once again it struck me how much simpler life was, even for people like me, after this invention became common property. I texted him, telling him my name, but not what I wanted, and asked him to call me.

My own half-sister had called Robert Høie Hansen 'a bastard'. While I was waiting to see if Andreas called back, I surfed the net to see if I could find any explanation for her expletive. All I saw was a name, address and tax data. I knew the name and address. The tax data was nothing out of the ordinary, but one thing did surprise me: Robert had assets worth six million kroner. I supposed that meant he owned his property in Sudmanns vei and had money in the bank on top. I found it hard to see how that tallied with the incomes of a porter and a nurse, even if both of them very probably earned more in a year than I did.

It was just gone three when I received a text back from Andreas: *What's this about?*

I replied: *Emma.*

A few minutes passed before the next message came: *Leaving school now. Where can we meet?*

I gave him my office address and wrote that I would meet him by the hotel reception desk.

He replied quickly: *OK. There in twenty.*

No sooner said than done, at just before half past three, the door to the street opened automatically for Andreas Høie Hansen. He looked around and I got up from the chair where I was sitting, walked over and said: 'Andreas?'

He clocked me without a smile: 'Yes?'

He looked younger than I had expected. He was an odd mixture of his parents. His hair was red like his mother's and his shoulders were narrow, but from the waist down his father's genes were in the ascendancy, which gave him a slightly unhealthy, pear-shaped build – a broad bottom and strong thighs beneath his dark-blue jeans. Over his chest he wore a blue-and-green all-weather jacket and on his head a cap emblazoned with *HALF-LIFE* on both sides.

'*HALF-LIFE* – what's that?'

'A computer game.'

'Right. Come with me,' I said, going to the lift.

He gave me a sceptical look. 'Where?'

'My office is on the third floor.'

He still looked sceptical, but after glancing at the receptionist and receiving a nod from her, he joined me in the lift and we were quickly up on the third floor.

In my office, his eyes swept the room. 'Do you run this hotel?'

'No, no, no. I'm a private investigator.'

'Eh? A detective?'

'Yes.'

'Why have you got your office here then?'

'It's a long story. But … I went to your parents' place yesterday for a chat.' I said nothing about how brief the conversations had been, but watched him digest what I had said.

'About her … Emma?'

'Yes. It was my understanding you had no idea you had a half-sister.'

'Dad hadn't said a word, no.'

'How old are you, Andreas?'

'Sixteen.'

'So … what did you think when you heard about her?'

'I had no idea who she was. I thought…'

'Yes?'

'Well. She stood at the door talking to Dad that afternoon. She was crying. I didn't understand anything, so I just went back in.'

'You're a computer whiz, your father said.'

He shrugged and made no comment.

'Then later – after your father had told you a little about Emma?'

'Dad? Nah. It was mum who told me the little she knew. It wasn't much, either.'

'But you must've been curious about … Emma's story?'

'Nah. Why?'

I looked at him. His face was pallid, with the beginnings of some pimples on his chin and cheeks. His eyes roamed from side to side, only stopping to rest on the floor, and not even settling there for very long. The hair I could see was longish and ragged. A couple of times he held the peak of his cap and shifted it from one side to the other, but didn't take it off.

'So … she didn't try to contact you herself then? Once she'd moved to Bergen?'

He looked straight at me for an instant, then his gaze whizzed out through the window to Bryggen, up to Mount Fløyen and back to the recently washed floor of my office. 'When?'

'Well … this autumn.'

'Not as far as I know.'

'Not as far as you know?'

'No! Are you hard of hearing or what?'

'No, not particularly, but … are you sure you're telling me the truth?'

'Are you saying I'm lying?'

'No, but … perhaps you don't want to talk about it?'

'She didn't get in touch. That's how it is. There's no more to say.' He fidgeted as if what he really wanted to do was get up and go. 'Anything else?'

I looked at him. 'So neither your father nor your mother said anything about why your father hadn't mentioned her and, as far as I know, hadn't had contact with her since she was two years old?'

'No, they didn't!'

'And you? Do you have a good relationship with him? With your father?'

He stared ahead. 'Dad?' He shrugged.

'I saw … Was that his motorbike outside your house?'

He nodded. 'That's the kind of stuff he does.'

'What kind of stuff?'

'Fiddling about with that bike. Riding with the other MC guys.'

'Right. He's in a motorbike club?'

He nodded.

'And what's it called?'

The same demonstrative shrug of the shoulders. 'Dunno.'

'You don't share his interest?'

'No.'

'And your mother … she runs the Stoltzen twice a day?'

Again he caught my eye for an instant, possibly impressed by what I knew. 'Ants in her pants.'

'It seems as if you all have very different interests in your family.'

'Yes, I s'pose we do.'

'So from that point of view it would be great to have a sister?'

'I've managed OK without one.' But he looked sad sitting there, not having smiled once since I met him.

'I'll tell you something, Andreas. Just recently I've experienced more or less the same as you. A woman appeared in the office and introduced herself as my sister.'

'And you didn't know about her?'

'I did, I knew she existed. Or that she'd been born. But she grew up with other people and I'd never met her, so I think I can understand how you must've felt with a young lady at the door saying … the same.'

'But she wasn't … she didn't grow up with other people.'

'No, she grew up with her mother.'

'That's still not the same,' he was quick to say. 'You could've contacted *your* sister.'

I nodded. 'Yes, I suppose I could've done.'

Our eyes met. Then he tore himself away. 'I have to go now.'

'Well, if you have no more to—'

He interrupted me: 'I have no more to say.'

'OK … Let's leave it like this, Andreas. If you hear from your sister, get in touch with me. Here's my card.'

He took it and put it in his pocket without looking at it.

'And if there's anything else you'd like to tell me…'

'Eh?'

'Get in touch, alright?'

He sent me a desperate look, the way only teenagers can when they meet an adult who is beyond their experience. Then he got up, threw his rucksack over one shoulder and went to the door.

'Bye,' he said as he left.

'Bye,' I said, but he had already closed the door behind him.

I was banging my head against a wall, once again. So why did I have the constant feeling that some of them knew more than they were willing to let on – whatever it might be?

As if to emphasise this point, I dialled Kari Sandbakken's number again, only to hear her voicemail. But I got an answer from Helga Fjørtoft this time.

'Helga here.'

'There you are! This is Veum.'

'Oh,' she answered, her falling tone audible.

'I've been trying again and again to get hold of Kari, but she doesn't answer. Have you seen her?'

'Yes. Well, I got a text from her.'

'Uhuh?'

'She didn't come home last night, and so … She just wrote that I shouldn't worry, she was sleeping over at a pal's.'

'A pal's?'

'Yes, that's what she wrote.'

'So you haven't spoken to her, either?'

'No.'

'And you've no idea who this pal could be?'

She hesitated. '… No.'

'You had to think there.'

'Yes. No. Yes, I did, I guess. I couldn't think of anyone.'

'No boyfriend from your block?'

'Not as far as I know.'

'Hm.'

Three single girls. One of them had vanished without a trace. Another was suddenly missing overnight. And the third not exactly keen to answer any questions. There was something about this that worried me, although I was unable to put my finger on precisely what.

We hung up. We had no more to talk about. Not yet.

12

Before doing anything else I rang my client – and half-sister – in Haugesund again. She was as quick to answer as the previous time. 'Any news?'

'No, I'm afraid not. But I need to know a little more about Emma's father. When we talked earlier today you called him a bastard.'

'Yes, well, perhaps I ought to be a bit more circumspect.'

'Not necessarily. But I simply have to ask you straight out: is he a sex offender?'

She paused for a long time before answering. 'Yes, he probably was, I think.'

'You think?'

'Yes, I imagine it was his word against someone else's.'

'Emma's?'

'No.' Another pause. 'Not as far as I know. But you have to understand … this is not so easy to ask someone about.'

'If I go to Haugesund and talk to her mother, will she tell me anything?'

'Maybe.'

'Does she know about this? About you hiring me to find Emma?'

'She knows I've contacted someone, yes. But not who you are. I mean with regard to you and me.'

'So it would be in her interest for everything that can help me in my work to come out?'

'Yes, of course. But surely you don't think this can have anything to do with the old business, do you?'

'Which old business?'

'Well, the business with Robert.'

'The business you won't tell me about?'

'I think it's better you examine it with fresh eyes. I can't understand how it can help you in this case anyway. The main thing is to find Emma.'

'Yes, that's true enough. It's just that it really isn't easy to get any concrete leads. She lived in Bergen only briefly, no one knows of any boyfriends, her fellow students didn't know her, and the girls she shared a flat with are not very forthcoming either.' I reflected for a moment. 'Did she have any boyfriends in Haugesund?'

'Nothing serious, I don't think. I'm afraid she was a rather solitary young person, Varg. The only friend she had was Åsa, but the two of them stuck together like glue. Did you get in touch with her?'

'Yes, we had a chat on the phone, but she didn't have a lot to contribute, either. They'd only had sporadic contact since they went their separate ways – to Bergen and Berlin.'

'Yes, that was how she described it to me as well.'

'More and more I feel a need to talk to Emma's mother. I'll follow up a couple of lines of enquiry I have here in Bergen first, but I may be down there in the very near future.'

'Just let me know and I'll take you to her place and introduce you.'

'Thank you. That sounds like an arrangement. You'll be hearing from me.'

With that we hung up.

I stared into space. I still didn't have a distinct picture of Emma, but it was beginning to resemble a kind of profile, a bit blurred at the edges, but clear enough for me to see a vulnerable young woman, someone it might be easy to lead astray, someone who was open to approaches, whether well meant or malevolent, someone who could easily become a victim.

This worried me and created a sense of urgency. Perhaps I would have to resort to a few short-cuts, however brutal they might seem to outsiders – or to those concerned.

I had four names on my list, and not one of them would be pleased to receive a visit from me.

13

I parked in Sudmanns vei, in a suitable location to see them when they appeared, either of them.

It was around nine in the evening but the house seemed uninhabited. I strolled back and forth, past the gate, without opening it. One window, facing the street, was lit, behind rolled-down blinds. I could imagine Andreas sitting inside, fully immersed in what was happening on his computer screen. The carport was empty. The motorbike I had seen the previous evening was gone. When I realised this, I decided to return to my car and wait for whoever came home first.

Liv Høie Hansen did not disappoint. She came from the north; I guessed she must have followed Fjellveien right out to Munkebotn before heading back and arriving in Sudmanns vei from that direction. Her stride was light and easy. The run from Haukeland didn't seem to have taken anything out of her. Once inside the gate she walked to the carport, leaned against the short wall and did a few stretches before continuing to the front door, taking a key from her tracksuit pocket and letting herself in. She didn't so much as glance in my direction.

Now it wasn't her I was most interested in, and I certainly didn't want to talk to her alone. I assumed she would go straight into the shower and some mental images of that flashed up that were not simply distracting. It was almost eleven when I heard the deep roar of a well-tuned Harley Davidson coming up from Formanns vei and right past where I was slumped behind the wheel of a not quite so well-tuned Toyota Corolla.

Robert Høie Hansen flicked out the stand, swung off the bike, opened the gate, got back on and powered inside, where he turned into the carport and parked. He walked back to the gate and closed it after him. After unhooking the tarpaulin cover from the ceiling, he spread it over the motorbike and pulled the strings tight. I let him reach the front door before following him. When he heard the gate go he turned round, holding the key in the lock.

'Jesus Christ', he said in very good English, as if that made it any better. 'What the fuck do you want? Didn't I make myself clear yesterday?'

'Yes, but I didn't feel we'd quite finished.'

'Oh, didn't you now? I'll finish you alright this time.' He was wearing full biking gear, from a legally acceptable helmet to a black leather jacket, grey jeans and chunky boots. On his back he wore a club emblem; I hadn't caught the name or the symbol in the middle from a distance, and now it was concealed.

Before we could say another word, the door behind him opened and Liv Høie Hansen peered out, dressed in a teddy-bear onesie for lounging in the corner of the sofa, with or without spouse. 'Robert?' Then she caught sight of me, and her questioning look vanished. 'I heard the engine, but when you didn't come in … Now I see why.'

'I'm happy to talk to you both,' I was quick to interject.

'You won't be fuckin' talking to either of us,' Robert said, visibly pumping himself up.

'Frightened something will come up you don't want to hear?' Before he had a chance to answer, I continued: 'The reason your first wife booted you out, for example?'

His face darkened. 'That's got fuck-all to do with you! Or anyone else,' he added with a quick side glance at his wife.

I looked at her, too. There was a strange blankness about her expression, as though what was being said didn't concern her, as though indefinable sounds were coming from far away while she was planning her next run up to the Sandvik weather vane. Even though she was in the doorway now and they were standing next to each other like caricatures of Winnie the Pooh and Piglet, there was still a visible distance between them, as if they came from two completely separate universes. But at last she turned her head in his direction, to hear what he had to say.

He opened his mouth to say something, but I was quicker. 'Your daughter from Haugesund has gone missing, Robert. That's what this is about. If you can just tell me if you have any idea where she is or if there's something she reacted to that might lead us in the right direction, then I won't be back here again once she's found. You can be quite sure of that.'

'Quite?' he repeated sarcastically.

'I—'

But he raised a hand. 'I can only repeat what I told you yesterday. When she showed up here I hadn't seen her for many years, and I didn't want anything to do with her, either. I made it as clear to her then as I'm doing to you now: piss off and don't show your face here again! Since then I haven't seen anything of her. Seen or heard!' He pointed to the gate. 'Now get out before I bloody throw you out.'

'And Andreas? Don't you think he wants to get to know his sister?'

'Half-sister,' Liv said pensively, as though she were only tasting the word and whatever it might involve.

'What you don't know can't hurt you,' Robert said.

'That's what the priest said, as he poured aquavit into the altar wine.'

'Piss off, Veum! Unless…'

'Yes, unless…?'

'Take it as a warning.' He turned round, put his arm around his wife and pulled her inside. Now I could see the emblem on his jacket. It was a stylised Viking head and helmet. The helmet had a sun cross on the side, and on the banners above and below it said: *MC BACCHUS NORWAY*.

As he closed the door I shouted after them: 'But they got him in the end, too. The priest, that is.' To the closed door, I added: 'And did him for driving under the influence.'

But no one was listening.

14

Rain and income tax arrears are among the surest signs of autumn in Bergen, as in so many other places. The following day there was thick cloud and the intervals between the showers were slightly longer. The rain clouds drifted over the town in a scattered formation and you never knew when they would be over you, just like the deadlines for tax arrears at this time of the year.

For the second time in two days I dropped by the Police HQ in Bergen, but this time I had an appointment with Inspector Atle Helleve. He spoke with a refined Voss accent and received me in his usual genial way, as though he had poured himself a tankard of freshly brewed Voss beer and was ready for the year's first sheep's head. His luxuriant beard suited a representative of the generations who had eaten sheep's head since the days when Odin, Thor and Freyr were celebrated as you approached the darkest period of the year.

The reason I wanted to talk to him today was that, to my knowledge, he was a central member of the group investigating biker crime in Norway. Such activities were apparently still peripheral in Bergen, but there had been a few cases in the media in recent years, which suggested there might be changes on the way in this part of the country as well.

He listened attentively to what I had to say, about Emma Hagland's disappearance and about my confrontation with her father the previous evening, which had culminated in a clear threat, or so I perceived it, not least because of the milieu to which he obviously belonged.

'MC Bacchus,' he said. 'Yes, we know about them. They're fairly new in town, although some of its members have a background in other clubs. It was founded about four or five years ago. They have a clubhouse down by the sea in Morvik, Åsane. They took the name from a Canadian club, and I assume they must be in contact with them as they're allowed to use the name, albeit with Norway attached. You know the expression a "one-percenter club", do you?'

'Yes. Most of the bikers are respectable, law-abiding citizens. It's the one percent up to no good who always appear in the media.'

'Exactly. Hells Angels are the most notorious of these organisations. The Bandidos are another. It's hard to say where Bacchus fits into this scenario. From an international perspective, it's a small club with its base in Canada, as far as I know. But there could be links not even we know about. In Canada it's considered a one-percenter, anyway.'

'And what sort of crime are we talking about?'

'Heavies. Debt collection. Related threats and criminal damage. If one of these gangs takes over a debt in the black market you'd better watch out when you leave the house, and they're not bothered about calling on you at home, either.'

'Fortunately it's been years since I could afford to go into debt.'

Helleve smirked. 'In recent years we've also uncovered drug smuggling and dealing activities among bikers. By and large the MC community distances itself from heroin, but the importation and sale of hash, amphetamines and cocaine have been linked to ... well, at least some members of such clubs.'

'Does that apply to Bacchus as well?'

He suddenly seemed hesitant. 'Not at the moment. But we have them under surveillance, so to speak.'

'Really?'

'I can't say any more than that, Varg.'

I waited, but he just motioned me on to the next question. 'Anything else?'

'A name. Robert Høie Hansen mean anything to you?'

'No, I'm afraid not. You know, in these clubs they try to keep most things a secret. It's almost impossible to obtain a list of members. So you have to use undercover officers, electronic surveillance, phone tapping and so on, but you need strong, well-grounded suspicions to get the court to support such activities, and we don't have them here. Yet.'

'So you're recommending I...?'

'I wouldn't recommend you fall out with anyone from these clubs, Varg. That's about as much as I can tell you. But as we always say, if you should stumble over anything you think could benefit us, we'd be more than pleased to hear from you.'

'And if I should fall under one of their front wheels?'

'Just give us a ring.'

Back on the street, I decided to have another stab at Møhlenpris. There were a small number of firms renting premises in the Industrihus and, funnily enough, one of them was called Bacchus Bergen, and was owned by Knut Moberg. According to the voicemail on his phone he should be back in his office by now. Perhaps it wasn't such a good idea to phone and announce my arrival in advance, so I decided to take the risk and visit.

I crossed the Nygårdshøyde part of town, walked through the pedestrian tunnel under the Historical Museum and headed for the Industrihus. It was on the slope between Torborg Nedreaas' gate and Professor Hansteens gate, with entrances at the top and bottom. I found the name Bacchus Bergen on a noticeboard: the office was on the second floor from street level, by the slip road to Puddefjord Bridge.

The door was locked, but there was a bell beside a sign saying *RING HERE*. Furthermore I noticed there was a little peephole in the door so that the person inside could see who was ringing. I followed the instructions and watched the little glass eye expectantly.

About a minute went by before the door opened and a person I assumed was Knut Moberg stood in the doorway. 'Yes?'

'Your voicemail said you were back in the office today. Have you got a moment?'

'What's the name?'

'Veum. I called you yesterday.'

He automatically stepped back and tried to close the door, but I could be the pushy salesman if I wanted, so I leaned against it and followed him in before he had a chance to complete his action. We ended up standing face to face.

'What the hell is this?'

'I'm sure we have something to discuss.'

Knut Moberg was like someone out of a Dressmann fashion advert – he wore a grey suit, white shirt and dark-red tie, and stood alongside a small, round picture of a chateau with the label *Cheval Blanc 1990* in the centre. He was about forty years old, with dark, slicked-back hair and a narrow, not unappealing face; I imagined he had more charm at his disposal than was in evidence with me. But he obviously knew his audience, and I was not among those in the stalls but firmly placed in one of the rows at the very back.

The office around him was furnished spartanly. A modest number of wine bottles was displayed on bare wooden shelves. On the walls there were large posters for a variety of wines, mostly Saint-Émilion, but I also saw some advertisements for products from Pomerol. Over by the window, which looked out onto the bridge and the mountain across the fjord, was a desk with a telephone, a laptop, a small printer and whatever else was necessary to run a wine agency single-handed.

I went for a punt from the side line. 'What's your connection with the motorbike club, Bacchus Norway?'

Bewildered, he looked at me. 'Who?'

'Haven't you patented your name?'

He splayed his hands. 'Bacchus and wine go hand in hand. There are restaurants and bars that use the name, but Bacchus Bergen is mine.'

'So Bacchus Norway is up for grabs?'

'I simply don't understand what you're on about, Veum. What do you want?'

'As I told you on the phone yesterday … I met your wife then, too. Didn't she mention it?'

'My wife? No.'

'But this is about your tenant from earlier this autumn, Emma Hagland.'

'Yes, I got that,' he answered with a taut expression. 'I've said all I have to say on that matter. I have no idea why she moved, where she went or anything.'

'My impression is that you have a good relationship with your tenants, Moberg.'

'Good relationship – what do you mean? I have no … relationship with them.'

'Take it positively! You don't want to be one of those crabby landlords no one has a good word for, do you? You give them wine, as well.'

'Do I?'

'Yes, you do. But perhaps you regard giving them a bottle of French wine as a present a marketing ploy?'

'Who said I … ?' He didn't finish the sentence.

'You gave one to Kari, didn't you?'

He clenched his lips together and said nothing.

'Kari Sandbakken. One of the three girls on the floor below you … where there are now two. And it's impossible to get in touch with Kari, incidentally.'

'Right.' Now his face was so taut the skin looked like it might tear.

'But maybe she's back now.'

He sent me a measured glare. 'I still have no idea what you're talking about. Could you please leave now?'

'Emma told a friend that her landlord – and that's you she was referring to – had been touchy-feely, but she'd put you in your place and afterwards everything was fine.'

'What? Touchy-feely!'

'That was the word she used. We know all about that, Moberg. It's not that unusual. You hear about it and read about it in the papers. A landlord trying it on, a bit of extra attention, maybe a slight reduction in the rent.'

His face went scarlet. 'OK! I didn't do that, and definitely not with…'

'Definitely not with … Emma?'

'Veum!' He pointed to the door.

'But with … Do you know if she's at home now?'

'Who?'

'Kari Sandbakken.'

He glowered at me. 'What the hell are you insinuating? And by the way … none of my tenants is obliged to register. You can find that out for yourself.'

'And, if not, I can talk to your wife again. She might've seen her.'

He took a small step forwards, still red-faced. 'Let me spell this out to you, Veum. If I hear you've been bothering my wife, or for that matter any of my tenants, I won't answer for the consequences.'

'Then you might ring MC Club Bacchus Norway?'

'As I said…'

'You can probably fix up a mutually beneficial sponsorship agreement.'

'Oh, what's the point? I'll ring the police.'

'Fine by me. They know what I'm doing.'

'The police?'

'Yes.'

I left him to chew on that. Perhaps it would force him to come clean. And perhaps it wouldn't.

15

Kari Sandbakken, it transpired, was an attractive, dark-haired young woman, dressed in tight black trousers and a rust-red blouse. But she opened the door to me with a look that came straight from the North Pole with no stop-over; and she wasn't particularly talkative either.

I explained to her who I was and why I was there.

'Yes, Helga said someone had been here.'

'That was me,' I said with a gentle smile, not that it helped in the slightest. 'Have you anything to add?'

'About Emma? I never got close to her.'

'Why not?'

'She and Helga got on best.'

'Any reason for that?'

'No comment.' With that she began to close the door.

'What are you studying? Comparative politics?'

'I beg your pardon?'

'You already talk like a politician.'

'Thank you and goodbye, *herr* Veum.'

I quickly countered: 'And why does your landlord give you such expensive wine?'

This time her look came from the far side of the moon. She opened her mouth, then decided not to dignify me with an answer. Instead she slammed the door and there I was, hoist with my own petard. Whatever 'hoist' meant and whatever a 'petard' was. This wasn't one of my finest moments, anyway.

For a moment I considered going upstairs to see Ellisiv Moberg in the hope of being asked in for a glass of wine. But from recent experience I suspected I would have the door slammed in my face there, too, so I quietly went down to the street, wondering if there was anywhere else I could go and make a fool of myself.

'MC Bacchus Norway perhaps?

Hardly.

I went back to my office, opened the bottle of aquavit I kept in a desk drawer, held it to my nose and lingeringly breathed in the aroma. But I put it back in the drawer without tasting it. Instead I rang Sølvi Hegge at her office in Bryggen, across the bay from where I was sitting, and asked if I could drive her home after work.

'You'd like some dinner, in other words?' she replied.

'I wouldn't say no. And some afters?'

'Let's see what we can rustle up.'

We chuckled in unison. It had been like this between Sølvi and me ever since the moment we met. A couple of years ago she had been involved in a case I was working on. Her husband had been killed and I managed to reveal the guilty party. We found the right wavelength and, afterwards bed – it had happened faster than I was used to, not that I was particularly upset.

We agreed a time to meet and I spent the interim searching the net for all the names I had come across so far. Most of the hits were for Liv Høie Hansen, but that was all the local race results. She had participated in the Stoltzekleiven run fifteen times and, according to one article in a Bergen newspaper, she had completed twenty-five marathons. That was four years ago. It was my guess she had increased the number considerably since then. MC Bacchus Norway was mentioned in a list of motorbike clubs in Bergen suspected of defining themselves as one-percenters, but that was all. Knut Moberg was interviewed briefly in a wine column where he introduced a selection of classic Bordeaux wines he had in his range. In the photo his hair was thicker and he was younger, but by no more than five years, according to the date.

I didn't get a lot further. I picked up Sølvi as arranged, by the Holy Cross Church at a quarter past four. She popped into a shopping centre in Morvik and emerged holding two plastic carrier bags, as heavy as telephone directories, with leeks poking out, revealing that she had primarily bought food.

Back in Saudalskleivane Helene was already home from school. She was eleven and had her own house key, which she told me about with obvious pride.

While her mother insisted on taking charge of kitchen operations, Helene and I went to the sitting room, where she brought me up to date on her progress in various school activities, and her enthusiastic chatter made me feel for the first time that day like a moderately alive human being after all.

A supper of oven-baked cod filets, leeks and a wide variety of root vegetables was on the menu, and actually there was afters as well, once Helene had gone to bed. Nevertheless I got up afterwards, kissed Sølvi goodnight and drove my car home at around midnight because I had made a decision. The following day I was going to Haugesund. I had no option.

16

When I left for Haugesund on Thursday morning there was a nip in the air and glimpses of sunshine between the showers. November hadn't made up its mind yet. Was it going to be autumn or winter?

What most people considered to be progress had reduced the number of ferries between Bergen and Haugesund to one. The crossing between Halhjem and Sandvikvåg was still long enough for me to swallow a cup of pitch-black coffee and a lukewarm hot dog while reading the day's *Bergensavisen*. The headline on the front page was 'BOXES GIVE GIGANTIC YIELD – and now there might be twice as many'. It turned out to be about automatic traffic cameras and the revenue from the grey speed camera boxes that had sprung up in and around Bergen over recent years, like wild plants the transport minister had sown. I noted that the stretch of road between Bergen and Os, which I had just driven, was the most lucrative and hoped I had kept to the speed limit.

In Stord there were the usual traffic delays because of road works, but by ten I had at least reached the bottom of the Bømlafjord tunnel, 260 metres beneath sea level, and could start the ascent to Sveio and the districts south of Haugesund. I passed Haraldshaugen at around eleven and took out the directions Norma had given me, to a white timber house in Gange-Rolvs gate, which, after a bit of to-ing and fro-ing, I eventually found.

It was clear that I was in the royal section of the town because the nearest street names included Magnus Berrføtt, Olav Kyrre and Queen Gyda. As far as I could remember, Gange-Rolv was identical with the legendary Rollo, the founder of Normandy, who was from Vigra, by Ålesund. Whether he had ever walked these parts, I had no idea, but

Haugesund at any rate was situated by the sound that in those days was called *Nordvegen*, the North Way, and was the origin of most of the foreign forms of the country's name – Norwegen, Norway, Norvège; simplified under Danish rule to Norge. For its part, Haugesund had registered the trademark of Harald Fairhair, the king who in the ninth century unified the Norway of the time into one kingdom and who died hereabouts, both of which were commemorated by the Haraldshaugen monument.

My half-sister opened the door and hesitated for a second or two before giving me a good hug, as though it were natural, we had been close family for years and it was always so nice to see each other again.

'Come in, Varg, and I'll put some coffee on. I suppose you'd like a cup?'

'Yes, please.'

I hung up my coat, kicked off my shoes and followed her through on my stockinged feet. We came into a clean, well-kept kitchen with a view of a trim garden, where only November's pale-red roses were still flowering, and even those wanly. Soon they too would be just memories.

She put on the coffee machine, took a tin of biscuits from a cupboard and set the table. 'Actually, it's unbelievable to have you here,' she said with a soft smile. 'I'll take you to Ingeborg's afterwards, and I've sorted out a room for you upstairs if you want to stay overnight.'

'Thank you. I don't know if that'll be necessary.'

'And I've invited a second cousin to join us this evening. Ruth Kjærstad.'

'A second cousin? How did you get in contact with her?'

'You know, Haugesund isn't such a big town, and we were both busy with the Norwegian Women's Public Health Association in the early 1960s. Even though she's almost twenty years younger than me we became close friends, unaware that we were related. When I returned from Bergen, after the meeting with our mother, I told her. She said her own mother had a cousin in Bergen, and when we exchanged names and she had mentioned this to *her* mother, it turned out that we were actually related. That came as a nice surprise to both of us, and thereafter we've been even closer than before.'

She smiled a little excitedly and carried on: 'It was when her aunt married that, well, *our* mother – yours and mine – came to Haugesund, in 1942. I thought it might be interesting to hear what she has to say … for us both.'

'Yes, indeed.' I hesitated, but had long realised that Norma Johanne Bakkevik was not the kind to take no for an answer, so I dismissed any further resistance and concentrated on the coffee and the biscuits that had now appeared on the table.

'Can you tell me a bit about this Ingeborg before we meet her, so that I'm prepared? I understood she wasn't in such good shape. Wasn't that how you put it?'

'Yes, I…' She stared into the distance, somewhat resigned. 'As I told you last time, Emma grew up on Karmøy, in a place called Velle. When she was in the ninth year at school they moved to Haugesund. So Ingeborg was alone with her from the time she was two, and Emma must've had a difficult childhood. She was bullied at infant school, and later too. It was only when she was in upper secondary that she seemed to be able to put that behind her. But this was hard on Ingeborg, of course. Time and again she tried to take it up with the school management, with other parents, with any authorities that were accessible, but no one seemed to take it seriously. She felt as if she was banging her head against the wall and gradually it began to take its toll on her as well. She went to the doctor and was prescribed tranquilisers. She became more and more dependent on them. In the end what the doctor gave her wasn't enough, and I'm afraid her main source for pills is now the black market.'

'Just pills though? Nothing stronger?'

'Not as far as I know.' She looked at me sadly. 'But … I promised my friend, when she was at death's door, that I would take care of her and I've tried as hard as I could … to support her. And Emma.'

'So how did Emma react to her mother's condition?'

'Well, there was a lot of arguing, and that was probably the main reason she left so quickly for Bergen after she had finished school.'

'Has the mother got a profession?'

'No. When she met ... Robert, she was working on a supermarket till, and she continued to do so after she was on her own. For a few years.'

'Surely she got child maintenance from the father?'

She heaved a sigh. 'No, that was the whole point. She broke completely with him. Reverted to her maiden name, gave it to Emma, and she refused to let him pay any maintenance, if he had ever offered it. I took this up with her, of course, but she said: "If he pays maintenance he has some rights of ownership over her. And he's not getting that!" She was very clear about it. Unmoveable. Now she's living off the dole.'

'I doubt that's sufficient for a large consumption of pills.'

'No...' She paused as if taking time to think.

'Has she any other sources of income?' When she didn't reply, I added: 'How old is she?'

'Forty-something.'

'Well...' I had met prostitutes who were fully active at that age, although I didn't mention this to Norma. 'We'll have to hear what she has to say.'

'I don't think you can subject her to an interrogation, Varg. She'll soon start bristling.'

'Yes, of course. But does she know about me? You said she did the last time we spoke.'

'Yes, she knows that I've asked for help. But she doesn't know who you are or what you do. I told her I would contact someone I knew in Bergen and get help like that ... to find out where Emma ... or ... what could've happened.'

'For the moment I'm actually a bit stumped. It's rare for anyone to disappear as completely as Emma has.'

'Does that mean ... Do you think she could be the victim of ... a crime?'

'I hope not. But you can never be sure, of course, before you have the facts.'

She finished her cup of coffee. 'Then I don't think we should delay. Let's go to Ingeborg's so that you can chat to her. Perhaps she can give us a lead anyway. Something that has wider implications than I've imagined.'

'There's one thing I'd like to know more about before we go to see her. What was the reason for the complete rupture between her and her husband seventeen years ago?'

Once again her face grew sad and she leaned forwards across the table as if to signal that what she was going to say was between us and shouldn't be passed on to a third party. 'She – Ingeborg – found out that he, Robert, had been involved in what was regarded as a rape case … It happened where he comes from – Buvik, in Ryfylke. But it never went to court because of the tragic circumstances. This is what suddenly came out, and when she asked Robert about it – well, demanded an explanation from him – they had such a bust-up that everything was lost in the process.'

'So what you're saying is that … previously everything had been fine?'

'I wasn't so close to them during those years, but … this was definitely the trigger.'

'Do you know how she found out?'

'Not the details, but it must've been pretty dramatic from what I gleaned.'

'Well, I'll have to see if it's possible to find out any more on that point.'

'But I still don't see how it could have anything to do with Emma's disappearance so many years later.'

'No, that's what I'll have to try and clarify.' I reflected for a moment. 'But he's got a new wife and a son in Bergen. What about Ingeborg? Has she found anyone new?'

'No, no established relationships at any rate. During the first few years after the break-up she was focused on doing the best she possibly could for Emma. Not least because she didn't even want child maintenance from him. Then she started to go to pieces, and the men she met were of the more unreliable variety, too. She's lived alone ever since. With Emma until this summer, that is.'

'And do you know any more about this rape case?'

'No, she never wanted to discuss it, and it's not very widely known. There was nothing in the papers because it was never reported.'

'And the victim?'

'The girl who was raped?'

'Yes.'

'She's alive. Lives on the island of Karmøy. That's what triggered the whole business. They met her. But I can't bear to talk about it, Varg. It's such a horrid story and it's obnoxious to think that the guilty person's still free – out there.' She looked out of the kitchen window. Outside, we saw an apple tree, all its summer leaves gone except for a few yellow stragglers, like splodges on a not always temperate painter's palette.

'The bastard,' she said under her breath.

'So if I want to try to find out more about this rape, who should I talk to?'

She stared into the air. 'Erm … I once talked to a journalist from the local Ryfylke newspaper. He's probably retired now. He was related to, erm, Veslemøy, I think her name was. A distant relative. You could try him, of course – if it's at all connected with this.'

I took out my notepad. 'Does he have a name?'

'Mm … what was it now? I'm so bad with names now. Ola or Olav, was it? And then Haugane. I think it was Ola.'

I jotted it down. 'You know, Mum came from Hjelmeland. We often went there in the summer and I remember her father very well, Sverre Moland, who'd been a vet there for ever. I can't quite place Buvik though.'

She looked at me sadly. 'Yes, I never got to meet him. My grandparents – in my adopted family, that is – came from Bokn and Haugalandet.'

'But I'm sure our paths have crossed a few times. Without either of us knowing.'

'I've thought about that, of course. Many times.'

'Buvik,' I repeated.

'Buvik, yes. It's further to the north. Between Strand and Nesvik, to stick with ferry terminals, and then towards the fjord. It's just a little village. I suppose if they went out, dancing and so on, they would've gone to Sand. The chapel, however, wasn't far away.'

'No, I seem to remember that. When did this rape happen?'

'In 1975 it must've been.'

I had a go at something I was poorly equipped to deal with: mental arithmetic. '1975? But then Robert can't have been more than … fifteen, can he?'

Her face went serious. 'Something like that.'

'Hm.'

'I apologise for repeating myself, Varg, but I can't see how this old business could have anything to do with Emma, unless it was what initially made her childhood and teenage years so difficult.'

'And it's exactly this kind of thing, my dear … sister, that can leave such deep scars, and create such deep ruts that it can be difficult to get out of them if you want to change direction. If you see what I mean.'

'Sort of.' She got up. 'Shall we go?'

'Yes, let's. Is it far?'

'We're going by car, I assume.'

'OK, let's do that. Thank you for the coffee and biscuits.'

'Pleasure. It would've been nicer if the circumstances had been different.'

On the front doorstep we felt one of the North Sea's freshest winds blowing into the town. You could say a lot about Haugesund, I supposed. The sky was high above the town, and the light strong, but there was invariably a wind there. There were no mountains high enough to protect the town, as in Bergen. The winds came straight in off the sea, like the shoals of herring in the nineteenth century, allowing Hauge-sund to spring up on the old historic sites and turning it into a town where the salty smell of fish never meant anything but money. The herring were still there, but the oil industry had taken over the stream of money – and made a return, little by little.

I held the car door open for her, got behind the wheel and followed her directions.

17

It wasn't far. We went down to Byparken and turned right twice. Then we followed Haugevegen past Skåre Church and on to the tired-looking blocks of flats at the end of the street, one green, the others originally white, now closer to a dirty grey. Norma explained that locally they were known as the 'Stack'em Inns'. 'In more polite circles the Council Tenement Quarter'.

'And which circles are we in?'

'You'll have to answer that yourself.'

'The funnier name was "Stack 'em Inn", anyway.'

'So you've made your choice,' she said in a caustic tone I hadn't noticed previously.

I parked on the opposite side of the street, and she took us to the yard between two of the buildings. On one side we were facing the busy street of Karmsundsgate, which I had driven along into the town earlier in the day.

She chose one of the entrances to the green building, and we took the stairs up a floor. There was no nameplate on the door, but Norma said this was the one and pressed the bell. After a while we heard a shuffle of footsteps inside and the door was opened a fraction.

The woman in the doorway looked first at me, without any kind of reaction. Then she shifted her gaze to Norma and smiled wanly. 'Hi, Aunty.'

'Hi, Ingeborg. Have you got time for a chat?'

She eyed me. 'Who's this?'

'Varg Veum. He's helping me look for Emma.'

'Oh, yes.' She nodded in my direction, as if to say she knew who I was. Then she opened the door wide. 'Come in.'

We hung up our outdoor clothes in the little hall and followed her into what was clearly the sitting room. It was furnished simply with a low, scarred coffee table, red furniture with obvious signs of wear and tear, a TV set that was at least ten years old in one corner and a bookcase on which there were some artificial flowers, family photos and a couple of porcelain animals. Among the photos I recognised one of Emma I had been given by Norma, cut from a strip and inserted in a frame with another childhood photo I assumed was her. In the middle of the coffee table was a big round ashtray, but there were only a few cigarette ends in it, as though it had been emptied recently. Next to it was a used coffee cup, empty as far as I could see. The only decoration on the wall was a calendar published by Haugaland Kraft, an energy company, with local photos as the motif. Over the dowdy flat hung an indefinable but nonetheless recognisable smell I thought I had experienced before: a mixture of coffee, smoke and damp clothes that had been left out to dry for too long.

There was an air of wounded beauty about Ingeborg Hagland. Her dark-blonde hair hung loose over her shoulders and was prevented from falling over her face by a couple of hairgrips. Her features bore the marks of slightly too many sleepless nights and her eyes were bloodshot and matt. With a pinched expression, she took a packet of cigarettes from the pocket of her loose, moss-green velour jacket, poked a cigarette between her lips and lit it with a small black lighter bearing the Statoil logo on the side.

'Sit yourselves down,' she said, pointing towards the sitting room. We did as she said, Norma only after brushing down the chair.

'Would you like some coffee?'

'No, thanks, Ingeborg. We've just had a cup,' Norma answered.

Ingeborg turned to me. 'I've got some beer as well, if you would prefer.'

'No, thanks,' I said, and added: 'I'm driving.'

She was still looking at me. 'Have you found Emma yet?'

'No, I'm afraid not. That's why we're here, fru Hagland.'

'Fru Hagland!' she snorted. 'That's a good one. Just call me Ingeborg.

Everyone does. But how can I help? I haven't heard a word from her since she left…' She waved her cigarette northwards, and the smoke lingered around her head, like a withered halo. '…For Bergen,' she concluded with a little yawn. 'Not so much as a single text!' she continued, slipping her hand into the other jacket pocket, fishing out a slim black phone and holding it out to me as a kind of proof.

'But you've texted her?'

'Course I have! I want to know how my girl is!' She swallowed. 'Sure you don't want a beer?'

'Yes.'

'Yes, you're sure?'

I nodded.

'I'll have one anyway, then!' She placed the glowing cigarette on the edge of the ashtray and got to her feet.

'Ingeborg,' Norma said.

But she was already on her way into the hall and the kitchen, where we heard the sound of a fridge being opened and closed, a can of beer fizzing and a glass being placed on the worktop and filled. Norma sent me a resigned look and shook her head from side to side.

Ingeborg Hagland returned with a full tumbler in one hand and the open can in the other. She held it out to me. 'Sure?'

'He's already said no, Ingeborg!' Norma said reprovingly. 'Several times.'

'Yeah, yeah, nagger! I'm allowed to offer, aren't I?' She looked askance at me, which in a different context could have signalled she was flirting with me, not that I considered it likely I would have responded with anything other than a cool distance.

She plumped down on the sofa, took a swig from the glass, placed the can on the table and focused on us again. 'I don't like it that you can't find her.'

'No, nor do we,' I said. 'I called on your ex-husband…'

'Ex-husband!' she exclaimed with contempt at what was clearly a much too refined title for him.

'And his family.'

She snorted, still offended by my terminology.

'And in fact she had visited them, not with a very positive outcome unfortunately.'

'No, I can imagine! Is he still with that bitch?'

'You're referring to…?'

'Liv Larsen! She threw herself at him the first moment she saw him out there on…' Another wave of her cigarette in the geographically correct direction. 'Karmøy.'

'Really? Mm, I could hear from her dialect that she was from there, too.'

'It was her that set it all off, and afterwards … Afterwards she bloody went off with him!' She took a long drag of her cigarette. 'Well, after I'd thrown him out, that is.'

'I see. And why did you do that?'

'Why?' She turned to Norma. 'Surely you've told him all that. About the bastard I was married to?'

Norma returned her look, but with a reserved expression. 'No more than the bare minimum, Ingeborg. Emma's my worry. And yours!'

'Emma!' Now she was waving her cigarette wildly. This time the smoke made me think of a bridal veil that had hung too long in the wardrobe, grey with dust and disintegrating. 'She's always missed her father – even if he never did her any good.'

'It's my understanding she didn't have the slightest inkling she had a half-brother in Bergen.'

'Slightest inkling! She was told many years ago.' She twisted her mouth to the side and raised her voice into a higher register. '"Oh, Mummy, can we go and visit them? I'd like to meet him so much! Fancy me having a brother!"'

I glanced at Norma. She was following everything Ingeborg said and for an instant a thought struck me: how many siblings are out there who never meet? Who don't even know about each other…?

'But the two of you never did? Visit them, I mean?'

'Visit them? I was absolutely determined to keep her as far away from that bastard as I could! He didn't even pay her child maintenance.'

'At your behest, I understand.'

'Yes, and so what?' She looked at Norma as if to provoke her into protesting.

'Well, he clearly wasn't interested in having any contact with her, either,' I said. As she didn't react, I added: 'At any rate he rejected her when she went to their house.'

'Yes! That was good anyway.' She seemed to be mulling over something.

'But ... could Emma have tried to contact them before? The brother maybe?'

'Half-brother!' she said, correcting me. 'Not as far as I know.'

'Sure?'

Her eyes flitted about and she shrugged.

'I've lost the thread here a bit, Ingeborg. You said Liv – who's married to him now – was the one who set everything off. And afterwards she ran away with him. What did you mean by that?'

'What did I mean? It was her who invited us down there, to that ... Veslemøy!' She had a talent for spitting out the names she didn't like. 'Down there in Skudeneshavn! I'll never set foot there again.'

'Veslemøy. The woman who...?'

'Yes! Her.' She tossed her head in Norma's direction. 'Aunty's kept you well informed, I can see.'

'Ingeborg,' Norma said forcefully. 'I was just thinking about...'

'Yes, I know.' She turned to her. 'You were just thinking about Emma. Everyone's thinking about Emma. No one's thinking about me!'

'Yes, they are, Ingeborg. I promised your mother...'

'Yeah, yeah, yeah. You promised my mother you'd take care of me. And how's it gone? You can see how I look. You know how I live. Where I live. Are you happy with the result, eh?'

'Well, I'm ... happy...' Norma looked at her in desperation. 'What should I say?'

'But,' I broke in. 'This incident your husband had been involved in ... As far as I understand, it was never reported.'

'No, thank Christ for that!'

'So why did you react so violently?'

'React? It was her who reacted.'

'Her? You mean Veslemøy?'

She gave a quick nod. 'As if the hounds of hell were after her! And that was when I saw. The state she was in. And then I didn't want … He wasn't going to get anywhere near Emma. Surely you can see that? She was only two years old.'

'Yes, but … Now, I don't know your husband or—'

'Stop calling him my husband!'

'Fine. I don't know either Robert Høie Hansen—'

Another interruption, but this time with the familiar contempt: 'Robert Hansen!'

'Or about the incident. OK, let's drop that side of the matter. It's my understanding that…'

Again she distorted her mouth, but this time it was my Bergensian phrasing she was parodying: 'It's my understanding blah blah blah. Is that the only way you can start a sentence? It's my understanding this, it's my understanding that … You haven't bloody understood anything at all!' She took her glass, drained it, smacked it down hard on the table and filled it again from the can.

'What I was trying to say,' I persisted patiently, 'is that I've heard she was bullied at school. Emma, that is.'

At once she changed character. Her face softened, and there was something sombre and baleful in her eyes. 'Yes. That's right. On Karmøy we changed schools twice. At the school for older kids it was even worse, but no one tackled the issue. Not the school, nor the parents.'

'That's what I heard.'

'It was only when we moved here and she went to a higher school that things got better. When she and a girl called Åsa became friends. They supported each other. They stuck with each other. I remember … they were obsessed with fashion and clothes, which girls are, and she came home with some wonderful designs she and Åsa had made. But then…' She paused.

'Yes?'

'It was me who had supported her, as far as I was able, throughout her whole childhood; it was me she turned against, when things started to improve. I was given the blame for everything that had gone wrong! And there was nothing wrong with Daddy – Robert.'

As gently as I could, I said: 'But she didn't know him.'

'No, she didn't, so why should he suddenly become her hero? Prince Charming. Daddy in Bergen. I'll tell you what he did ... That's what I should've said. This year wasn't the first time she'd been to Bergen. When they were sixteen they caught the coastal bus up there – her and Åsa – to find him.'

'Right.'

'But ... she came home pretty disappointed. They hadn't found him. Or no one was at home. What do I know? We never talked about it again.'

'I've talked to Åsa. I can ring her again to find out what she can tell us.'

She looked at me in silence, as if to say she had said everything she wanted to say.

'This Skudeneshavn business,' I said.

She fluttered a hand in Norma's direction. 'You'd better ask her. She can tell you as well as I can.'

I looked at Norma. She nodded slowly while raising a hand in defence.

'You can both go now,' said Ingeborg Hagland.

I leaned across the table. 'But you want us to find Emma, don't you?'

That kindled the fire in her eyes again. 'Of course I want you to find her! My daughter!' she said with a stifled sob. 'I want her back of course, don't I.'

'Good. I'll do everything in my power to make sure that happens.'

But leaving the flat in Haugevegen, I was even less sure about what was what in this case. For some reason it seemed more complicated now than it had done when I took on the job, and I was no closer to working out where Emma was. Norma didn't appear to be particularly upbeat, either. She didn't say a word until we were in the car and I had started the engine. And she didn't take the initiative then, either.

18

'She called you Aunty,' I said.

'Yes, the poor dear.' She waited a while before continuing. 'Ingeborg didn't have an easy childhood, either. She grew up with a single mother, there was no father at all, she was frowned upon by the family and had no security net. I got to know her mother simply because I was an active volunteer worker, through NWPHA, as I told you before, and so I often visited them. That was how I became a kind of aunty.'

'Sounds as if Emma has quite a pattern to follow. By which I mean growing up without a father and being a typical victim of bullying.'

'Yes, I'm afraid that was the case with Ingeborg, too.'

'I didn't want to draw attention to it there, but I noticed her eyes. And she had a very short fuse. Do you know what's she's on?'

'Various tranquilisers, I believe. Valium, Vival, what do I know? And maybe other drugs, too. But, to my knowledge, only pills, often accompanied by alcohol. You saw for yourself...'

'Yes, I did.'

'I don't think she's ever injected herself. I would've noticed.'

'And how does she get hold of this stuff?'

'A variety of places. Even pensioners deal in drugs, I've heard.'

'Yes, they probably do.'

'Anyway ... Haugesund's had the reputation of being a bit of a drugs town for many years, you know.'

'Yes, I do. As a child welfare officer, and as a private investigator, I've been here several times looking for teenagers who've left home and come here, for precisely those reasons. I've been to the saddest places, on Risøy and elsewhere, searching for them. Sometimes I found them, sometimes I didn't.'

'I see.'

'But you assume that a woman like Ingeborg Hagland would look for supplies in this sort of milieu?'

'Yes, as far as illegal drugs go, definitely. She might have a liberal doctor as well.'

'They do exist, people say.'

As I turned into Gange-Rolvs gate, she said: 'What are you going to do now? I'd like to make a little something to eat. Well, it'll be more like a dinner. Hot rissoles at any rate with some garnish.'

I parked by her house. 'I suppose it's too far to go to Skudeneshavn and back, is it?'

'Skudeneshavn? Surely not to Fredly?'

'Fredly?'

'Yes...' She looked a little ashamed. 'That's where she lives, the woman I was talking about earlier, and Ingeborg mentioned – Veslemøy.'

'Yes, that's exactly the person I'd like to have a chat with.'

'But why on earth would you want to? For what purpose, Varg?'

'Well, Ingeborg seemed to suggest there was some kind of link between her and Robert's new wife, Liv. My experience is that in cases like this one, where a young person has gone missing, the strangest things can jump out and hit you along the way. And sometimes they're linked to the disappearance. I like to examine every possibility, let me put it like that. But I can hear you know something about a place called Fredly.'

'I do indeed.' Resignation was in her eyes. 'It's a kind of a home, an institution run by the Inner Mission – the evangelicals – where they take care of people who have come off the rails but whose problems fall outside the health service's usual responsibilities, to put it a little long-windedly. Some are there for shorter periods, as a kind of convalescence or like at a rest home. Others are there for life. Like this Veslemøy.'

'Have you met her?'

'No, never. I've just been told about her. I doubt it would be worth your while going there.'

'Well ... I'd like some background for the questions I'm going to ask Liv Høie Hansen when I return to Bergen. Did you know anything about this link between Robert, his new wife and Ingeborg?'

'Yes, she's spoken about it before, but I couldn't see that it had anything to do with this. By which I mean, Emma.' She sent me a regretful look. 'But if you're really planning to go to Skudeneshavn, I think you should definitely wait until tomorrow, Varg.'

'Alright. So I might call Åsa in Berlin. To hear if she has any more to say in the light of what I know now.'

'Yes, that sounds sensible. Are you coming in?'

'Yes. Thank you.'

This time she put me in the sitting room while she went to the kitchen and rustled up some food. I looked around me. It was a cosy, slightly old-fashioned room with a dining area at one end. The pictures on the walls were mainly oil paintings of various landscapes, some of them mountains, some seascapes.

On one wall there were some family photos that aroused my curiosity. Without any assistance from Norma it was difficult to say for certain who was who, but I assumed a double portrait of an ageing married couple was probably her adoptive parents. There were several photos of a girl at different stages in her life. Judging by the quality, these were more recent pictures, and I presumed they would be of Karen, the grandchild. I spotted a young man in a sailor's uniform on a wedding photo. I guessed that would be Petter, her son, who had died in the Alexander Kielland oil rig accident. In a third photo an easily recognisable Norma was standing between two young women, one of whom I identified from the wedding photo while the other was vaguely reminiscent of Norma herself. If I wasn't much mistaken, one was her daughter-in-law and the other her daughter, Ellen. An older wedding snap showed Norma with her husband, who obviously wasn't alive any longer.

I tore my attention away from the photos, sat down in a nice comfortable chair and rang Åsa Lavik, but this time I didn't get through. All I got was the recorded reply telling me to leave a message or ring back later. I considered the options, then hung up.

Now that I had the phone in my hand I tried Emma's number once again. No answer. I could have carried on down the phone list, from one to the next, but I concluded that enough was enough.

The mobile phone had made it easier to communicate with people, if they were willing. However, for the potential interlocutor it was also easier to see who was ringing and make a decision about whether they wanted to answer or not. Over time I'd had the feeling very few people wanted to talk to me, however nice and friendly I tried to sound. Unless it was my profession that put them off. If someone would accept the bet, I would wager a krone on that.

19

Ruth Kjærstad turned out to be a pleasant lady in her late fifties, not very tall and somewhat rounded at the edges, but with a big smile and open eyes, in which she veritably swallowed me. With an amused side glance she said: 'Fancy having a detective in the family, Norma. A genuine detective.'

'Well, not exactly a Sherlock Holmes,' I said.

'No, but *nevertheless*! This is the first time I've met one anyway.'

'Perhaps you should be pleased about that.'

'I am, of course. It means I've never needed one,' she trilled, spelling out the logic. She placed a welcoming hand on my arm and said: 'What's more we're second cousins, Varg!'

'I've also worked that one out.'

'Mum always talked about her cousin in Bergen with a tone that suggested she was talking about the Merry Widow.'

'Oh, yes?'

'Yes, because now they're all dead, family secrets can be revealed, can't they.' Again I had the sense she was swallowing me with her eyes – from the side, like a freshly smoked bloater.

Norma interceded: 'I suggest we sit at the table first. The food's ready.'

After the failed attempts to contact anyone by phone I had gone for a stroll in the town, down to Smetha Sound, along the quays to Risøy Bridge and finally back along Haraldsgaten. Under the bridge I had seen a gathering of down-and-outs sharing the day's booty, suspiciously eyeing me as I passed. A new undercover officer in town? Or a competitor?

During the walk I had stopped by the not unattractive sculpture of

Marilyn Monroe sited in front of one of the town's most popular hotels, based on the premise that her father had family from Haugesund, which had later been disproved. But Marilyn was sitting there now, like a guest of honour at every single annual film festival since she was unveiled in 1994. Further up, there was a town hall with a pink façade, in a style that made me feel I had been transported back to a 1950s comedy, with Marilyn in the main role. Below the Church of Our Saviour, built in red bricks, stood a verdigris sculpture of two fishermen in sou'westers pointing to what had brought the town its fortune in earlier times: the sea yonder and the mid-nineteenth century's apparently endless shoals of herring.

From there I made my way back to Gange-Rolvs gate, where we now sat around Norma's so-called supper: an abundance of hot rissoles and onions so fresh they were still steaming, a classic shrimp dish with egg, peas and asparagus, a broad selection of herring, as was appropriate in Haugesund, an overflowing cheeseboard and various kinds of jam and marmalade. Our second cousin Ruth's hungry eyes strayed to the table for a while. She clapped her podgy little hands and expressed her speechless admiration for what Norma had served – although speechless was not exactly a word I would use to describe the impression she had made thus far in our acquaintance.

It wasn't long before we were discussing family connections.

'We heard lots of times that Aunty Asta and Uncle Atle were not the only family we had in Bergen, there was also a rather distant cousin of mother's and Aunty Asta's. My mother's name was Tora, and I think she went to visit your mother once when she had been referred to a specialist for an examination at Haukeland Hospital. She always spoke with pleasure about this reckless cousin of hers from Hjelmeland.'

I glanced at Norma. Reckless was not a term I associated with my mother. 'And what did she mean by that?'

Now it was Ruth's turn to glance at Norma. At once her expression changed from being cheerful to something far more serious. 'Well, there was of course the fact that she became pregnant at a very young age. It was her maternal grandmother who helped her when she came here and gave birth at the Spring-Spawning Herring Tariff Foundation Hospital, as it's known.'

'Spring-Spawning Herring Tariff Foundation!' I said. 'That's a mouthful.'

'And the child was of course Norma, who grew up without any contact at all with either her mother or father.'

'But in a good home!' Norma added sharply. 'My adoptive parents were the nicest people in the world.'

'By all means, yes. I haven't said a bad word about them!'

'Perhaps it wasn't the result of any frivolity,' I said. 'Her being seduced by an itinerant preacher.'

'Well, there were enough of those brutes up and down the coast. We've heard many stories about them. I prefer a proper priest from the state church!' Ruth said, looking firmly at both Norma and me.

Norma smirked and half leaned across to me: 'Ruth's married to one.'

'Yes, and what about it?' said our red-cheeked second cousin.

'Just telling Varg.'

'Right.' Ruth took a mouthful of food before continuing: 'But it was probably the wedding during the war she talked most about. In January, 1942. When Aunty Asta and Uncle Atle got married here in Haugesund, before moving to Bergen. Mother was only a year younger than Aunty Asta, and I suppose she'd already started dreaming about getting married herself. In those days, though, when Ingrid came down from Bergen...'

'Alone?'

'Yes.' She looked at me. 'Your father wasn't with her. And this must be where the frivolity comes in. But mother often said ... perhaps this was how it was in big towns.'

Frivolity was not a quality I associated with my mother, either, and Ruth's story seemed more and more fanciful with every word she said.

'There was that saxophone player, of course.'

'Who?' I leaned forwards, my body suddenly rigid.

'You know, my uncle Atle was from Bergen as well. He played in a band himself, and for the wedding he'd invited the musicians he played with to perform at the dance. Mother said she thought the saxophone player was very good-looking, but later, when the young ones got together for a kind of party, he only danced with Ingrid and they left together...'

'I see?'

'Yes, but not in any unseemly way! He accompanied her to her grandmother's house, where she was staying. No scandal at that point. The day afterwards however...'

'Yes?'

'Mother and Grandmother had accompanied Ingrid to the Bergen boat and they couldn't help but notice that the only musician taking the same boat was this saxophone player.'

'Naturally enough, as they came from Bergen.'

'Yes.' Again she turned serious. 'But we all had our own ideas in autumn that same year when we heard that Ingrid, after many years of marriage, had given birth. A little boy, born in October!'

I immediately felt a sort of dizziness come over me, as though I had ventured onto the edge of a precipice I had never been close to before and looked down – not over a bottomless chasm but a landscape I had never previously seen. I could see my sweet mother in front of me, always caring, and my father, Anders Veum the tram conductor, immersed in a book about Norse mythology, much more distant in his demeanour than my mother, bordering on absentminded. Behind them both I glimpsed the shadow of a saxophonist, someone whose photo I had found in the papers my mother had left behind, together with the other musicians from the jazz quintet, the Hurrycanes.

'This uncle Atle ... what was the rest of his name?'

'Atle Eliassen.'

'And did he and your aunt...? Well, they stayed in Bergen, didn't they?'

'Yes, for as long as they lived.'

'They're dead?'

'Yes, they died several years ago. They would've been, erm, in their late nineties now, if they were alive. Aunty Asta was born in 1907.'

'But they have children, I imagine?'

'Yes, a son and a daughter. I can write down their names and addresses, if you want. They're our second cousins as well.'

'The family's growing, I can see.'

I met Norma's eyes. She nodded sadly in return. 'Yes, I've felt that many times,' she said.

'But you're on your own, I understand?' Ruth said.

'On my own? Yes, I don't have any siblings. Apart from Norma. And it's a long time since I got divorced. But I have a son, a daughter-in-law and a little grandchild. They're in Østland.'

'Østland, oh, horror of horrors, my husband used to say, and then he shuddered. He became the resident curate in Mysen, Østland, after he finished his theology studies, and I think the shock of that stayed with him for the rest of his life.'

From then on the conversation moved on to more general topics, and at around ten Ruth politely thanked Norma and said her good-byes, hoping this would not be the last time we met. Before she left she grabbed my arm and whispered, almost confidentially: 'I hope you weren't too shocked by what I told you. About your mother, I mean.'

'Shocked, no … but it did come as a bit of a surprise, I must say. It'll take some time to digest it, for both Norma and me.'

'It wasn't meant nastily.' Her eyes were almost pleading.

'No, no, I understand that. Thank you.'

But after she had gone I wasn't at all sure how I felt. I was left with a numb feeling in my brain, with distant childhood memories once again forcing themselves to the forefront. Was this why I had never seen my mother or father exchanging a caress for as long as they lived, and definitely not while I was watching? Was this why I had sometimes observed some annoyance on my father's side at something she had said, completely out of proportion to her comment, while she had just looked down without answering? And was this why he always turned down the radio as soon as there was anything reminiscent of jazz on, whereas the *Folk Music Half Hour* was played at full blast and resounded around the walls?

When we returned to the sitting room Norma made a beeline for the corner cabinet, opened the door and took out a bottle. 'After that I think we need a *digestif*; what do you reckon, Varg, eh?' She unscrewed the top. 'It's just port, but ... Do you want a glass?'

'Yes, please.' I took out my phone. 'I'll just try and ring Åsa again in Berlin. I didn't manage earlier in the day.'

She nodded, and I tapped in Åsa's number. This time she answered. On hearing who was at the other end she instantly asked: 'Is there anything new? Have you found her?'

'No, I'm afraid not. Nothing.'

'But what could've happened?' She sounded absolutely desperate. 'She can't just have vanished into thin air! She must've left some traces.'

'There'll definitely be some traces. We simply haven't found them yet.'

'What about the police then? They must be able to locate her.'

'Yes, but they're not taking the case very seriously yet. They think she'll turn up. She might just have found herself a ... man.'

'I refuse to believe that. Not Emma. She's not like that. And anyway she'd never have done anything like that without telling someone. She'd definitely have told me – we were such good friends.'

'Yes, that's exactly why I'm ringing you, Åsa.'

'Do you know what? This is making me very nervous indeed! I'm so frightened something might've happened to her.'

Norma placed a well-filled wine glass on the table in front of me, sat down at the other end of the room, raised her port in a toast and sipped with a mellow expression on her face.

'Yes, we're worried, too. Naturally. But ... I'm in Haugesund and earlier today I met Emma's mother. I assume you've met her, too.'

'Yes, I have. Several times. But Emma wasn't happy about inviting me to her place. Where they lived ... I think I'm the only person to have been there, and even I went very few times over the years we knew each other.'

'Her mother said the same – that you and Emma supported each other. You almost took over her role. She was blamed for everything that had gone wrong.'

Åsa was silent for a while. Then she said: 'Yes, but it was her mother who broke up with the father. In fact, she kicked him out. And Emma was never really given a proper explanation as to why. She knew sexual abuse lay at the bottom of it – a rape. And that was why her mother wanted to keep her away from him at all costs.'

'So he never molested her?'

'No, absolutely not! She would've told me. If she'd known.' After another silence she added: 'Unlike *my* father.'

'I see. And … was *he* punished, Åsa?'

'I don't want to talk about it. Not to … a total stranger.'

'No. Fine. But Emma's mother told me you and Emma went to Bergen once to trace her father.'

'Yes, that was an idea we had. I wanted to help her. Things being the way they were with my father, I passionately wanted her to have hers back. To get to know him. Perhaps, despite everything, he had a better life than her mother did.'

'And how did it go?'

There was such a sharp intake of breath that I heard it across the mobile network all the way from Berlin. 'It was dreadful! He refused to talk to us.'

'I see. Did you meet him?'

'No, only the woman he was married to.'

'Liv?'

'I have no idea what her name is. But she opened the door when we rang the bell, somewhere out in Sandviken, I think it was.'

'That's right.'

'When Emma said who she was, the woman told us she would go back in and talk to her husband, and she closed the door in our faces. We stood waiting, and after a while she came back. Emma's father didn't want to speak to her, he'd said. We should just go on our way. What! A sixteen-year-old girl, alone or with a friend, comes all the way from Haugesund and he refuses even to say hello. What kind of father's that? As useless as my own? He would love it if I went to meet him, wherever he is!'

'No explanation?'

'Not a word. The woman just said: "You'd better go". She seemed fine, a bit resigned maybe, as though it hadn't been her decision.' She paused again. 'Emma was utterly shocked. We walked back to the gate and stood there looking at the house, talking about what to do. A head appeared in one of the windows and peered out. It was a boy, around twelve years old. That hurt me so much! It must've been her brother. Or half-brother, to be precise. And they – her outside; him inside – they looked at each other and couldn't exchange a single word because their father was an idiot.'

'And then…?'

'Well, we caught the bus back. Emma hardly said a word all the way home, and later she never wanted to talk about her father. It was as though she had written him off for ever.'

'Nevertheless, she visited him again this year when she came back to Bergen to study.'

'Yes, but isn't it what all you lot always say? Time heals all wounds.'

I thought I just about understood what she meant by 'all you lot', so I refrained from asking her to be more precise. Instead I said: 'And the brother … she didn't try to contact him?'

'No. Or at least she didn't tell me. It wouldn't have been so easy anyway. I doubt he had his own phone at that time, and his mother and father would probably have shielded him if she'd tried to ring him on the landline – or write to him.'

'But now … She called on her father when she came to Bergen. Do you think she could've tried to contact the brother as well?'

'If she had, I think she would've told me.'

'And she didn't?'

'No, I told you that when you called a couple of days ago, didn't I?'

'Yes, you did. I just had a feeling when I met him that there was something he wasn't telling me.'

'OK. In which case I know nothing about that.'

'No. I apologise for disturbing you again, Åsa, but—'

She interrupted me. 'Just ring me whenever, if there's anything at all I can help you with.'

'Thank you.'

We rang off, I put down the phone and seized the glass of port like a drowning man a lifebelt. I raised my glass in a toast to Norma and knocked it back in one.

She arched her eyebrows. 'Another one perhaps?'

I nodded and pushed my glass in her direction. 'Yes, please.'

She poured me another drink, and I said: 'What do you think about what we found out this evening, Norma? About our mother, I mean.'

She slowly shook her head, as if to signal she hadn't digested the information properly yet, either. 'What should I say? I still have the same father and mother, biologically speaking. It must be worse for you having to hear something that casts doubt on who your real father is.'

'Most of all, it's confusing. I mean ... my father, or the one I've always thought was my father, died when I was fourteen, and he always was a little distant. I never really had any proper contact with him. Nonetheless he *is* my father, not this saxophonist I only have some photos of in old newspaper cuttings.'

She nodded. 'A bit like my relationship with my adoptive parents. *They* are *my* parents the way I see it. I arrived as a newborn baby and never called them anything else but Mum and Dad.'

'It also makes me think about my present case. Emma's dad moved out of his home when she was two, and she didn't see him again until she came to Bergen this year. Emma's mother didn't have any new men in her life later, from what I've gathered?'

'No. At least no one fixed, if I can put it like that.'

'There's one thing I'm becoming more and more curious about, and that's this: what was it that led to the dramatic break-up between Emma's father and mother seventeen – yes, seventeen – years ago. And to what extent does that have anything to do with what happened in Buvik in 1975.'

'I just don't understand what it could have to do with Emma's disappearance in 2003.'

'No, nor do I. But maybe I can find out. There are a couple of places...'

'A couple of places...?'

I nodded. 'I'm planning to go to both places tomorrow. To Buvik and Skudeneshavn, if not necessarily in that order.'

It depended on what arrangements I could make, and clearly it was too late to make any now. So I had another glass of port with my hospitable half-sister before withdrawing to the guest room she had prepared for me on the first floor.

Before I went to bed I looked out of the window. The clouds had cleared and there was a vaguely starry sky over Haugesund. But the stars weren't easy to see through the haze of lights from the town, in the same way that young people's dreams were often eclipsed – sometimes disappearing for ever – by the glow from life itself and everything in its wake. During the course of my career, in social services and as a private investigator, I had come across many such fates as Åsa's, and I might well have stumbled across some like Emma's, too, on the odd occasion. They were life's lost souls, migratory birds that had overstayed, unaware that winter was right around the corner, and when it came it was merciless.

20

On the top of Karmsund Bridge you pass right over Nordvegen, the North Way. On a clear day you can see in all directions, so far that you have the feeling the whole of the Norwegian coast is spread out beneath you. This is where they trudged across the ice, the very first migrants to Ultima Thule, clad in furs, frozen, hungry, hunting the fleeing herds of reindeer. This is where later generations came in their rudimentary craft carved out of tree trunks and with primitive oars. This is where the Viking chiefs came, under their broad sails, gathering to fight Harald Fairhair in the ninth century. And this is where bigger and bigger vessels came in the following centuries, driven by sail, steam and, thereafter, diesel engines and electricity. This is where aircraft came and landed at Haugesund Airport, which is safely located on Karmøy, and this is where I was driving my Toyota Corolla one November day in 2003 on my way to Skudeneshavn.

For many Vestlanders Skudeneshavn was a ferry terminal they passed on their way to or from Mekjarvik and Stavanger. Many had been pitched and tossed through heavy sea across Bokna Fjord, one of the many exposed ferry crossings binding Norway together, from Kirkenes in the north down to Randaberg. Many had clung to the railings and drawn the air deep into their lungs when they finally saw land in Skudeneshavn, where they could get behind the wheel of a car or stagger onto land, relieved to have survived another fjord cross-ing between Stavanger and Karmøy. Now plans were well under way for underwater tunnels on this stretch as well. Before very long these ferries would be history and the experience of Skudeneshavn Harbour reserved for those who knew what they were missing.

Like a Sørland town that had drifted up the coast and stranded on the southern side of Karmøy, Skudeneshavn lay facing the greyish-blue sea, a late-summer idyll, even in November. The long, narrow street of Søragadå with its well-preserved, white timber houses, warehouses and marine buildings gave you the feeling you had travelled at least a couple of hundred years back in time, to when there were sailing ships and fishing smacks filling the harbour rather than today's cabin cruisers and island-hoppers. Now the herring shoals had been replaced by tourists, who flocked through Søragadå during the high season and were only very rarely at risk of being hung up to dry or canned.

I had phoned in advance to warn I was on my way. The woman I had spoken to hadn't sounded overly enthused by the purpose of my visit, but as she herself said: 'We don't turn anyone away from Fredly.'

Fredly was discreetly set back from the main road to the ferry, and I had to stop the car, roll down the window and ask a passing young lady with a pram if she could direct me. She smiled and pointed, as if she was directing me to the Lady in the Park, a local tourist attraction. But this was no galleon figurehead from clipper times I was visiting; this was a living woman so damaged by the shipwreck of her own life that no one would dream of erecting her on a rock for public consumption.

I found the two-storey, white timber building at the end of a side road and so high up on the crag that even from the front entrance you could see across the countryside to the west and towards the North Sea, to thousands of fishermen's graves, but also the source of the sudden wealth that had been washing across Norway since the mid-1970s.

Fredly had once been the private residence of the town's richest shipping owner; later it had been left in a will to the Inner Mission, or so I was told by the severely dressed woman who welcomed me after observing me enter through the open door of what a sign informed me was an OFFICE. She introduced herself as Laura Lothe and was wearing a grey skirt that was reminiscent of a uniform, but it wasn't one. She had short, grey hair and sharp eyes looking over her half-moon glasses. On a chain around her neck she had a small, round device, not much bigger than a doorbell, from which I assumed she could receive signals from the residents' personal safety alarms.

She invited me into her office, in which a large picture of Jesus holding a shepherd's crook and surrounded by lambs in a field dominated one wall; bookshelves and filing cabinets the other. Through the window we looked south, towards the outline of Skudeneshavn, where I could make out some tall cranes against the sky, high above the old wooden houses.

'I have to warn you, *herr* Veum, Veslemøy has had an anxious day. For what reason we don't know. Not that she is easy to communicate with on calm days, either.'

'She's been here a long time, I've been given to understand.'

'Yes, the longest of all our residents. So you can see the effect abuse can have!'

Initially she had seemed merely sad; now the colour of her complexion changed to something angrier, almost reproving, as though I were being called to account for everything my gender had committed against her sisterhood over the centuries.

'Yes, I understand it was a traumatic experience for her.'

'Traumatic? That's much too gentle a word. It was a catastrophe. It made her catatonic. What she experienced on that awful day in her youth paralysed her with horror for ever. And it is many years ago now.'

'1975, I have written here.'

She nodded. 'She's a woman of over forty now. Her whole life, from when she was fourteen until today, lies behind her, unused. She has nothing to look forward to. There is as much life in her as in a galleon figurehead!'

It struck me then that there was perhaps a connection with the Lady in the Park after all, however inappropriate it might seem. 'But … is it possible to meet her?'

She nodded, but her lack of enthusiasm was obvious. 'You will meet her. But as I said, she has nothing to say. She doesn't talk to anyone, not even to us, and we work here!' And she still wasn't finished with the reprimand. 'If unscrupulous males had any idea what they put women through when they commit such violations against them!'

'But … has she got any family? Does anyone visit her?'

'Her parents are dead, both of them. It must have been a heavy burden for them to bear – their daughter turning out as she did. She has two sisters who come to visit her, but months can pass between visits and they always come alone, as if they're ashamed to show her to others in the family. And then she has a brother who comes once or twice a year when he's in the area. He lives in Bergen.'

'Really? What's his name?'

'Vetle.'

'Vetle and Veslemøy. Powerful names, I must say. What's the surname?'

'Valaker. I thought you knew.'

'No, I was only told Veslemøy.'

'Right.' She got up. 'Shall we see how she is?'

'Please.'

She led the way and I followed her down a corridor that seemed to end in a large common room with heavy furniture. Before we reached the end she knocked on a door to the left and waited for a few seconds, then she opened it and went in.

I waited a little before entering.

Veslemøy Valaker was sitting in a chair by the window, in a strangely crooked position with her arms folded firmly around her upper body, as though she were cold. She wore strong glasses, with thick lenses; they had slipped down her narrow nose with its pointed tip, like a short ski jump. I could make out her eyes through the lenses. She was staring stiffly ahead through frozen, light-blue irises, and didn't react visibly to our coming into the room.

Her hair was fair without any signs of grey, but lifeless and cut in a style that was girlish in a slightly geriatric way, as though this was how she'd had her hair since she came here and no one had seen any reason to change it. The clothes she was wearing gave the same impression: a blouse with blue and white stripes, grey slacks and a pair of light-brown slip-ons.

The room was furnished simply with a bed, a table and two chairs, all in white wood. On the wall hung a picture of the same kind as the one in Laura Lothe's office, but the motif this time was Jesus in intimate conversation with small children. They were looking up at him with eyes full of gratitude, unaware of what was awaiting them in later life, perhaps even before they were adults.

'Hello, Veslemøy,' I said from where I had positioned myself inside the door.

Laura Lothe sent me a sour look, and Veslemøy gave no hint of a reaction now, either.

'My name's Varg. I wish you no harm.'

This time there was a tiny reaction, as though she were trying to turn away, to avoid looking at me.

'She reacts like that to all men,' Laura Lothe whispered. 'No matter who they are. The parish priest. Her brother. A doctor. She doesn't want anything to do with any of you.'

I looked at Veslemøy. I felt an internal fury building up, as irreconcilable as the reaction Laura Lothe had shown me in her office. For some moments I forgot why I was there. Emma Hagland was miles from my thoughts. All I felt was an immense urge to track down the person who had done this to young Veslemøy almost thirty years ago, stand him against the wall and call the nearest police authority before I behaved like some warped Western hero and took the law into my hands.

A sound came from between her lips as she sat with her face partly turned to the window. 'Uh-hu.'

I looked at Laura Lothe questioningly.

She met my eyes. 'She wants you to go.'

I nodded. I cast a final glance at Veslemøy, then slowly walked through the doorway. Behind me I could see Laura Lothe lean over the middle-aged woman, gently stroke her hair, pat her cheek and say a few well-chosen words to her, far too softly for me to hear from where I was.

Then she straightened up, followed me out and closed the door carefully after her. On the way out neither of us said a word.

She accompanied me to the front door. Before I left, there was one matter I wanted cleared up. 'I've been told there was an incident here involving Veslemøy. I understood it took place in 1986.'

She looked at me, waiting. 'Yes.'

'Someone brought the person who had committed the assault here?'

She pressed her lips into a thin line, but she was unable to stop her muscles twitching.

'Is that correct?'

When she did finally answer, her mouth seemed to be distorted into a grimace, as though what she had to say was so hard to communicate it hurt. 'In all my years here that is my worst experience ever. She was sacked that very day!'

'Who?'

'It was one of our employees. She'd invited a friend to visit her here. It was an unusually beautiful summer's day and many of the residents were sitting outside in the sun, among them Veslemøy. Suddenly she went into a fit. She was absolutely hysterical: she stood up, spat out some sounds, in such despair and so desperate that it was terrible to hear. We – the staff – ran over and it turned out that this female, the friend, had brought a man along. And it was this man that Veslemøy reacted so strongly to. We had to send them packing and it took us several days to calm her down. She cried like a small child – long, painful sobs, gasping for breath and pinching her eyes shut. It was quite a few days before she opened them again. We had to feed her intravenously; otherwise we wouldn't have been able to get any nutrition into her. It was an absolutely horrendous experience, Veum.'

'Yes, I can well imagine.'

'It wasn't until the following day – after we'd done a bit of investigating and found out the name of this man – that we realised ... the actual perpetrator of the villainy himself had been here. It must have been pure thoughtlessness or ... clearly neither of them knew who he really was, in relation to Veslemøy. That was what we were told at any rate ... by our employee. She realised the error of her ways and bitterly regretted her action. Neither she nor her girlfriend, who furthermore was married to this man, had any idea about what he'd done. But she had to be dismissed. There were no two ways about that.'

'And her name was ... Liv Larsen?'

She eyed me sternly. 'I'm not at liberty to say.' But she added, almost as an afterthought: 'But I appreciate that you're well informed. She never showed her face here again, understandably enough. And I have no idea what happened to her afterwards.'

I could have told her. But I refrained. I wasn't completely sure how she would take it, and it wasn't something she needed to know anyway, neither her nor Veslemøy.

But Liv Høie Hansen was at the top of the list of people I would have to have a serious chat with as soon as I was back in Bergen.

21

I met Ola Haugane where we had arranged on the phone, at a café by the ferry terminal in Sand, in Ryfylke. The retired journalist preferred to meet me there, and there was no need for him to go with me to Buvik afterwards. He had bad memories of the place, he told me, without going into any detail.

Fargeriet Kafé was situated in what I took to be the main street in the old beach resort. It occupied an ochre timber house with burgundy mouldings, and the room inside was furnished in rustic style with the woodwork in the walls visible and original, as well as small-paned windows facing the street. Ola Haugane was sitting at a table by the wall next to the door, and he realised who I was as soon as I entered. I didn't belong there.

He was in his early seventies and the little hair he had was combed back diagonally across his narrow scalp. He wore slender, steel-frame glasses and continually peered over the top of them, as though they were unable to cope with the distance between us at the table, each sitting over a cup of coffee and homemade *lefse* pancakes with whipped cream. He was wearing a shiny grey suit and a red-and-black checked cotton shirt, and the whole of his upper body leaned forwards, as if he were sitting and thinking over the keyboard that was no longer there. But his eyes were sharp enough. There wasn't much this man missed, I guessed.

'Private investigator?' he said tartly. 'Hm, I must've met a few in my time as a journo, but they were mostly from the capital. I think you're the first from Bergen.'

'There still aren't so many of us. For many years I was the only one, but now some have begun to appear, largely ex-police officers who think retirement has come far too soon or they leave early.'

'Yes, it was mostly that type that came from Oslo as well.' He looked at me, waiting. 'But what on earth has piqued your curiosity about the nasty Buvik case? That one passed under the radar for the police and the media when it was topical. Now it must be well past the statute of limitations.'

'Yes, actually this is about something quite different. A young woman's disappeared and her roots are here, at least on the father's side.'

'And the father's name is … ?'

'In those days he was called Robert Høie.'

A shadow seemed to fall over Haugane's narrow face and his mouth seemed to sag as though he had eaten something that tasted bad.

'Now he's added a Hansen.'

'Yes, he probably needed something to hide behind, I imagine.' After a pause for reflection he went on, somewhat irked: 'So you're here working for Robert Høie, are you?'

'No, no, no. He hasn't had anything to do with his daughter for many years.'

His ears seemed to prick up, he turned his head to the side and looked at me over his glasses. 'No?'

'Perhaps you haven't followed how he got on after he left home?'

Again the same expression of a bad taste in his mouth. 'No, you can be damn sure I haven't. Good riddance to him, I say, and I'm hardly … I know I'm not alone in thinking that.'

'In principle, I know what this is about. Earlier today I was in Karmøy and met … Veslemøy.'

For the first time he looked genuinely surprised. 'What! You met Veslemøy. Well I never. How is *she*?'

'Not very well, I'm afraid. She's catatonic, doesn't speak to anyone and rejects any attempts at contact.'

'Bloody hell!' He stared down at his coffee cup, stood up suddenly, took the cup and glared at me as if he wanted to throw it at my head. 'I need a refill. Do you want one, too?'

I breathed out and pushed my cup towards him. 'Yes, please.'

I took a bite of the *lefse* in front of me while waiting for him to return.

The cream melted on my tongue and tasted of freshly churned butter and vanilla.

Ola Haugane came back and put both cups down with an angry expression. As he slumped onto his chair he exclaimed: 'That was a terrible business! And worst of all, the guilty party was never caught. A case was *never* brought, for Christ's sake. Veslemøy's life was ruined for ever, as you've seen yourself, and her family imploded. Her parents took it so badly they died long before their time, her brother took off as quickly as he could and her sisters made sure they married a long way away from Buvik. Their farm down by the sea is falling to pieces – that's the last I heard about the case.' He sighed heavily, as though the effort of being reminded of this had been much too much.

I leaned across the table. 'Could you tell me what you know about what happened?'

He sent me a fierce look. 'Yes, I can tell you. But I warn you, from now on you might wake up in the middle of the night unable to sleep for thinking about what can happen to a young girl whose path is crossed by wolves, and they don't bloody pretend to be lovable grandmothers either, I can promise you that.'

'I regret to have to say this, but I've been through pretty tough times myself and to a large extent I've retained my beauty sleep.'

'OK. Don't say you weren't warned.'

I motioned him to carry on.

'It all happened one late-summer's evening in 1975. There'd been a dance at the youth club in Buvik, and Veslemøy, who's actually from a completely different background, had sneaked away to be with someone many knew was her boyfriend.' He shot me an eloquent look. 'Robert Høie.'

I nodded.

His voice took on a lecturing tone as he continued. 'There are some myths about the distribution of the population out here in the country, whether Ryfylke or on Karmøy ... or very probably in your neck of the woods, in Vestland.'

'Indeed.'

'One of them is that you can divide the population into two groups: they either belong to the chapel folk or they're the Wild West. Either they go to church and hold bazaars to collect money for the poor people in Africa, or they drive big cars and check out the girls walking beside the road. What no one talks about is the huge stratum in the middle – ordinary working people and families of the kind you see everywhere in Norway, in big and small towns. But the point is, of course, that here in the sticks there are fewer of us, so it's hard to keep a secret from your neighbours and those who are on the outer fringes are more visible.' His expression was ironic, and he added: 'Especially for those looking in from the outside.'

'Thank you for the lecture. What happened in the youth club that summer's night?'

'In the youth club? Nothing. But Veslemøy, who in fact came from the chapel community, did something she'd never done before, at least not that anyone had seen. She stepped out onto the dance floor. Mostly with Robert, but she danced a couple of numbers with others, too.'

He gazed pensively into the air. 'I remember her quite well, Veum, because I wrote some articles on the school she went to, and we're distantly related. You immediately noticed her because of her strong glasses. She was very short-sighted, had been from early childhood. But she was a sweet girl – in an almost childish way – and, glasses aside, you could easily understand how kids of her age could fall in love with her.' He seemed to brace himself before going on: 'It happened on the way home.'

'She was subjected to a sexual assault.'

'Yes.'

Something appeared to be in the way of what he had to say, as though the words just piled up behind his teeth and refused to let go of his tongue. He took another large swig of coffee and rolled the lukewarm liquid around his mouth, then swallowed it.

'Her parents started to be concerned when she wasn't at home by ten, which was the usual deadline if she went out. And they had no idea where she had been, of course. She hadn't said a word at home about going to the youth club. But soon it was eleven, then it was getting on for midnight and now they were seriously frightened. They rang around her friends, but the majority of them were chapel folk and knew nothing. Then they stumbled on someone who was able to tell them she had seen Veslemøy at the youth club and she had left with Robert. So Veslemøy's father went to the house where Robert lived and rang the bell. It was well after midnight. There was a terrible rumpus, of course, and Robert was hauled out of bed and had to go down and explain himself in his pyjamas.'

'Right. And what did he have to say?'

'He had to admit he'd persuaded Veslemøy to go to the youth club with him, despite her not having permission, and that he'd left with her. But he insisted – and he always stuck to this afterwards – that he'd accompanied her to the crossroads where they could see up to her parents' house, but she didn't want him to go with her, understandably enough, and so they had parted there. He'd gone home and that was the last he saw of her – that night, and for all I know, he's never seen her since, not immediately after and not later.'

Oh, yes, he has, a voice inside me said. *At least once, in 1986.* But for the moment I kept that to myself.

'Soon a large-scale search was under way, but they didn't find her until dawn, in a little hay shed a kilometre from where Robert said he'd parted company with her. She lay huddled up in a corner, as though trying to hide, and when they went towards her she cowered away, wrapped her arms around her knees and screamed with terror. Her clothes were dishevelled and torn, they could see blood on her skirt, and there was no doubt about what she'd been subjected to. Her glasses were missing as well – they weren't found until many days later, in the brushwood nearby. Broken in the middle.'

'But ... an investigation was started?'

He looked at me gloomily. 'We-ell, certain mechanisms kicked in, and the keyword is shame.'

'Shame?'

'Yes, the people who found her – her father was one of them – several of them wanted to report it to the police at once, but her father ... he said no. He wanted to take care of this himself. This wasn't anything for the authorities.'

'He wanted to take care of this himself?'

'Yes. For him, an avowed chapel man, this was a sign from above. Not only had his daughter been disobedient and gone somewhere he'd absolutely forbidden her to go, she'd also been subjected to something so unmentionable and shameful that for him it seemed like a voice of thunder, a judgement from God, on Sodom and Gomorrah, which his daughter had knowingly and intentionally sought out. So, in other words, he forbade anyone to do anything at all. He wanted to take care of this himself.'

'Yes, you said that before. So ... did he take care of it himself?'

Once more he heaved a sigh. 'What no one knew, at least not that night, was how badly damaged Veslemøy was. Perhaps not physically, because no medical examination was undertaken and so there was no documentation anywhere, but psychologically. You've told me how she is today and I can tell you how she's been every single day since that accursed summer's day in 1975. The person who committed this rape destroyed her life. For ever.'

It was as though I could hear the echo of Laura Lothe's voice in Skudeneshavn. 'OK, but let me repeat: did her father take care of it?'

'Not as far as I know. No one knows what happened inside the four walls of the house, but ... Veslemøy just disappeared. She never showed her face outdoors. I know from other quarters that her school was worried and made enquiries. After a while child welfare was summoned as well. The local doctor. But no one could help, and bit by bit it leaked out – reports of her condition. She'd locked herself in her own world. Like in a shell. She didn't speak, they could barely get any food down her, it was impossible to get any information at all about what happened that night. The GP – and this is confidential information, Veum, but I got it out of him at the time – he considered her completely traumatised and in his opinion she would need intense psychiatric treatment to recover. And so ended that side of the case. After eight or nine months she was taken from home and moved to an institution.

She never returned again. Many years ago I heard she'd been taken to a new institution where she would remain as a patient in a nursing ward for the rest of her life.'

He raised his voice and slammed his fist down hard on the table sending the coffee cup in front of him into the air. 'All that because … Well, what do I know? But someone did this to her, and most people afterwards pointed the finger of blame at Robert Høie. No one believed his story. No one!'

'And he himself? How did he take it?'

'As I said before, he obstinately stood by what he'd said the night they went to his house, and he didn't change his statement one jot. But you know how it is in such small communities. Everyone gradually found out what had happened and most drew their own conclusions. Robert and his family were given the cold shoulder. He himself left as soon as he started at a higher school, and not many years afterwards his parents moved, too.'

'He was just fifteen!?'

'Yes, and Veslemøy was fourteen! She was just a child, Veum.'

'Robert, too.'

'Ye-es…'

'And there was no one else who might've committed the crime?'

'There are kiddy-fiddlers molesting boys and girls everywhere, as you know. And naturally enough there was one in Buvik too – a bit of a boozer, in his fifties, but he had an alibi. He'd gone fishing with two pals, across the fjord to a cabin in Nedstrand. Both of his friends vouched for him and there were other witnesses as well.'

'Alibi, witnesses? So there was an investigation after all?'

He placed a hand on his chest and grinned. 'Investigative journalism, Veum. It was me who found out about that. I became very committed to the case because I heard about it from someone in the family and I remembered Veslemøy so well from the newspaper report on the school. But, as I said, he was in the clear, no question.'

'Any others?'

'There were two brothers, Torfinn and Åsmund. Some people called them the *Vangsgutane*, the two well-behaved boys in the eponymous cartoon, but they were more like Larris, the uncouth slob.'

The reference to the cartoon, which continues to appear in Christmas comics even today, made me think. 'In other words, their name was Vang?'

'No, Vangen.'

'And where do they come in?'

'Well, that's the Larris bit. Whatever devilry or nastiness there was in the area, nine times out of ten, one of these two – and more often than not both of them – was involved. They were outsiders, of course: that played its part. Broken family, it was rumoured. The father took over a smallholding and turned it into a kind of workshop. Åsmund still runs it. Boats, cars, motor bikes. There have been rumours of other activities as well: dealing in stolen goods, maybe ditto illegal substances – alcohol, drugs and so on.'

'And in this case?'

'Well ... the workshop is next door to where Veslemøy grew up. On the other side of the road and not so far from where she and Robert parted company that night, if we can take him at his word.'

'OK. Were they confronted with this case?'

'That's the whole damn trouble! There was no case. I assume the police station heard about it, via the jungle telegraph, but as there was no formal complaint, no medical examination to base an investigation on, so there wasn't a lot they could do.'

'What about you then? You made enquiries about this other guy. Didn't you make any progress with these two brothers?'

He looked down. For the first time he seemed unsure what to say. It came eventually, slow and hesitant initially, then with greater conviction. 'Yes, I did make an attempt. I called on them – on some other business. As a journalist you can always make something up. I camouflaged it as some report on what it was like to run a workshop in such a depopulated area.'

'You spoke with the father?'

'Yes, but the boys were hanging around the workshop the whole time, and on the way out I struck up a conversation with them and mentioned – almost by the bye – what had happened to Veslemøy. And there was quite a reaction, I can tell you. They literally went for me. Pushed me up against the wall and … Torfinn even pulled out a knife and brandished it in front of my…' He held his nose. '"Don't you come here trying to blame us!" Obviously they'd been blamed for enough in the area. If I as much wrote one single word of this in the newspaper they'd personally look me up and flay me alive, they said.'

'And you didn't pursue the matter? You didn't contact the local chief of police?'

He hunched his shoulders and thrust out his hands. 'It wasn't worth the hassle. But I will say one thing while we're at it: right from the time he was small Robert was fixated with engines. He got a moped as soon as he was old enough to ride one, and he was often in the Vangens' workshop and either getting help or tinkering around himself. So … they weren't exactly strangers, even if Torfinn and Åsmund were a couple of years older than him.'

'Hm.' I stared at our cups and plates. Empty, and further refills were looking unlikely. 'You said this Åsmund still runs the workshop?'

'Yes. Are you thinking of paying him a visit?'

'I've developed a nasty habit of walking into the lion's den, with or without back-up. Fancy coming?'

He made a show of looking at his watch. 'No, Veum. I have neither the time nor the inclination.'

'What about the second brother? Torfinn. What's happened to him?'

'The last I heard was that he'd settled in Bergen.'

'OK! By the way, Veslemøy's brother did, too. Vetle. Do you know anything about him?'

'Her little brother? No. I only remember he moved away as soon as he could, and her sisters … yes, I've already told you.'

'Yes, and in a way that closes the circle.'

We left the café together, got into our separate cars and drove off in separate directions. I had no idea where he was going. I was headed for Buvik. But one thing was beginning to dawn on me. Those who maintained all roads led to Rome were wrong. From here they led to Bergen.

22

The first thing I saw as I approached what my map said was Buvik was the classic white chapel with a cross carved into the top of one gable end. Five hundred metres away there was a red house. From the posters on the outside I inferred it was the local youth club. It was as if the colours of the two buildings symbolised what they stood for: heavenly peace amid white clouds in one place; blood ceaselessly pumping through the body and awakening desire in the other.

A notice pointed down towards Buvik Quay, but I doubted there would be any ferries moored there now. The rest of the village was scattered across the slope leading down to the sea. On one side of the street there was a disused shop with empty windows, on the other a sale in a nationwide supermarket chain, plus a notice advertising *Post Office in Shop*. An apparently empty school building reinforced the impression of dereliction and centralisation, and there weren't many people out and about on an early Friday afternoon in November. I saw a few chatting outside the supermarket, but that was all.

Ola Haugane had explained to me where Åsmund Vangen's workshop was – south of the crossroads and afterwards down a bylane towards the sea. It was beginning to get dark as I turned into the forecourt by the workshop. There were a few run-down old cars outside, a couple of them with price tags inside the windscreen, prices that said dirt cheap, extra discount for anyone who liked to live dangerously. A rusty snowplough completed the scene. Even the workshop was a superannuated wooden building with the appearance of an abandoned cowshed, but the smell that met me as I knocked on the door and stepped inside was heavy with diesel and oil, seasoned with a faint *après*-stench of welding gear.

The man stooped over a partly dismantled motorbike straightened up when I entered, holding a blowtorch in one hand. He was thin, lean, with several days' bristles around his narrow mouth and was wearing dark-blue overalls that hadn't seen the drum of a washing machine this side of the millennium.

'Åsmund Vangen?'

'Who's asking?' he said in the local dialect.

'Varg Veum.'

He waited for me to continue.

'I'm here to … I'm an investigator.'

'Cop?'

'Private.'

'Ex-cop then, I reckon.'

'Ex-social worker.'

'Oh yeah? I thought only women with sagging breasts and purple scarves did that sort of stuff.'

'Then you were wrong.'

'Well, if you're from child welfare, there are no kids here! I don't get any bloody benefits even if I break my arm. So what the fuck do you want here? That's what I'd like to know.'

'You know someone from the old days called Robert Høie.'

Immediately he was on his guard. He searched my face with suspicion. As if to gain time he said: 'Robert … yup … Donkey's years ago.'

I waited.

'He grew up here. Over there.' He glowered towards the door I had come through. 'Is it … has something happened to Robert?'

'What do you think could've happened?'

'How the hell should I know? I think it's time you started talking.' He waved the blowtorch in the air, as if that was meant to motivate me to start. Then he seemed to realise what he was holding in his hand. He put the blowtorch down on the bench beside him, took a handkerchief from a pocket in his overalls, about as clean too, and wiped his hands while moving a step closer. 'Don't *you*?'

'Robert spent a lot of time here, I'm told.'

He came even closer. 'A hundred years ago, yes.'

Now he was so close I could smell the stench of oil on his overalls and see the saliva at the corners of his mouth. There was a glint of irritation in his eyes, which revealed something was bothering him, a nervousness that became apparent in his face. The skin above his nose and on the upper part of his cheeks was dotted with open, black pores and now twitched visibly. In the blond bristles I saw glistening sweat mixed with oil.

'There was some drama right here.'

His jaw started churning. 'What are you referring to?'

'I think you know.'

He took another pace forwards. If he came any closer we would collide. But I didn't give way. He didn't frighten me, not someone as skinny and frail as he was. 'No, don't think I do.'

'Her name was Veslemøy, and her life stopped that night.'

He looked me straight in the eye, with a slight squint. 'And what has that got to do with us?'

'Us? I'm talking about you.' When he just glared in response, I carried on: 'You'd like Torfinn to be in this with you, would you?' He opened and shut his mouth wordlessly, and I added: 'But he's in Bergen, isn't he, so I can talk to him when I'm back home.'

Then the gift of speech returned. 'You can talk to Old Nick, you can!'

'Yes, I probably wouldn't notice much difference.'

He raised a fist, clenched and ominous. 'You can go to hell!'

'You'd know the way, I imagine.'

This time he came so close I was forced to take a step backwards, if for no other reason than to avoid the smell. It was a long time since I had met such a disgusting specimen of humanity. For a moment we stood glowering at each other, until I realised I wasn't going to get any more out of this oaf without resorting to violence, and that wasn't in my job description.

So as not to miss out on a last word, I served up an old classic. 'See you when our paths cross again.' Then I turned and walked towards the door.

'Oh, yeah?' he shouted after me.

'Just don't feel too safe,' I added and went outside, where darkness was falling in earnest. And out of the darkness came the fallen angels.

I heard the roar before I saw them, coming on big black motorbikes down the bylane and onto the forecourt. There were five of them, one at the front and four in arrowhead formation behind him. When they started circling my car I opened the door, got in, turned the ignition key and started the engine.

For a moment it looked as if they were going to hem me in. In my rear-view mirror I saw Åsmund Vangen in the doorway and the biker who had been at the front pull up by him. They exchanged a few words, then he waved to the others; they moved aside and I left, feeling like Moses crossing the Red Sea, without a life jacket.

I buckled my seat belt and turned up towards the main road while keeping an eye on my mirrors. There were no Egyptian soldiers or black-clad biker heroes in my wake. But before leaving I had noticed the logo on their jackets: *MC BACCHUS NORWAY.*

23

I kept an eye on my rear-view mirror as I drove. When I turned onto the main road they had gone. If they decided to follow me a little later they had three ferries to choose from. If they chose the right one I was trapped. I drove to the closest one without seeing any sign of them.

From the Nedstrand ferry I called Norma's number, but she didn't pick up. All I got was a voicemail saying she couldn't answer the telephone right now, but I was welcome to leave a message. I complied with the suggestion and asked her to ring me back.

The drive westwards reminded me of a book I had read many years ago when it came out in Norwegian translation for the first time: *Journey to the End of the Night.* It was pitch-black and the road wound through the nightscape with a potential surprise at every single bend. The beams of my headlights cut through the darkness and were reflected on the markings on both sides of the road. On the slope to the right tall, dark spruce trees towered up, to the left, far beneath me, I could make out the sea with the occasional flash of light from a boat or a building. Sometimes I passed a little cluster of houses, an isolated farm or an area of unlit holiday homes. Most of the time I was in a virtual tunnel, created by the darkness around me.

I had put a disc with Gene Ammons on tenor sax into the CD player, and so perhaps it wasn't so strange that my mind went to the totally unknown saxophonist who had been in Haugesund and played for a dance at a wedding in January, 1942, nine months almost to the day before I was born, in October that same year. All I knew about him was his name: Leif Pedersen. I didn't know if I wanted to take this extremely private investigation any further. I had no idea if there was any more to be found out. There was a lot to suggest it would be better to let buried saxophonists lie, lift my head and concentrate on solving the far more acute investigative tasks that lay ahead. But one day when things were quiet, maybe...

Driving conditions didn't improve until I reached the E134. The intervals between lit buildings were becoming shorter and I began to lower my shoulders. As I still hadn't heard from Norma by the time I arrived in Våg, I decided to turn off to Haugesund again. I wanted to talk to her face to face, first of all to report back on my meeting with Veslemøy and what I had learned from the conversation with Ola Haugane.

Haugesund unfolded like a golden jewel along Karm Sound when I crested the last hill before the town. The low cloud cover reflected the light in a way that made it seem as if the whole landscape was packed into a duvet, and under that duvet I lay with a torch reading a book I was desperate to finish. But there was a lot to read and I was afraid it would take most of the night.

It was getting on for eight as I swung in and parked in front of Norma's white timber house in Gange-Rolvs gate. Light shone from the windows in the sitting room and the kitchen. I went up to the front door and rang the bell. No one opened. I took my phone and dialled her number again. I got the same answer message as before.

OK. So she might be busy doing something. It irritated me that I hadn't noted down her daughter's number.

I stood looking around. Gange-Rolvs gate was set back and quiet. Through several of the windows around me I glimpsed the flickering of TV sets. I weighed up the pros and cons. Should I just get in my car and postpone the conversation until the following day, or should I attempt to find out where she was?

Not wishing to leave any stone unturned, I grabbed the door handle and pushed the door. It opened.

With a feeling of unease I stepped inside. 'Hello! Norma! Are you there?'

No answer. There was total silence. No radio, no TV.

I quickly orientated myself in the cosy hallway. The door to the sitting room was ajar, but the one to the kitchen was closed. I pushed the sitting-room door completely open. No one there. No cups or glasses on the table, nothing to suggest that someone had been there during the evening at all. Then I went towards the kitchen and opened the door.

Norma was lying supine on the kitchen floor. Beside her a stool had been knocked over, as though she had tried to grab it in her fall. Next to her right hand was her coffee cup. There was a brown stain on the floor where the liquid had spilt. Her head lolled at an angle against a cabinet and blood had run from the back of her head down onto the floor.

I leapt forwards and went down on one knee beside her. I felt for her pulse, but couldn't find anything. I saw her glazed eyes and could feel her skin was cold and clammy. I had come across enough dead bodies in the course of my life to know that there was little else to be done here.

With a new, deep sorrow in my heart I stood up straight, took out my phone and rang two numbers. First of all, the ambulance service, to be on the safe side. Then the police.

24

The duty doctor was the first to arrive, but the young man with the foreign appearance could only confirm what I had observed: Norma was dead. 'We'd better contact the police,' he said.

'I've already done so,' I said, still numb from the shock.

He looked at me with concern in his eyes. 'Is she a close acquaintance?'

'My sister,' I answered, and everything I was unable to say rose like an acrid, black liquid inside me: *Whom I've only known for a few days even though we'd been alive for more than sixty years. Whom our mother, because of circumstances, left to guardians and another life rather than the one she could have offered at that point, and this a long time before she had me, also under dubious circumstances, it now seemed.* With a dull ache, it struck me there would never be any more than the few days I'd had. The big sister I had just met was gone for ever.

I looked down at her thinking, as I had so often before, how quickly life departed, how fast a personality was gone, what some called the soul, leaving only an empty, lifeless husk. There was already a bluish-grey tinge to her skin as a precursor of the decay that was in the process of taking place and, unless something was done within a short time, it would change her body totally, in a way you would prefer not to think about if you yourself were at an age when you were approaching the final frontier – which the conclusion of life is for us all.

Strangely enough, it was as though the conversations we'd had over the last few days had somehow erased the long vacuum when we barely knew about each other, so that we still had memories of a shared life, however separately we had lived. So there probably was something in the old proverb that states blood is thicker than water, even in diluted form.

'Hello?' We heard footsteps in the hall and immediately afterwards two uniformed officers and a plain-clothes policeman stood in the doorway.

'Is this where a dead body…?' The man who was speaking, the plain-clothes officer, broke off when he caught sight of Norma. 'Right, OK.'

The detective glanced from me to the doctor and back again. He had a narrow, elongated face and was bald, or as good as. Just a few thin tufts of hair around his ears were visible.

He eyed me suspiciously. 'Haven't we met before?'

I nodded. 'I was thinking the very same. It was around ten years ago, on the coast, south of Ryvarden. The name's Veum.'

He screwed up his eyes in thought. 'Ah, yes, *that* case. Well, I'm Inspector Liland. You were some sort of investigator, weren't you?'

'Yes. A private investigator.'

'Exactly.' He tasted the two words and didn't like them. 'Was it you who found the dead body?'

'Yes.'

The doctor coughed. 'Do you guys need me any more?'

Liland glanced at him and didn't particularly like what he saw, either. 'No. We need a death certificate, of course, but we can deal with that later. The ambulance to transport the deceased will have to wait though.'

'Right.' The doctor nodded to me and went on his way without another word.

Liland turned to one of the uniformed officers. 'Gjessing, call in the SOC officers. We'll have to carry out the necessary examinations.'

The officer nodded and went out.

Then he turned back to me. 'Are you here on a case?'

'Yes and no. This is my … half-sister.'

'I see. So you knew her well then?'

'No, I'm afraid not. We met for the first time on Monday this week.'

He raised his eyebrows in surprise. There wasn't much hair on those, either. 'And why was that?'

I shrugged. 'She was adopted from birth in Haugesund. My mother kept it a secret for the rest of her life. I didn't find out until she'd died.'

'And that was recently?'

'No, it was almost thirty years ago.'

He shook his head slowly. 'I don't understand.'

'No? But it doesn't have anything to do with this anyway.'

'This?' he said, pointing to Norma.

'Yes. She was my half-sister, Norma Johanne Bakkevik, which is her full name. She came to me about the case I'm investigating. She was my client, in fact.'

'Really?'

'One of the leads brought me here to Haugesund, and that was why we met here. I stayed over yesterday, but today I've been first to Kamøy, then to Buvik, Ryfylke. Now I was actually on my way home to Bergen, but there was something I wanted to talk to her about, and then … Then I found her like this.'

'Did you have a key?'

'No. The door wasn't locked.'

'Hm.'

'Yes.'

'At first sight this seems to be your typical accident in the home. Elderly lady has a turn with a coffee cup in her hand, reaches out too late, falls and hits her head on a kitchen cabinet. Unfortunately, I've seen this all too often, Veum.' Then he added with force: 'But we will of course investigate this thoroughly – get forensics in, talk to any witnesses there might be, see if the neighbours have heard anything. In short, do our job. But before you go…'

'I'm in no hurry.'

He eyed me patronisingly. 'No, but we don't need a private investigator here. We can manage this on our own.' After a short pause, as if he was waiting for a protest, he continued: 'Before you go I'd just like to know who you talked to in connection with the case you're dealing with, so that we can contact them too – in so far as we might deem that relevant.'

'There weren't many people. A relative by the name of Ruth Kjærstad, but we just talked about family. As far as the case is concerned, the mother of the young woman I'm trying to track down: Ingeborg Hagland. I also visited an institution in Skudeneshavn called Fredly, but frankly I can't see what that has to do with this. Finally, I've been to Sand to meet a journalist – Ola Haugane – and then Buvik and had a kind of confrontation with someone called Åsmund Vangen, who runs a car workshop out there. But I've come straight from there now, and if Vangen has anything to do with this, he must have wings.'

He noted down the names as I mentioned them. 'So this Vangen isn't a prime candidate,' he said, looking up from his notebook.

'You don't think he...?'

'For the time being we don't think anything, Veum. What's this case you're investigating?'

'As I mentioned, a young woman in Bergen who's gone missing. Student nurse. Her name's Emma Hagland and she comes from this area.'

'But aren't the police involved?'

'Not yet. But if you could encourage them to be involved I'd be eternally grateful.'

'Eternally?'

'For a couple of weeks at any rate.'

'And am I correct in thinking your sister commissioned you for this job?'

'Yes, you are. She was Emma's godmother.'

He nodded. After further reflection, he smacked his notebook shut. He looked down at Norma. 'Well, her contract clearly ran out here. Sad business, Veum.'

'Yes.' Again I felt the sense of loss growing in me. There was so much we should have talked about, and now those conversations would never take place. Perhaps it would have been better if she had never contacted me. At the back of my mind a thought presented itself: what about if there was actually a connection? Was the woman lying on the floor in front of us a victim of an accident in the home or of murder? And, if so, did it have anything to do with the case I was investigating, and was something I did or said the trigger?

Liland coughed. 'Did your sister have any family, Veum?'

'Her husband and son are dead. But she has a daughter, and then a daughter-in-law and a grandchild, from what I gleaned.'

Again he sent me a resigned look, as if to mark his distance from such loose family connections. 'Would you like to inform the relatives yourself?'

'I've never met any of them. I don't know what she told them or if they even know anything about me at all. I think one shock for them is enough, so…'

'In other words, you'll leave it to us?'

'Yes … please.'

'Or the priest.' He glanced at his watch. 'I think you should be getting home, Veum. I have to wait here until the SOC people arrive. Afterwards we'll get down to the investigation.'

'You'll keep me informed, won't you?'

'We'll contact you if we find anything unusual. If not, you'd better get in touch with the deceased's relatives.' His expression was sardonic.

I nodded. I looked down at Norma for the final time. *Farewell*, I said inside me. *Fare well, Big Sis.* I hoped she was alright where she was now, if it was somewhere different from the minds of those left behind.

I nodded to Liland, went outside and got into my car, paused, then inserted the key into the ignition and started up. I put the volume on the radio down to zero and decided not to put another CD in the player. I needed silence for some reflection, some peace time to say a proper farewell.

25

There wasn't much traffic on the roads that evening. In the Bømlafjord Tunnel I didn't see a single car – neither in front of me, nor behind. When I had crossed to Stord there was the occasional vehicle, but none going as far as Sandvikvåg. North of the Leirvik turn-off, after I had passed a sign warning drivers of the danger of deer crossing, I suddenly noticed a motorbike in my rear-view mirror. It stayed behind me for a kilometre or two, but on the incline down to the ferry terminal in Jektavik the biker accelerated, swung out to the side and overtook me at a speed that was way over the limit. But not so fast that I was unable to recognise the emblem on his back. It was identical to the one I had seen in Buvik.

On the ascent from Jektavik the biker shot away from me. Afterwards I checked my rear-view mirror at regular intervals to see if the rest of the clan had appeared, but all I could see were the headlights of a handful of cars on their way to the same ferry as I was. After arriving in Sandvikvåg and parking in the queue I saw the biker a couple of places ahead of me, still wearing his helmet.

I saw him again when we were on the ferry, the same couple of places ahead of me, but this time in the cafeteria queue. Now his helmet was under his arm and I could see who it was: Robert Høie Hansen. As far as I could make out, he still hadn't spotted me.

He ordered stew and a Coke. As for myself, I invested in a portion of cod and a bottle of alcohol-free beer, put it on a tray and followed Høie Hansen to the table where he was in the process of settling down next to a west-facing window. It was then he saw me.

'Mind if I sit here?'

His face went red. 'Mind if … Yes, I bloody do.'

'I have a couple of questions I'd like you to answer.'

'I've got nothing to say to you. Just piss off!' He plumped down on the bench by the table, poured Coke into his glass and began to wolf down the stew while staring out of the window to demonstrate how much he wanted company.

I shrugged and moved to the adjacent table, behind his back but with him firmly in sight.

We both ate in deepest silence. After I had finished I went to the counter and got a cup of coffee. On my return I sat at his table without asking for permission this time.

I got straight to the point: 'I went to see Veslemøy today.'

Again he flushed, but not just with anger this time. The look he sent me spoke more of despair than fury. 'Didn't I tell you to—?'

'Afterwards I was in Buvik and talked to Åsmund.'

His jaw dropped. 'What the f—!' He leaned over. 'I thought Emma was your assignment, Veum.'

'And while I was there, bugger me if a whole gang of you didn't turn up, all dressed the same.'

His face wore a very eloquent expression, revealing a mixture of concern and despair. 'So what?'

'Well, was it a kind of family outing to Haugaland?' When he didn't answer, I went on: 'Because it's obvious you were on home territory.'

'So?'

'Visiting family maybe?'

'Family?'

'Yes?'

While he was giving that some thought I tasted the coffee. It was as bitter as a row over a family inheritance in Sunnmøre.

Suddenly he leaned across the table again, his eyes flashing, but his voice still low, and said: 'Where I've been and what I did has got fuck all to do with you! If you don't...'

'If I don't...?'

He sat back on the bench, crossed his arms and flexed his biceps as much as he could under the tight jacket. 'If you don't stop, you may have to deal with much tougher guys than me.'

I met his eyes, but still felt a cold tingle go down my spine. 'The Wild Bunch?'

He nodded, and there was a hint of a tiny smirk. 'You can bet on it.' Then he got up clumsily. 'Now I have to go for a piss. Were you planning to follow me to the toilet as well?'

'No, thank you. I think I'll stay here.'

He snatched his helmet from the bench where it had been lying and took it with him, as though afraid I would steal it. There was no danger of that. But it might come in handy if the Wild Bunch should come knocking one fine evening.

The ferry slowed down and glided into the narrow sound leading to Halhjem. The exclusive summer houses on both sides looked empty and abandoned, with little more than cosmetic lighting in a couple of them. Over the tannoy system passengers were told to go to the car deck to prepare to drive ashore, and I saw no reason to pursue any form of civil disobedience in this respect. I had no wish to return to Sand-vikvåg, where even the hot-dog stand was closed on a Friday evening in November.

I didn't see any more of Robert Høie Hansen. But I heard him. He revved up and roared ashore as if he had the devil and the whole of the police force on his heels, and he was up by the Bjørnen turn-off long before I had even started the car.

Still off balance after all I had experienced in the last few hours, I told myself: *You have to think about something else. You still have a job to do.* It didn't matter that my client was dead or that my fee was down the drain. Quite the contrary. Now finding out what had happened to Emma Hagland and discovering where she might be had become a matter of honour.

As I drove I wondered what my next move should be. I had several names on my list. I suspected both Kari Sandbakken and Helga Fjørtoft of holding something back. I also felt I hadn't talked to Knut Moberg enough. An attempt to speak to Liv Høie Hansen was high on the list, and perhaps I should have a chat with her son as well. Furthermore, I wanted to track down Veslemøy Valaker's brother, Vetle, who also lived in Bergen and possibly – in due course – Torfinn Vangen from Bergen. But I had to admit to myself that the latter two were definitely on the periphery of what I ought to be doing and for that reason could hardly be prioritised.

Back home in Telthussmuget, I called Sølvi and told her I had returned from my expedition to Rogaland safe and sound. She was at a hen party and the noise level was way above the falsetto limit, so we quickly brought the conversation to an end. I didn't even tell her about Norma. Afterwards I treated myself to two glasses of Simer's Taffel Aquavit and listened to Duke Ellington's 'Second Sacred Concert', then went to bed with two powerful images as the clearest memories of the trip: one of an unhappy woman with her face turned to the window and no interest in speaking to anyone; the other of a woman who would never speak again on the floor of her kitchen.

*

The following morning I was woken early, at eight, by my phone. I could see from the display it was Åsa Lavik calling. Still drowsy with sleep I answered: 'Yes?'

'Veum?'

'That's me.'

'This is Åsa Lavik.'

'So I see.'

After a tiny pause she continued: 'I've hardly slept a wink all night. I just keep thinking about Emma and what might've happened to her. I'm wondering whether to travel home and search for her as well.'

I rubbed my eyes, still not completely awake. 'Oh? Well, if you think that might help, then … For the moment we're getting nowhere, but … If I'm honest, after what you've told me so far, I doubt there's much you can do right now. But thank you for offering.'

'I've been turning things over and over in my mind. Trying to piece together the last conversations we had, on the phone, to see if anything she'd said could reveal what was troubling her … or was happening.'

'Oh, yes?' I could feel I was waking up.

'In the end I remembered a word I barely reacted to at the time because for some reason we started to talk about something else. She asked if I knew what the word moribund meant. I didn't, and then we carried on chatting.'

'Moribund?'

'Yes. And now I've looked it up on the net. And ... it means dying.'

'Yes, there's a song by Jacque Brel called "Le Moribond".'

'Who?'

'Someone I listened to a lot in my younger days. She didn't say anything else?'

'No, I'm afraid not. I thought it was so awful to remember that now, with her missing and not even answering her phone.'

Yes, I said to myself. *Nowadays not answering your phone is probably in reality tantamount to being dead.*

There was an audible tremor in her voice as she went on: 'I hope you find her soon!'

'Yes, I ... Thank you, Åsa. I'll ring back if there's anything else. Let's keep in touch anyway.'

'OK. Thanks.' She hung up, and I sat in bed with the phone in my hand.

Moribund?

I couldn't deny that I felt a bit uneasy as well.

26

I drove to Møhlenpris and parked as near to Konsul Børs gate as I could. I reckoned my chances of meeting the two students on a Saturday morning were greater than on any other day of the week. Knut Moberg might be at home from the office as well, sitting with his wife for once and sipping expensive red wine. It transpired that this wasn't so far from the truth, even if the picture had been upside down and someone had put a foot through it.

I rang the external doorbell beside the names of Fjørtoft, Sandbakken and Hagland (crossed out). After a while a voice I recognised as Helga's came over the speaker: 'Yes, who's that?'

'It's Veum. I have to speak to you both again.'

'There's only me here.'

'That's fine.'

'But—'

'I have to speak to you, Helga!'

'OK, OK!' she shouted. A second later the door lock buzzed, and I pushed the door open.

When I emerged on the second floor I saw she had opened the door a little and was standing in the doorway with a determined expression on her face, as though she had no intention of letting me in. She was wearing the same grey sweater as before, but this time with red velvet trousers and she was barefoot. Her hair looked, if possible, even more dishevelled, slightly askew, as if she had just got up. 'What do you want?' she asked before I had even reached the top steps.

I breathed out for two seconds. 'Moribund – does that mean any thing to you?'

She opened her eyes wide with surprise. 'What!'

'The word moribund.'

Her eyes were focused on somewhere to the side of me, as though someone had come up behind me. 'Never heard it.'

'Never heard the word?'

'No.'

'It means ... dying. Doomed maybe. Or simply dying. Emma had mentioned it on the phone to a friend in Berlin.'

'Oh, her.'

'But it doesn't mean anything to you?'

'I've already—'

A sudden noise came from inside the flat, as though something had fallen to the floor. I tried to see past her, in the direction the sound came from, but she closed the doorway even further. 'I thought you said it was only you here.'

'I didn't say ... I didn't mean it like that.'

'No? How did you mean it then?'

'I meant that ... Only I can talk.'

'Oh, yes? And who's making the noise in there then? Kari?'

She pressed her lips tight, as though refusing to answer, but once again events inside caught up with her. I heard the sound of a door opening and a pitiful voice shouting: 'Helga! Are you there?'

Helga half turned and shouted. 'Yes, but I'm busy. Go back in!'

I felt a strong urge to lean heavily against the door and force it inwards, but I knew I had no right to do so, not yet.

The voice from inside came again. 'Is it that hysterical woman again?'

'Go back!' Helga said, louder this time.

After a silence – during which Kari was probably thinking – we heard the door inside close with a muffled bang. Helga came all the way out into the corridor this time, pulled the door to, glanced up the staircase and said in a low, almost confidential tone: 'There was a terrible row here last night. That woman up there came down and rang our bell until I opened the door and then...' Another long stare at the floor above. 'Then *he* came down and they started fighting.'

I adopted the same tone as her. 'I know who you're talking about. Can you tell me any more?'

This time she opened the door behind her. 'Come in.' I followed her, but almost bumped into her when she stopped inside the door. 'Only into the hallway!'

She leaned past me and closed the door. We were standing so close we could have been a couple about to kiss. The same thought seemed to occur to her and she retreated half a metre, but not so far that I would have been unable to extend a hand and stroke her cheek, if that kind of thing had been on the agenda.

She spoke in the same low tone. 'Last night. Kari'd been out – at a party, she told me. I'd been in bed, but then there was such a racket outside I had to get up and see what was happening. She was lying … there.' She pointed to the spot where I was standing. Then she rolled her eyes. 'She was … pissed.'

'I see. But you helped her inside and into bed?'

She nodded. 'After she'd …' She motioned towards a door with a red heart on and made a graphic gesture with her hand from her stomach to her mouth while grimacing and sticking her tongue out as far as she could. It would have been hard to be more descriptive. 'But in the end I got her into bed.'

Now she pointed to the front door. 'But when I was about to go to bed myself I heard more noise from outside, as if someone was staggering down the stairs. I listened and after a while heard it continue – upstairs.' She met my eyes. 'I had a suspicion about what was going on, but … it was none of my business, so I went back to bed.' She looked at the ceiling above us. 'Then I heard loud voices from upstairs. Shouting and screaming. And then … she came down here.'

'Fru Moberg?'

'Yes. She just leaned on the bell, letting it ring and ring. I didn't know what to do. And then Kari started screaming from her room: "Get them to stop! Get them to stop!"' She glanced at one of the closed doors. 'In the end I had to open the door, but as I did, Moberg came down too, and there was one hell of a to-do. She just shoved me to the side …

with an almighty push to my...' She held her shoulder. 'She shouted into the flat: "Where's the bitch? Where's the bitch?" But then Moberg staggered in, not exactly sober, either. He grabbed her and pulled her backwards. She kept screaming: "Bring that bitch out! I'll talk to her. I'll force the truth out of her."'

Helga gulped and looked at me with widened eyes. I could see she was reliving the night's events so intensely it was as if it was happening again. 'Kari's room was as silent as a tomb. Moberg and his wife were on the floor fighting. I didn't know what to do! Should I have intervened?'

I shrugged and splayed my hands: *Who knows?*

'She hissed in his face: "Don't you know I saw you two? You thought you were being so clever, but I saw you from the window, smooching in Olaf Ryes vei. You'd probably been under a bush in Nygårdsparken..." Then she used...' she blushed '... a very rude word for sleeping together.'

'Yes, there is quite a selection.'

She pulled a face. 'And she carried on: "And then you thought you'd better not arrive together. So you sent her off first and you followed five minutes later. But you had no idea I was watching you with the light off. I saw what you did with her through the binoculars!" And then he whacked her.'

'He hit her?'

'Yes, he slapped her several times – like this – across the face. Hard! And she went quiet – at first – and then she began to howl like a siren! He slapped her again to make her stop, but it didn't help. He got up and dragged her after him. He twisted her arm to the side so that she was forced to follow him out and upstairs.' She stared at the door.

'Friday's entertainment in Møllaren,' I said.

A door right behind her opened and out stumbled Kari Sandbakken, wearing black underwear and nothing else. Her hair was pressed flat to her scalp, she was wearing yesterday's lipstick and her mascara was smudged across her face. When she spotted me, her eyes widened. 'Ohh! It's him isn't it!' she cried, disappeared back into her room and slammed the door hard behind her.

Helga met my eyes again, almost apologetically.

'Might be a good idea to find alternative accommodation?'

She nodded mutely with a resigned expression on her face. Then she said: 'The last words I heard as he as good as carried her up the stairs were a scream: "Either she leaves or I do. Her or me! You can choose!"'

'So there's no longer any doubt, Helga. There's been something going on between Moberg and Kari.'

'Yes, I'd begun to suspect there was something.'

'I have another important question. Did he ever try anything on with you?'

She opened and closed her mouth. 'Moberg? No.' After a moment or two she added: 'He probably didn't think I was exciting enough.'

I looked at her. 'What about Emma?'

She shrugged, a little sullenly, without answering.

'She told her friend in Berlin he'd been touchy-feely – I think that was the term she used, but she'd put him in his place, and then nothing else happened.'

'OK.'

'OK? You aren't sure?'

'I didn't know anything about Kari and him, either … until last night! Not for certain.'

'Are you trying to say you suspected that Emma and he could also—?'

'No,' she interrupted. 'Emma wasn't like…' She glanced at Kari's door. 'She'd never … But when you say that, she might've told her friend that he … tried it on, but she rejected him.'

'Did she mention anything to you?'

'Never.'

'Well … I'd like to have a few words with Kari as well, but something tells me I ought to come another day.'

'Probably best.'

'Erm … I did give you a card last time, didn't I?'

'Yes, you did.'

'Could you ring me if the two of you have been evicted … at once? I should talk to her.' Again I looked at the door behind her.

'Yes, I promise. And you've got our phone numbers, haven't you?'

'Yes.'

She accompanied me out. I started walking downstairs, and she closed the door after me. Then I stopped and looked up the stairs. It was hardly the right day for it, but...

Then I heard the sound of a door opening upstairs. 'Hello?' came the voice of Ellisiv Moberg.

'Er ... yes?'

'Is that the police?'

She swished down the stairs in a rust-red silk dressing gown. On her feet she wore some elegant high heels. Every step she took could have been the prelude to a fall. Her gaze was heavy and what I could see of her sea-green eyes was so turbid that they reminded me of brackish water. A substantial bruise had collected around one eye and she had bluish-green marks on one cheek and the side of her chin.

When she saw me, a sense of disappointment spread across her face. Then she recognised me. 'You! You were here earlier this week, weren't you?'

'Yes, I was asking after...'

She had reached the landing on the second floor now. With a quivering finger she pointed at the door. 'Those girls ... they're tarts! They've turned the place into a brothel. It used to be a respectable house. Look here! Look what he did to me!' First of all she showed me her face. Then she opened her dressing gown and pulled it down over her shoulders. 'Look!'

Fortunately she had her panties on, but she uncovered her breasts, and there were big bruises at the top of them as well and what appeared to be a bite mark on one of them. She met my eyes, in a kind of masochistic triumph, then covered up again. 'I've rung the police!'

'Sounds sensible,' I said, nodded, turned round and continued down the stairs. As I opened the front door, I saw them outside, two officers, a man and a woman, him with a shaven head, her with a long blonde plait.

I held the door open for them and nodded, but he pulled out a truncheon and held it horizontally in front of me as though demanding a toll. 'Hang on there!' he barked. 'There's been a report of a domestic disturbance. Have you had anything to do with that?'

'Not at all. But she's waiting on the second floor for you. The woman who called you.'

The female officer nodded and passed me. She looked up the staircase and shouted: 'Hello?'

'Are you the police?' a voice said from above.

'Yes.'

I nodded to her male colleague. 'Have fun,' I said, and continued down the steps outside. He glared at me, replaced his truncheon in his belt and followed his colleague up the staircase inside.

A normal Saturday morning in Konsul Børs gate, for all I knew.

27

I found Vetle Valaker in the Yellow Pages – he lived in Vognstølbakken. I rang his number and when he answered, I introduced myself, said who I was and asked if he was available to meet me.

'What's this about?' he asked.

'I went to see Veslemøy yesterday.'

'Really?' He sounded surprised. 'For what purpose, may I ask?'

'Her name came up in a case I'm investigating. A young woman who's disappeared. The daughter of someone I assume you know. Robert Høie, now with a Hansen attached.'

It seemed to take him some time to digest this, but when he answered he was clear and articulate. 'I know who Robert Høie is, yes. But I don't understand how I can help.'

'If we could have a chat, I'll explain.'

'Well, I don't want to be difficult. I'm going into town anyway in about an hour. Where can we meet?'

'By the Seamen's Monument? I'll be wearing a black leather jacket.'

He mumbled something I didn't catch and hung up.

I left in good time and arrived punctually at the monument to find a man approaching me with an inquisitive expression on his face. I nodded slowly and it turned out he was Vetle Valaker.

He was around forty years old. He wore a grey cloth cap with a discreet check and most likely a retail price far higher than the item suggested. What hair I could see was short and dark blond. He had very little neck and his chin area was fairly rounded. The rest of him looked bog standard. Not exactly a fitness freak, but not a couch potato, either. He was wearing a light-brown leather jacket with a belt, which made him appear older than he was. The brown slacks and knotted grey scarf around his neck reinforced the impression.

He shook hands without any particular enthusiasm. 'My name's Valaker.'

'Veum. Shall we go for a cup of coffee?'

He nodded. 'Where do you suggest?'

It wasn't like in the old days when there were traditional Norwegian restaurants in every other street. Now the modern cafés had taken over, but generally speaking they were small and so cramped that it was difficult to have a discreet conversation. I pointed to Galleriet, a 1980s shopping mall. 'On the fourth floor maybe?'

He nodded, and we walked together through the bookshop on the corner and into the atrium, which had once been the central yard of the original housing block before Galleriet occupied all the buildings around it. From there we took the escalator up to the fourth floor and the café. We found a free table with a view of Torgallmenningen. I was in a generous mood and treated him to a currant bun as well as a coffee, and had the same myself. I kept the receipt; in due course I would make sure to add this to the final bill for whoever was going to pay.

'I heard you go to see Veslemøy when you're in those parts.'

'Yes, but it's only a couple of times a year. Not that she gets much out of my visits.'

'It…' I started.

'But…' he said.

We both paused, and I motioned him to carry on.

He nodded. 'What … I wanted to say … Why did you visit her? Surely you don't believe that what happened to Veslemøy so many years ago … could in any way be connected with Robert Høie's daughter going missing today?'

'I'm the type that … Well, when I stumble over some peripheral information during a case, an investigation I'm doing, my experience is that it might well end up having some significance. So when I heard about what your sister suffered, I was … I don't want to use a word like "curious", but I was … interested.'

He pursed his lips and slurped his coffee at the same time, which struck me as highly impractical. He had to get a paper serviette and wipe his chin afterwards.

'How old were you when it happened?'

'Me? In 1975?' He appeared to have to do a mental calculation. 'I was twelve. Veslemøy was fourteen.'

'So you remember ... the events?'

'I remember everything afterwards, yes. How Veslemøy stayed in her room for days and later refused to go out. How Mum and Dad didn't want to tell me anything about what had happened, beyond saying someone had been ... bad to Veslemøy.' He swallowed. 'You have to understand ... ours was a strict Christian home.'

'Yes, so I've heard.'

'My school friends told me what had happened to her. That she'd been raped by ... well ... you know. By Robert.'

'He never admitted it, did he?'

'No, I ... I don't know. Not officially anyway, and there was no police investigation. But Veslemøy was never the same person again. You've seen that for yourself.' There was more colour in his cheeks now; he had become animated on behalf of his sister, just like everyone else I had discussed the case with.

'And no one tried to do anything about it? I mean ... it's one thing reporting a crime to the police and quite a different matter taking the law into your own hands.'

'Your own hands? You mean ... revenge?'

'Yes. Or ... if not revenge then setting things straight. As you know, Robert left the area as soon as he had the opportunity. I suppose that was because he felt unsafe there.'

'You'd better ask him that.'

'You also departed as soon as you could.'

He looked at me in surprise. 'Who have you been talking to? How much work have you invested in this actually?'

I splayed my hands. 'Not that much, but as I said: I'm the type that gets to the bottom of cases. Right to the bottom.'

'OK. If you get to the bottom of this one, you'll get an award!'

'A star in a Sunday school book?'

'Yes, go on, make fun of us believers as well, but if you knew—'

I interrupted him. 'It wasn't meant like that.'

'Oh, yes, it was. That's how people behaved at home as well. The others. That's how it's always been. "Whoever is not with me is against me", Jesus said. Luke, Chapter 11, Verse 23.'

'But…'

'But what I wanted to say was this. My parents … they suffered so much as a consequence of this that they sickened and died long before their time. Life at home was never the same from the day Veslemøy was assaulted. The atmosphere was so oppressive that … It was quite simply no life for a young boy. My sisters followed suit – left as soon as they could. If I wanted to carry on at school I had to move to a bedsit, so I applied to Haugesund and got in there.'

'When was that?'

Again he appeared to have to do some mental arithmetic. 'I went there from 1978 to 1981. After doing compulsory national service I moved up here and started at university in 1983.'

'And what were your subjects?'

'I majored in IT.'

'Computers?'

He smiled condescendingly and nodded. 'Information Technology.'

'And where do you work?'

'I have a sixty-percent job at Bergen Teacher Training College. For the other forty percent I'm a supply teacher at secondary schools.'

'Where?'

'It varies. I doubt there's a school in town where I haven't temped. At the moment I'm at Tanks.'

'Sounds good. But back to what we were saying. So you left home. You never considered confronting Robert Høie with what – as far as we know – he'd done at that time?'

'Confront? It's not in my hands. "May the Lord see you and call you to account!" Second Chronicles, Chapter 24, Verse 22.'

'Well…' I looked down at my hands. The answer to everything wasn't there, either. 'What about…? Do you remember the two brothers, Torfinn and Åsmund Vangen, from home?'

He pulled a face. 'The Vangen brothers? Yes, I do. What about them?'

'Well, Torfinn lives in Bergen as well, I've been told. You've never run into him here?'

'Torfinn Vangen?' He looked at me in bewilderment. 'No, I've barely given him a thought since I left.'

I nodded. 'OK. Just a shot in the dark.'

He leaned forwards. 'Are you trying to suggest … those two had something to do with what happened to Veslemøy?'

'I'm not suggesting that or anything else.'

'I don't understand why you've asked to talk to me at all, Veum. How could I help if it's Robert Høie's daughter you're searching for? What sort of girl is she actually?'

'Her name's Emma, and she came to Bergen to train as a nurse earlier this autumn. But then she disappeared.'

'Just like that? Disappeared?'

'Yes.'

'Without a trace?'

'Yes, in fact. So far anyway. That's why I'm casting the net wide. Perhaps too wide. Perhaps it will pay off. That's where you come into the picture.'

'I see. I understand.' He raised his palms. 'But I'm afraid I can't help you with anything.'

'OK, thank you for meeting me anyway.'

'Mm … thank you for the coffee and currant bun.'

We went back downstairs and parted in Torgallmenningen, roughly where we had met an hour earlier. 'Head out on the highway', I remembered from a song in my younger days. But I was getting nowhere. In life I had discovered that it was the byways you learned from, not the highways. Perhaps this was one such byway. And perhaps it wasn't.

28

It was Saturday and early afternoon, but I still didn't feel it was time to take the rest of the weekend off. I decided to try another foray against Robert, Liv and Andreas Høie Hansen.

I parked the car near the end of Sudmanns vei and strolled back to their house. When I opened the gate I noticed the carport was empty and the motorbike gone. I crossed the gravel and rang the doorbell. No one answered. When I stepped back and faced the house again I noticed a curtain twitch in one window. I walked over and knocked hard on the pane. After a few seconds Andreas appeared behind the glass.

I pointed to the front door and gestured that I wanted to talk to him. He stared at me despondently. Then he nodded sullenly and disappeared from the window. I walked to the door and waited for him to open up.

Through the crack he said: 'What do you want?'

'Are your mother and father at home?'

'No. Otherwise they would've opened themselves. Dad's out on the bike and Mum's … up there.' He glanced up the steep mountainside to the Sandvik weather vane.

'But you're at home,' I stated. 'And I've got a couple of questions for you, too.'

'Hm,' he grunted.

'I've been speaking to your sister's friend in Berlin, and she told me that she and Emma had travelled to Bergen to meet you all when they were sixteen and you were twelve or thirteen.'

'Hm,' he grunted in the same sullen way.

'Do you remember them coming here?'

'Yeah, but … I didn't speak to her.'

'No. That's what Åsa said. They'd just seen you through the window … to your room maybe?'

He nodded. 'I'd forgotten that until she reminded me.'

'*She* reminded you?'

He went red. 'Yes. Or … I was reminded when she came here again this autumn. When Mum and I turned up, and she was talking to Dad.'

'And he just sent her packing?'

'Yes.'

'Didn't you think it odd of him to react like that?'

He shrugged.

'But the last time we talked, Andreas, you said it was only this autumn that you realised you had a half-sister.'

He gave that some thought. 'Yes.'

'But you just said you were reminded the second time.'

'Yes!' He glared at me. 'But Dad never said anything. Dad didn't say anything then. Mum opened the door, and when I asked afterwards they both looked awkward and said someone was at the door selling something. But then she…' He bit his tongue.

I studied him. When he didn't carry on, I took over. 'There you go again, Andreas. You *have* been in contact with her.'

He chewed his lips, as if to stop himself saying any more.

'When?'

'Alright!' He looked down. 'She rang me.'

'Rang you? On your phone?'

'No, here. She'd tried before, she said, but put the receiver down if Mum or Dad answered.'

'I see. And when was this?'

'This autumn.'

'After she'd been here?'

'Yes.'

'What did she want?'

He looked up again. 'Well, she said who she was and she wanted to get to know me.'

'And what did you answer?'

'I said … that was fine.'

'We're getting somewhere now, Andreas. You didn't say anything about this last time.'

'No, because … it was supposed to be a secret.'

'Between her and you?'

'Yes.' He quickly added: 'We definitely didn't want Mum and Dad to find out!'

'So you met as well, did you?'

'Just the once.'

'Where was that?'

'At a café. Dromedar, in the pedestrian area.'

'When?'

'It was straight after she came here. At the beginning of September.'

'That's the only time you've met?'

'Yes.'

'Didn't you get on?'

'We were busy with other things.'

'Did you talk on the phone?'

He hesitated. 'We emailed. I've got IT at school and she had my email address there. If she sent me a message there no one else could read it. But it wasn't often. I mean we didn't email much.'

'And when was the last time you heard from her?'

'Mm … about a month ago.'

'Middle of October?'

'Something like that.'

'Did you save these emails?'

'At school? Are you out of your mind? I delete them at once so that no one can see them.'

'I'll have to ask you then: was there anything at all in the emails that could help us to find out what's happened to her?'

He shook his head slowly. 'I don't know what that could be.'

'Nothing about her meeting someone? Or that she was thinking of moving?'

'Surely the people she lived with could tell you that?'

'No, they can't either.' I turned my palms upwards. 'We're totally in the dark, Andreas.'

He looked at me as if expecting more.

'Surely you must … Aren't you worried about her? After all, she is your half-sister.'

He shrugged. 'I don't know her. We've never had any time to get to know each other.'

'Are you sorry?'

Again the same roll of the shoulders. 'What you don't know, you don't miss.'

'Really? Do you mean that?'

He didn't answer; his eyes looked past me. I had heard the gate go behind us and I turned.

Liv Høie Hansen was on the gravel, jogging up and down, wearing a spring-green tracksuit with white stripes down the sleeves and sides of the trousers. On her head she wore a blue-and-orange hat, on which was written *UP STOLTZEKLEIVEN* in diagonal letters at the front, like a logo.

Beads of sweat pearled on her forehead, and she inhaled as she stopped in front of us. 'What do you want?'

'To talk to you.'

'About what?'

'About Veslemøy.'

'Eh?' I heard Andreas say behind me. 'Who?'

Liv Høie Hansen met my gaze with even greater defiance than her son had shown me. 'I have nothing to say!'

'You do.'

We stared at each other for a few seconds. Then her eyes shifted. 'Alright then. You'd better come in. But I have to shower first.' She looked at her son. 'Andreas, take him to the sitting room and … keep an eye on him.'

'Keep an eye on him?' Andreas said meekly.

'Yes. Make sure he doesn't start sticking his nose into things that don't concern him.'

'OK, right,' her son answered, although he didn't seem to understand exactly what she meant by that.

29

The sitting room had a view of the sea through panoramic windows, but dusk was beginning to fall and the most visible feature in the landscape was the luminous chain of pearls that marked out Askøy Bridge, a kind of virtual hammock for sylphs of the air. Liv Høie Hansen stood in the doorway watching us until we had sat down in the classically inspired drawing-room suite, which wasn't very comfortable. Andreas didn't appear to be particularly comfortable, either.

For the first few minutes we sat in awkward silence. He looked down; I let my eyes wander to take in whatever there was to observe.

A conspicuous item of furniture in the room was the large glass cabinet along the facing wall, filled with trophies and statuettes of all sizes. I assumed that Liv had brought most of them home, but didn't exclude the possibility that some of them were associated with motorbike activities. One of the statuettes was in the shape of a silver motorbike, at any rate.

The pictures on the walls reflected the same mood. A big black-and-white poster of Marlon Brando in *The Wild One* stared at us from one wall, framed in red and gold. A corresponding photo of Brooklyn Bridge dominated the other, although in colour. The road across the bridge seemed to be covered by a multi-coloured woven rug. Even without getting up to take a closer look I presumed it was a photo of the New York Marathon, possibly featuring Liv Høie Hansen. In stark contrast to these two photos there was a series of pictures of flowers, as if taken from an old-fashioned herbarium, spread across both walls by the hallway door. The furniture was otherwise relatively un-modern, and I noticed there wasn't a TV set, a sound system, a radio or any form of reading material in the room.

In the hallway we heard a door open and close, and not long afterwards a low rushing in the plumbing. I considered it time to break the silence. 'So ... what do you do on a Saturday, Andreas?'

'Nothing special.'

'No? You don't do any form of sport?'

Again he eyed me with disbelief. 'Eh? Sport?'

'Yes, your mother's obviously very active. She hasn't taken you with her on anything similar?'

'And become as crazy as her? Not likely!' After a little thought, he mumbled: 'But she did try a few times when I was small.'

'Football ... athletics ... anything else?'

He just heaved a sigh. 'I can't be bothered to talk about it.'

I tried a different angle. 'Parties, then? You must have a few school pals you knock about with?'

For a second or two an indefinable expression flitted across his face, a kind of mixture of envy and extreme loneliness. He didn't answer, just shook his head.

'So you're happiest in front of a computer, I suppose?'

A flicker of light illuminated his face, then it went out too, and he reverted to the same sullen tone of voice. 'Yeah.'

'You've got pals there, I take it?'

He sent me a look of contempt. 'Pals?'

'Yes. Like when you tried to get to know ... Emma.'

Once again he heaved a sigh to signify how bored he was by this conversation. From the hallway came the sounds of a door opening and closing again, and he looked hopefully in that direction. But it was another minute before his mother appeared in the doorway, wearing a one-piece casual outfit in roughly the same colour as her tracksuit – green and white – except that the white was concentrated on her chest, as with squirrels. Her face and neck were still dripping from the steam in the bathroom and her short red hair stuck out in all directions, still wet.

As she entered, Andreas jumped into the air, faster than I had ever seen him move before. 'Can I go now?'

'Of course.' She nodded, but stayed by the door until he had passed her, although she didn't look at him. Her face didn't lie. It showed a mother's concern and a resigned sense that she no longer knew if she had her son under control. We heard his bedroom door slam hard in the hallway, as if making a point.

She crossed the floor. As she sat down in a chair facing me, she asked: 'What did you talk about?'

'Andreas and I? Nothing special. About Emma, of course.'

She glared at me. 'And why have you come here to torment us with this again?'

I met her eyes. 'Wouldn't a more natural question be: Is there any news? Had I made any progress in the search for Emma?'

She rolled her eyes and mimicked my voice: 'Alright. Is there any news? Have you made any progress in the search for Emma?' As I didn't answer at once, she added: 'But that wasn't what you said you wanted to talk to me about ... outside.'

'No, but to take second things first: No, I'm afraid there's no news. There's still no trace of her.'

For a moment she revealed a more human side. 'That's incredible! No one can vanish into thin air nowadays, can they? With all the electronic trails we leave.'

'Not unless something serious has happened, no. And even then they turn up in the end.'

'Yes.' She nodded, serious now.

'As for the other matter ... I went to visit Veslemøy Valaker on Karmøy yesterday.'

At once she was tense. 'Right.'

'I didn't know you and Ingeborg knew each other so well. In fact, all three of you, I was told. You, Ingeborg and Robert.'

'So? What's surprising about that? We...'

'Yes?'

'We went to school together, in Haugesund. Ingeborg and I were in the same class. Robert was in the one above. But ... they were the ones who got together.'

'You were both in love with him?'

'Maybe. You fall in love so easily at that age. And it's gone just as quickly.'

I put on a weak smile. 'Yes, I suppose we've experienced that, most of us. But ... Robert wasn't as quick to go, I gather.'

'Yes, he was. But ... Well, I went away after finishing my exams at school to train as a nurse – yes, here in Bergen. Then I got my first job after training – on Karmøy – and moved back home in 1983.'

'And that was at Fredly?'

'Yes.' She paused. This wasn't a subject she wanted to broach. 'Then I met them again.'

'And...?'

'And, and, and! What are you after actually?'

I had to think that through. 'I suppose what I'm after is a kind of causal connection.'

'Causal connection? Between what happened then and this now?'

'For example. What did actually happen then?' She didn't answer. 'When you invited Robert and Ingeborg to visit Veslemøy?'

She reddened. 'It wasn't like that! You don't understand. It was chance. I had no idea then about Robert and Veslemøy, that he was suspected of having...'

'But you knew the background? Her story?'

Her eyes narrowed. The skin of her lean face tightened as though she was passing the finishing line of the – I looked up – New York Marathon. But what did I know? 'Everyone at Fredly knew. It was just awful. Such a ghastly business, not least because of the consequences it had for Veslemøy, all the years afterwards. But how could I have known...?' She looked at me almost accusingly. 'I couldn't possibly have known!'

'Let's take it from the beginning. You'd met your old school friends, Ingeborg and Robert, again.'

'Yes.' She gazed into the distance, way back in time. 'They'd had Emma and were so happy. I may as well admit it – I was envious and perhaps even jealous when I saw how they were.'

'So that was why you...?'

'No, I've told you! I didn't know. Not then. Time passed. We began to hang out, Ingeborg even tried to play matchmaker and find me a suitable partner.' She grimaced. 'Without success though. And then ... well, we'd talked about it many times – that they should visit me in Skudeneshavn, at Fredly. And so one Saturday, it was in June, one of the first really hot summer days that year, we had moved most of the residents into the sun. Veslemøy, too. And then they arrived, without any arrangement or warning. He just parked outside and they crossed the lawn in front of the house, where Veslemøy was sitting ... and then it happened.'

'She recognised him?'

'Recognised him!' She gaped at me as though what I had suggested was an understatement. 'That's just for starters. There was such a reaction, an explosion – it was so intense, I don't think I've ever experienced anything like it. She went absolutely hysterical. Ranted and raved. At first she stared at Robert as if he were from outer space. The expression on her face was ... indescribable. She was terror-stricken. Then she covered her eyes with her hands and refused to remove them. She sort of toppled out of the chair she was sitting in and lay on the ground in front of us howling. The rest of the staff raced over, it was total chaos, and on the side lines there was Robert.'

'And how did he react?'

'If I could describe the living dead, that would be him. He just stood there, like a frozen shadow, staring at her, incapable of moving, incapable of uttering a word. Ingeborg, on the other hand ...'

'Yes?'

'She looked from Veslemøy to Robert and back again. Veslemøy was helped back into the house by other staff, but Robert was transfixed, as immovable as before, but now he wore an expression of ... hm, a bad conscience, what do I know? ... It was so clear that everyone must've realised who he was and what he'd done ...' Her voice cracked. '... To Veslemøy.'

'So you're convinced as well?'

'Convinced about what?'

'That it was him who'd sexually assaulted her.'

'Me?' She looked at me as though she hadn't understood what I had asked. 'Ingeborg was convinced anyway.'

'Oh, yes?'

'She grabbed him and dragged him down to the car without a sideways glance. They drove straight home to Velle, where they were living at the time, and what happened there I don't know, but it must've been a terrible showdown because it ended up with him being kicked out. She told him she never wanted to see him again, he was out of her life for good and he could just forget any kind of contact with Emma. She even refused to accept any child maintenance from him!'

'That was quite a reaction.'

'Reaction? If you ask me it was a sort of hysteria as well.'

After a little pause I asked her: 'And what happened next?'

She sent me a puzzled look. 'What do you mean?'

'I mean ... how, after all this, did Robert and you ... get together?'

She nibbled at her lips as though she didn't know what to say. In the end she said: 'Well, I lost my job at Fredly because of all this. Had to leave at once as well. Then I got a supply job at Haugesund Hospital and ... I met Robert at a pub in Haugesund a couple of months later. It was an uncomfortable encounter, at first. But we sat down, had a beer and then I got his version of the whole business.'

'His version of...?'

'The Veslemøy story – what happened back then.'

'Right. And what...?'

'Because it *wasn't* him who did it!'

'No?'

'There were some others involved.'

'Some others?'

'Two of them.'

A feeling of unease went through my body. 'And these two, what were their names?'

'I have no idea. He's never told me.'

'But why ... How does he know, and why didn't he report them?'

'Because…' Now she seemed quite desperate. 'Because they threatened him. Threatened to kill him.'

'But…' My head was spinning. Thoughts tumbled around in my brain. The meetings with Ingeborg, Veslemøy and – not least – Åsmund Vangen forced themselves to the forefront of my mind, intertwined and became a chaotic nightmare. 'How could he put up with this for so many years – take the blame for something other people had done? Not even when he lost his wife and daughter did he stand up and tell the truth. Why not? Can you tell me that, Liv?'

Now she looked resigned. 'No, in fact, I can't. I'm afraid you'll have to ask him.'

'But you believed him – enough to marry him, move to Bergen with him and start a new life?'

'We didn't marry until we came here.'

'No, but—'

'Yes,' she interrupted. 'I did believe him.'

'Where is he now?'

'Robert? He's a member of a bikers' club.'

'Yes, I know that.'

'They're supposed to be having an open day tomorrow, Sunday.'

'And that means?'

'They open the doors to anyone who's interested. Neighbours, others.'

'The police?'

'Them too, I'm sure, if they can be bothered. So today the bikers are getting things ready, tidying up the place.'

'I see. You don't know when he'll be home then?'

'No, but I'm sure it'll be late.'

'Perhaps I should drop in on them tomorrow as well?'

'Yes, why not? Was there anything else?'

'No, I don't think so.' I got up from the little sofa I had been sitting on, if that was the right term for such an item of furniture.

'I still don't understand what this has to do with Emma's disappearance.'

'No, but…' On the way to the door I stopped. 'Emma was here in 2000, wasn't she? With a friend?'

'Yes, just out of the blue. There they were at the front door ringing the bell. I barely knew who they were. They looked very similar, the way young girls do – same hairstyle, same clothes, same stubborn expression.'

'But she introduced herself and asked to speak to her father?'

'Yes, she did, but Robert refused to allow them in.'

'He couldn't even be bothered to go out and say hello to them.'

'Yes. It … It was something he just had to put behind him, like a trauma. For him his daughter didn't exist any longer. Hadn't done since Ingeborg booted him out in 1986.'

'And you two didn't tell Andreas who she was?'

She squirmed. 'No. That was Robert's decision. And I did as I was told.'

'But…?' I raised my hands in the air.

'You'd better ask him about this as well, when you meet him,' she said, in a slightly sarcastic tone this time.

'I suppose I better had.' I continued towards the front door. Then I pulled up again. 'By the way, does the word moribund mean anything to you?'

'Moribund? Of course. It's still occasionally used in medical records. It means that the person in question won't survive.'

'Exactly.'

'Why do you ask?'

'Actually, Emma brought the word up with a friend.'

'Really?'

Our eyes met for a final time before I left their house that Saturday afternoon, and it was as though I saw a reflection of my own, almost unconscious, reaction in her – a feeling of uncertainty and concern, brought on by one word: moribund.

30

I got into my car and rang Sølvi. 'Recovered after the girls' night out?'

She chuckled. 'Sort of. Might've imbibed slightly too much wine.'

'Feel like going to an open day in your neighbourhood tomorrow?'

'Whose open day?'

'MC Bacchus Norway.'

The same light chuckle. 'Don't think so, no. Tomorrow, you said?'

'Yes.'

'But you're more than welcome to come here this evening. Then it isn't so far to drive.'

'Would that be the only reason?'

This time her chuckle went down a register. I took that as confirmation it wouldn't be, thanked her for the invitation and started the engine.

In Saudalskleivane she met me at the door, gave me a hug and a kiss on the cheek. She was wearing blue denims and a casual shirt in a small check, which hung loose over her hips, and at the neck I could see a black vest.

She stood watching me while I disposed of my outdoor clothes, and as I was about to go into the sitting room she held me back. 'What's the matter, Varg?'

I looked at her. 'Nothing, I...'

'I can see there's something. Have you found her? The young girl you were looking for?'

'No, unfortunately not.'

'But I can see something's happened. Tell me what it is.'

I sighed loudly. 'I think I told you when I was here on Wednesday about the woman who commissioned me for this job? Norma?'

'Yes? The half-sister you'd never met before.'

'She's dead.'

'What?' She stared at me in amazement. 'But … how?'

'It looked like a domestic accident, but you know … lots of murders look like accidents and consequently are never defined as murders.'

'But has it got anything to do with the case?'

'That's what I'm wondering myself. Primarily though it was a shock. The first time we ever sat face to face was last Monday. Now that'll never happen again. And we didn't have time to get to know each other properly.'

Again she gave me a hug. This time she stayed close to me, as if to share my grief.

'It's not that … I don't feel any profound grief, precisely for that reason – she was a person I didn't really know. She came to me because of a job. So in a way she wasn't even contacting me because we were family. But that's what makes it so agonising.' As I spoke I felt the lump in my throat growing and it was becoming harder to get my words out. It seemed as if for the first time I was assimilating what had happened and how tragic it was. 'I'm just imagining how the years ahead of us could've been. Years when we could've got to know each other. I could've met her family, become a kind of belated uncle … or great-uncle.'

'You still can.'

'Yes, but not in the same way. If I do, it'll be without her.'

She kissed me lightly on the mouth. 'But now at least you have a bit of extra family here in Saudalskleivane. Let's go in, shall we?'

'Yes.'

In the living room there was a cosy Saturday atmosphere already. Helene was watching children's TV, but sent me an excited wave when I appeared. On the coffee table there was a bowl of tapas. Sølvi already had a glass of red wine. She poured me one and ensconced herself in the corner of the sofa where she had been sitting before I arrived, with a pile of inch-thick Saturday newspapers beside her.

I filled her in on the details of my experiences in Rogaland, including the new information I had gained about my mother and the thoughts that had set off.

She watched me with a furrowed brow. 'My goodness! And no one had told you any of this before?'

'Who would have been able to do that? If that's really how it was, I don't suppose it was exactly something my parents wanted to talk about. Not even Norma knew anything about it before our second cousin told us on Thursday.'

'This saxophonist ... do you think can he be traced?'

'That remains to be seen, and I'm not so sure I'm interested. First of all, I have to concentrate on the case.'

'And you can do that?'

'I have to put all the personal stuff on hold. Although, that said, it inspires me in a way. Both Emma and I have an issue about an unknown father. And there's something in the case about a half-sister too. In a way she's related to you, and in a way she isn't – and I can sympathise with that.'

Sølvi stroked my cheek. 'I'm not surprised you're confused. I think my brain would've been tied in knots.' After a while she asked: 'Was there anything else you found out down south?'

'Yes, but I'm at a loss as to how to interpret it.' I gave her a brief run-down of my visit to Veslemøy and what I knew so far about the events of that summer's day in 1975.

'What a story. But does it help you with your present case?'

'Well ... you have me there; but I have a strange feeling there is a connection, somewhere.'

She smiled. 'You've been right about that a few times before.'

'A few times. Not always though. So my idea of going to the open day at MC Bacchus tomorrow is to find a lead.'

'That's the only reason?'

'No. Something tells me Robert Høie Hansen is a key figure in both of these stories, a knot where all the threads meet.'

'But tonight you're here.' She stretched out a hand and gently caressed my neck. 'And you can relax, away from all of that.'

'I'll try. But my brain never rests. And I can't get them out of my mind ... Least of all Veslemøy. Also Emma, though, whom I haven't even met. To me she seems like a – what shall I say?' – an abandoned child? A victim of such an intense conflict between her parents that it ends in a rupture so total that even when she's tried twice to contact her father, she's been snubbed at the door … both times. He didn't even go out to say hello to her the first time!'

*

This was exactly the image I had in my head as I got into my car at around twelve the following day, leaving Saudalskleivane after a family evening with the two women there, one of eleven and one of over fifty, and a night with the older of the two. Both parts had done me good. Now my break was over and it was back to reality. The black angels were waiting, but not with raised swords of fire. Today they had their swords in their scabbards and were welcoming all and sundry inside their walls with open arms.

Usually MC Bacchus Norway met in a run-down factory by the sea, protected from unwanted attention by a tall wooden fence mounted with barbed wire, a gate with a robust locking system and a sign proclaiming in large letters: NO TRESPASSING! To avoid any misunderstanding they had painted a big, black skull above the text.

But today all the gates of hell were wide open. They had created a provisional car park in front of the gate, where I was shown a space by a man with shoulder-length hair and a sparse beard, wearing black denim jeans, a T-shirt sporting the club emblem and a thick leather waistcoat with a sheepskin trim. He regarded me with obvious scepticism as I got out of the car, but retained his composure and made no comment.

Inside the gate, visitors were thin on the ground. For the moment, the black-clad bikers constituted the majority. Most of the visitors appeared to be fathers with their sons, come to see the bikes. The few women there were mainly constituted the refreshments committee and stood behind small, makeshift counters, under canvas in case of rain, where they served homemade cakes, waffles with jam, hot dogs, and coffee and juice to those who wanted it for a small contribution to the needy in black biker uniforms.

But they had been lucky with the weather. There was even a glimpse of the sun between the drifting, greyish-white clouds.

The few visitors in attendance concentrated on the motorbikes on display, admiring their polished surfaces and assiduously studying the shiny metal parts. Enthusiastic owners extolled the virtuosity of their vehicles in traffic and how fast they could go 'in speed-restricted areas, ho ho', as one of them said, winking at the closest fathers, who chuckled conspiratorially.

The club members were as different from the rest of the gathering as flies on a sponge cake. They looked conspicuously similar. Most had shoulder-length hair; many of them had relatively trim full beards. Others made do with a variety of whiskers from small to large moustaches to hefty sideburns. Some had mutton chops in a style I couldn't remember seeing since the early seventies. Nonetheless I identified Robert Høie Hansen without a problem. He was standing beside what I assumed was his motorbike, sullen and taciturn; any contact was an uninviting prospect. That must have been the vibes others also got, because they walked past without stopping.

I was making a move in his direction when something else caught my attention. One of the club members had climbed up onto a rock. He clapped his hands and was met with a round of applause and shouting from the other members. Everyone present turned in his direction and, when he gestured for them to do so, drew closer.

The man on the rock wasn't much different from his colleagues. The outfit was the same, his hair shoulder-length and untidy, and he had gone for the droopy-moustache variant leavened with two-day stubble.

'Hi there, folks!' he shouted from above the gathering. 'My name's Torfinn Vangen, and I'm a – what should I say – a kind of general manager of this place.'

The club members chuckled and laughed, and some of the visitors joined in, warily. *Right*, I said to myself. *So this is where you hang out.* It shouldn't have been a surprise after what I had seen of his brother in Buvik.

'Every six months we hold an open day here. The last one was in May. Now we have the Winter Blót before we're all consumed by Yule hysteria.'

'Yesss!' shouted someone from the inner circle, and further bursts of applause followed.

'We do this basically for you children and young people.' Here he inserted a dramatic pause while he ran his eyes over the audience, stopping at representatives of the new generations present, and giving a wolfish grin, as though his greatest pleasure would be to eat them. 'It's you who in a few years' time will be riding your first motorbikes and who will have a totally wrong impression of what we do if you listen to the news, watch TV or read the papers.'

A rather more tentative round of applause this time, coming by and large only from the members.

'They say we smuggle drugs and commit other types of crimes, but that's lies! All we want to do is tune our bikes, get them in tiptop condition and then go on long trips in this wonderful country of ours, from Gulen to the Swedish border, from Lindsnes to the North Cape.'

Greater enthusiasm now.

'Normally if you see a *NO TRESPASSING* sign on our gates it's because we have so much valuable material here – new bikes and old, not to mention our stock of very rare spare parts – that we have to keep trespassers out. It's no secret that many criminals – not only from Norway, but also the whole of Europe – would like to get their hands on some of this. And we never see the police busting a gut to deal with the break-ins and thefts we have. Quite the contrary!'

Again a little scattered applause.

'But today all the doors are open. You can see for yourselves...' He raised both arms. 'You're very welcome to visit our club rooms in there...' He pointed to the open factory hall doors. 'Yes, go wherever you like in the whole area. But ... a tiny word of warning to children. There are steep slopes down to the sea, so we'd prefer it if you didn't wander too far in that direction. You won't find any bikes there.' He seemed to deliberate before rounding off with: 'Have a nice day, everyone!'

He received more applause from the audience, then raised a strapping fist in the air and jumped down from the rock. There he was met by a handful of his club mates, who patted him on the back and congratulated him on his refulgent speech. Over the shoulders of a couple of them I watched him scan the audience before his eyes rested on me and lingered a little longer than was natural. But perhaps he was just wondering who I was. Now at least I knew where Torfinn Vangen was, if I needed some answers later.

I continued on my way towards Robert Høie Hansen, the reason I was here at all. He spotted me before I quite reached him and, if possible, his expression became even colder than it had been.

When I stopped and greeted him with a nod, he eyed me sullenly and said: 'We have nothing to talk about.'

'I spoke to your wife yesterday.'

'So I heard,' he said in a barely audible mumble. Then he raised his voice again. 'I told you. I've got nothing—'

'So Torfinn Vangen's your club leader, is he?'

'That's—'

'You were pals back in Buvik.'

His face went crimson. 'Now you just…'

'Is there anywhere we can talk without being disturbed?'

'How slow on the uptake are you? Haven't you understood? I don't want to talk to you.'

'We can do it here and now if you like. It is an open day after all. Perhaps the visitors would like to hear what really lies behind at least one of the façades here?'

'You wouldn't dare…' Then he took a decision. 'Yes, there is. There's a storehouse at the back. We can talk there.'

'OK,' I said, and noticed that I was changing my mind now. I took a long, hard look around me, but there was nothing to suggest anyone was keeping an eye on me.

'We don't have to talk. It was you who were so bloody keen.'

'In fact, I still am.'

He leaned forwards and took the key from his bike, looked around and beckoned with his head. I followed him around the nearest corner. As we moved into the shadow I felt instantly how much colder it was. Even when the sun was at its zenith there wasn't much warmth in it at this time of the year.

Roughly in the middle of the wall there was a large, grey sliding door. I looked up and observed a CCTV camera high above, focused precisely on this door.

'Someone's watching us,' I said, pointing in its direction.

'Not today. Everyone's busy with the open day.'

He took a solid bunch of keys from his waistcoat pocket, to which it was attached by a chain. He quickly found the right key, inserted it in the lock, twisted it and pushed the door aside with a grating rasp.

I followed him in. He switched on the light in the ceiling and pushed the door to behind us. Then he turned to me with an expression on his face I couldn't quite place, but I didn't like it.

31

It occurred to me that I might have chosen the wrong place to meet him after all. Standing just inside the door, he towered over me, many kilos heavier and a couple of decades younger – as compact as a prime bull and about as genial. His big, dark beard moved as though he were chewing something – his own tongue for all I knew.

I cast around me. The storeroom was spacious and empty, except for a few broken folding chairs that had been slung in a corner. I turned back to him.

'Well?' he growled. 'What was it you wanted to talk about?'

'As I told you when we met on the ferry on Friday evening, I'd been to see Veslemøy, and I'd been to Buvik.'

His eyes smouldered. 'And what the fuck was the point of that? Who the hell commissioned you to dig up this shit? Ingeborg?'

'No, as I said when I was at yours—'

'You said Emma, my daughter, had gone missing and that was why you were there. What the fuck has Emma going missing now got to do with what happened then? It was long before she was born.'

'Yes, but what happened then has had big repercussions on her life, hasn't it? It was why Emma's mother broke up with you, gave you the bum's rush, wasn't it?'

He didn't answer, just glared back.

'Yes, it was,' I continued. 'And I wouldn't mind betting that in some way it's the root of all the misery in this case.'

'All the misery? This case? You haven't got a fucking clue what's happened to Emma! She's probably just run off as well.'

'As well?'

'OK, I meant anyway.'

'Hm, is this something you know?'

'Know? For Christ's sake, I don't know anything.'

'Have you had any contact with her at all since she came to Bergen, apart from the sad meeting on your doorstep in September, when you rejected her?'

He met my gaze squarely. 'No contact. Haven't you got that into your head yet? I didn't want anything to do with her.'

'Why not? Because you were embarrassed?'

'Embarrassed?'

I took a step closer to him. 'I know all about what happened to Veslemøy in 1975, Robert!'

'All…'

'And your wife gave me your version of events.'

'What? Have you talked to Liv about…? And she…' He opened and closed his fists in a way that didn't bode well for Liv Høie Hansen when he went home. 'She doesn't have a fucking … I'm the only person who knows what really happened!'

'Oh, yes. Only you? Wasn't anyone else involved?'

'I…' He half turned and didn't complete the sentence.

The door behind us was pulled open with the same grating rasp. Through the doorway came five black-clad bikers, Torfinn Vangen at their head. The one at the back slammed the door shut. The others spread out behind Robert Høie Hansen as though he had suddenly sprouted big, black bat wings.

Torfinn Vangen came alongside him. He stared intently at me while partly turning his head to Robert. 'And what are we discussing here then?'

'The good old days in Buvik,' I said. 'Veslemøy Valaker – that sort of thing. Anything to add?'

His narrowed eyes glittered darkly. Then he squared up to Robert. 'What the fuck did you tell him?'

Robert paled visibly, and I could see beads of sweat bubbling up on his brow. 'He's lying! I didn't say a word, Torfinn! I swear to you.'

'And who the hell led him to Buvik? We took note of his car

registration number on Friday when he'd been to see Åsmund. The same car is parked outside here and we've checked him out. This guy's a cop, Robert, and he's digging up old shit.'

'I didn't tell him about ... anything, Torfinn!'

'You've already said too much. Why the hell did you bring him here?'

'It's an open day, isn't it?' I said.

Torfinn spun round to face me. 'And you shut your mouth!'

Robert was almost whimpering now. 'He wanted to talk. He said ... if I didn't he was going to shout it out so that everyone could hear.'

'Everyone could hear what, Robert?'

He held back for a moment, but then he couldn't keep it in any longer. 'About Veslemøy.'

Torfinn Vangen made a gesture with one hand. One of the bikers behind Robert stepped forwards two paces and swung a baseball bat through the air. It hit Robert on the back of the head so unerringly and with such a hollow ring it sounded as if he had hit a billiard ball. Robert's eyes widened, then the pupils disappeared beneath his eyelids so that all we could see were the whites of his eyes. With a sound that reminded me of air being released from a balloon, he crumpled to the floor in front of me and stayed there.

Torfinn Vangen made another gesture and three bikers came towards me, two of them brandishing baseball bats. The fourth stood by the door with a big grin on his mug.

I moved backwards while trying to hold their eyes. Two of them went so far to the side of me that I had difficulty following their movements. The third shuffled towards me with his bat in the air.

Torfinn Vangen stood by the felled Robert Høie Hansen and smirked. 'Just give up, Grandpa. You won't be going anywhere unless it's feet first.'

I cupped my hands to my mouth and yelled: 'Help! Heeeelp!'

He gestured to his pals and instantly they were on me. I held my arms above my head in defence, but received a blow to a bicep that paralysed it. At the same time the bruiser in front of me stepped closer and rammed his bat right into my stomach with such power it knocked all the breath out of me. As I folded over I felt the other bat hit me on the back of my head, not with the same power as the blow that felled Robert, but more than enough for me to see stars. My legs buckled beneath me and I fell to the floor.

Before losing consciousness, I felt them turn me over, open my jacket and rifle through my pockets. One of them found my car keys and held them up in the air triumphantly. 'Here!' he said.

'Good,' I heard Torfinn Vangen say from a distance. 'We'll dispose of them as soon as the coast's clear.'

'Both of them?'

'I'm sure that'd be nice for them. Have some company on their final journey, eh?'

'Ho ho ho,' guffawed one of the men in a way I thought I recognised.

'Heh heh,' laughed another.

Ha ha, I said to myself, but there was no one to hear.

32

My head felt as though it was full to the brim with slivers of glass – the remains of a smashed mirror. It stung and tingled all over, and when I opened my eyes my vision was diffuse and fragmented. It took me several minutes to focus.

What I saw first was Robert Høie Hansen. He had a thick rope around his waist and under his armpits. The rope was tied to a large sling hook hanging from a pulley in the ceiling, and he had been lifted five metres off the floor like an animal carcass ready to be carved up. Broad strips of gaffer tape had been wound around his legs, from his ankles to his crotch, and also around his arms. Hanging there, his hands held devoutly together at waist height, he reminded me of the blessedly departed ascending to the heavenly vaults. His head was slumped forwards as if in silent prayer on the way up.

As for me, I was sitting on the floor with my hands behind my back, tied to a concrete column, my arms and legs bandaged in similar fashion. I could barely move, however hard I tried to jiggle the rope and tape.

I looked around. We were in a concrete cellar, lit only by the dim daylight leaking in through the wired glass in some narrow windows high above. Wooden and cardboard boxes of various sizes lined the walls, and there was a strong smell of oil, like in a military arms store. At one end of the room there was a solid iron door that made me think of bunkers and air-raid shelters.

But it was an effort to move my head. I was dizzy and felt an acute urge to throw up. I had terrible pains in my back and head, and fear was gnawing at me with such intensity that I had to resist with all my strength not being sucked into what would ultimately hurl me into the great darkness long before I had planned.

I closed my eyes and concentrated, breathed in deep, breathed out, breathed in, breathed out. When I opened them again, I focused as hard as possible on Hansen in an attempt to make contact with him before all hope was gone.

'Robert,' I said, and just the vibration of my own vocal cords sent another wave of pain through my head, as if everything inside was smashed to pieces.

He didn't react.

'Robert!' I said, louder this time, causing a clap of thunder to roll behind my forehead.

'Aagh,' came a faint, drowsy sound from him.

'Wake up!'

'Eh?'

A thousand drummers ran amok in my head, but I clenched my teeth and went on: 'You have to wake up, Robert! Robert Høie Hansen! Am I getting through to you?' Under my breath, I mumbled to myself: 'Mayday, Mayday, Mayday...'

In an odd screwing motion, as though it was dislocated, Hansen raised his head. His eyes swirled around the room, blinking again and again until he finally managed to focus, and when his vision encompassed me, he seemed to experience an acute urge to be sick as well. 'Jesus,' he groaned. 'Jesus,' he repeated. 'Jesus,' he said with real feeling, as if to stress that all good things came in threes.

'Are you the kind that thinks you can conjure Him up by saying His name three times?' I muttered.

'Oh, Christ.'

'Yes, that's his other name,' I riposted, trying to keep my spirits up.

'Whose name?'

'Forget it. Do you know where we are?'

He answered with a question. 'Can you see what you've got us into now?'

I pondered that one. 'Yes, I can see that I'm in trouble, but I don't understand why they insisted on dragging you into it.'

'What?' He was struggling to keep his eyes focused. 'What are you drivelling on about?'

'Too many words? I'd better give you the short version: Yes, I can see.'

'See what?'

I groaned aloud. 'Do you know where we are?' I repeated.

This time he twisted his head a few notches further to the side. His mouth moved, but no sound emerged, as though he were talking to himself.

'What? I can't hear.'

Then he twisted his head back and looked at me again. 'By the Oster-fjord. Old Local Defence depot. We took it over a few years ago.'

'So this is where you store the contraband?'

He didn't answer.

I sniffed the air demonstratively. 'Weapons, too, eh?'

He stared at me, poker-faced.

'Well off the beaten track?'

'A dead end down to the sea. Barbed wire around it.'

'So there's no point shouting for help?'

'We can shout till we lose our voices. No one'll hear us.'

'We've got to get out, Robert. Before they return.'

There was a glint in his eyes. 'Yes … out.' But he didn't seem to believe it possible.

To demonstrate what I meant, I wrenched at the rope tied around me and tried to pull my hands apart, hoping the tape would give a little.

I stared at Robert. 'You know you're here because of Veslemøy, don't you.'

'Eh? What do you mean?'

'Torfinn's frightened you've told me what really happened to her.'

'Torfinn…'

'You told your wife you were innocent. You hadn't done anything to Veslemøy. But they'd threatened to silence you.'

'Yes…'

'But I don't believe you.'

'What?'

'I don't think you were innocent. Not *so* innocent. You would've told

Ingeborg when she found out. You wouldn't have just let her kick you out and you wouldn't have accepted never being allowed to see your daughter again. You didn't want that, did you. The entire break is not only because of Ingeborg's disappointment and fury. It's also because of your own shame at what you'd done.'

'Been part of.'

'OK. Been part of.'

He kicked desperately with his taped legs, like a fish on a hook – not yet dead, but still with enough energy to wriggle in protest.

'You can tell me now, Robert. Doesn't look like either of us is going anywhere. You can tell me everything.'

He started speaking, oblivious of me, as though he were talking to himself, a monologue he had repeated again and again over all the years that had passed since that August night in 1975. 'I … walked her home, but not to the door. Her parents. She didn't want them to see us. So we'd stopped at the crossroads, then they suddenly appeared from nowhere.'

'Torfinn and Åsmund?'

He nodded. 'The Vangen boys. Suddenly they were there. They grabbed her. Covered her mouth so she couldn't scream for help. She looked at me in desperation. Shouted for help, but nothing came out. They … They were my pals. I was often in their workshop fixing my bike. They'd always helped me. And they said: "You've never had a girl, have you, Robert? Look!" And then they lifted up her dress and pulled her knickers down and said: "Look! Never seen anything like that before, have you, eh?" And then … I don't know what got into me. I've never understood. But Torfinn said: "You can have her first, Robert. Come on. In the forest here, and then…" And so I joined them and did what they said, and afterwards I had to hold her, first for Torfinn and then Åsmund and finally Torfinn again. They … We … were like wild animals, and afterwards … She just lay there, not moving. At some point she'd lost consciousness, and I said we have to … But they said they'd make sure she got home, I should run along, and Torfinn said: "We'll kill you if you say anything, Robert! We'll kill you!"'

The long speech seemed to have woken him up and he locked his eyes on me, as if begging for forgiveness, an appeal to me to understand how he felt all those years afterwards, especially when he thought it was all forgotten and he bumped into her at Fredly with Ingeborg, and everything came out.

I had no forgiveness to give. He wasn't innocent. He wasn't hanging here like a slaughtered animal almost thirty years later for no reason. There was some poetic justice in it. But it wasn't forgiveness he wanted. Not now. I didn't either. What we wanted was to get out before the black angels returned to finish off what they had started.

'Robert! Now you've told me all this, there's one more question: Emma. Do you know anything at all about what's happened to her or where she is?'

He shook his head in despair. 'No, Veum. I've told you time and time again. I don't know anything about what's happened to Emma.'

'All the more reason for us to get out, don't you think?'

'Yes, but how?'

'Hm,' I said. 'How indeed ... ?'

33

I studied the hook he was hanging from. 'If you could move your body…'

'Move?'

'Yes. If you could build up some momentum and swing, maybe the rope around you will come off the hook and then…' I looked from the soles of his feet to the floor and omitted to add what I was thinking: *Then you'll fall five metres to the concrete floor. And if you're lucky, you won't break your legs.*

'And then what?'

'You'll be down here, and then…' *We'll see what happens.*

He still looked dubious, but he began to swing his body back and forth as best he could.

I watched and cheered him on. 'That's the way! Go for it, Robert! From side … to side. Side … to side!' I could see the loop at the top was moving. 'It's working. More!'

But then he seemed to give up. He slowed down, breathing heavily, and in the end hung there, with a downcast expression and a tight-lipped grin.

'What's the matter? Don't give up. It was working.'

He sent me a desperate look. 'Can't do it. We're going to … We're going to die here, Veum. Do you understand?'

'Are we hell!'

Once again I started to squirm and twist inside the ropes around me. Was there a tiny millimetre of give in the rope holding my arms behind me, one on each side of the column? And I noticed something else at the same time. The light in the room was fading. Outside the narrow windows, darkness was falling.

From Robert I heard more groaning. When I looked in his direction he had started swinging back and forth on his own initiative with a new and more determined expression on his face. I urged him on while continuing with my own exertions.

I could feel it clearly now. There was some give in the rope behind me. I yanked my arms, hard. Then I stopped and tried jiggling instead. *Yes! Maybe…* I squeezed my fingers into as small a space as I could. Then I pulled – *Gently, gently does it…*

'Ugh, ugh, ugh!' Robert groaned, swinging from side to side. Now there was no doubt things were happening for him, too. The loop on the hook was moving in synchrony with his movements: into the wall, away from the wall, into the wall, away from the wall, a few centimetres more each time.

Once again he gave up. 'Grrrr! Fuck, fuck, fuck!' he shouted.

'You can forget that particular activity, if you don't keep trying,' I said, moving my right hand a fraction. The rope cut into my wrist as I pulled; it felt as if my skin was being peeled. My head was pounding. Fiery dots of light danced in front of my eyes, so intense that I was dazzled. There! Suddenly my hand moved more easily, and then it was free. 'Yesss!' I shouted, so loud that Hansen lifted his head from where he was hanging and looked down at me in the darkening room.

'Are you free?'

'One hand is, at any rate.'

But there was still some way to go. With my free hand I managed to find the end of the gaffer tape around my legs and pull at it until I could kick one foot free, half turn and get a better grip on the knot behind the column. I stretched my muscles as far as I could, felt a sudden, new pain when a fingernail broke, but once again I could sense progress. At the back of my mind I had an unpleasant feeling time was racing away from me, second by second, minute by minute, but then – at long last – I managed to loosen the main knot at the back. I jerked again and then my left hand was free as well. Now I could move more easily and I set about the rest. After a couple of minutes I was completely free and standing on the floor, the blood throbbing in my head, my muscles aching as if I was breasting the finishing line in a triathlon, oblivious of where I was. What I wanted to do most was slump down, curl up and let the tears flow.

However, there was still a lot to do.

I assessed Hansen's situation. 'Listen,' I said. 'If I can move some of the boxes over there and stack them up I might be able to get high enough to free you.'

'Really?' He didn't seem to believe me, and I wasn't at all convinced myself, bearing in mind his body weight and the exertions I had already subjected my body to.

I dashed over to the nearest boxes. I tried to lift one of them, but it weighed a ton and the smell of oil was stronger. I tried another. The same.

'The cardboard boxes,' Robert groaned.

I scanned the room and spotted a pile of cardboard boxes. I ran over, grabbed the top one and tried again. This was lighter. Running back to Hansen, I could hear metal rattling against metal. Bullets, I guessed.

I placed the box underneath him, but realised I would need at least one more on top and maybe one under that to give better support. After building this pyramid I could see this wasn't enough, either.

Now I could feel my desperation growing. 'There must be a stepladder here somewhere, isn't there? Or a ladder.'

'Maybe in the corner,' came an answer from above.

'Where?' I peered into the darkness, made out the direction he was nodding to and ran over. If possible, it was even darker there. I stumbled over various bits of junk: some discarded cardboard boxes and equipment I couldn't identify in the gloom. By the back wall I groped my way forwards. There I finally found what seemed to be an aluminium ladder. I felt at the back. It was a stepladder. I lifted it up, carried it under my arm and dashed back to Hansen.

He watched me, like a starving child waiting for his turn in the food queue. Quickly I positioned the stepladder beside him and climbed up until I was level with his upper body.

I grabbed him, trying to get a good hold on his belt in order to lift him. It was hopeless. He was much too heavy, and all I could do was raise him a little and slacken the rope, but not enough to dislodge it from the hook.

I had to employ another strategy. I reassessed the situation. 'Listen, Robert. I'll put your feet on the ladder. If I can push you up a step I might be able to stretch far enough to loosen the rope.'

Again I grabbed his belt, but this time to pull him sideways towards me. It was no good. I had to go down several steps and hold his legs around the ankles. Now I managed to pull his legs towards the ladder and place his biker boots on one step. I went down another step, held his ankles and pushed upwards so that his knees bent. Then I lifted him; the effort went down my spine like an electric shock, but it worked. I had managed to get his boots onto the next step up.

'Now, Robert. Straighten your legs, so you're a bit higher.'

He gave a loud groan, but did as I said.

'Don't move.'

I forced my way past him and up to the top step. I looked up. I could just make out the hook in the darkness. I groped for the rope, but almost lost my balance and had to go down a step. Then I made a fresh attempt and this time I succeeded. I held the rope and slid it up the hook … up a bit more. Suddenly it was off and falling past me. I quickly went down a few steps while still holding onto Hansen.

But it was too late. He was off balance and in free fall. I clung to the ladder with one hand and tried to catch him with the other. My arm jerked, as if it was being wrenched out of its socket. My grip on the ladder was weakened, but I managed to slow our fall. Like Siamese twins we slipped down step by step, tumbling onto the concrete floor and finally lying still after the most painful release imaginable.

Once again I felt like giving up, falling into a deep sleep and for-getting everything. But I picked myself up by the scruff of the neck, struggling first to my knees, then to my feet.

I bent over Hansen. 'Robert! Are you awake?'

He groaned from the floor. 'Yes.'

'I'll try and remove the tape.'

'OK.'

I would have given a year of my life for a knife right then, but I had to press my fingernails into service again. Slowly, and with difficulty, I managed to tear off the tape wound around his arms and legs. It seemed to take an hour, but in reality it wasn't such a long time. At last he was free. I straightened and stretched, then held out a hand to help him up. Shakily he got to his feet, and I wasn't that steady on my legs, either.

'Now to get out.'

'Mhm.'

In the darkness I crossed the room to where the iron door was. Once I had found it, I grabbed the handle, forced it down and tried to push the door open. It didn't budge. I tried the opposite direction, pulling it towards me. Nothing. I suspected they had closed it from the outside, most probably by putting something heavy against it. I tried again several times, but it wouldn't shift.

I turned to Hansen. 'The windows. That's our only chance.'

I could barely make out his face in the darkness, but the way he was standing made it clear that he didn't hold out much hope for this, either.

'We have to try!'

I went to the ladder, lifted it and moved it to where the dim light told us the windows were. I clambered to the top. If I stretched up on the tips of my toes I could reach the edge of the window. I ran my hand along the frame, searching for a metal catch, and in the middle I found one. I held it and pushed it open. It gave and I pushed the narrow window outwards.

Fresh air streamed into the room and I heaved a sigh of relief.

This feeling lasted for approximately five seconds. Through the open window I could hear the roar of motorbikes on their way down through the forest and I saw the flickering lights of their headlamps on the crowns of the trees.

34

I turned and stared into the darkness beneath me. In a shrill voice I shouted: 'Is there anywhere we can hide?'

Hansen didn't answer, and I hurriedly slid down the ladder. I stumbled towards him. He was standing stock still where I had left him. 'Robert! They're on their way here. Is there anywhere we can hide?'

'Here?'

'Yes!'

Now the bikes were outside the building. The din was subsiding. Some of them had already switched off their engines.

I grabbed him and pushed him further into the room. 'Come on!'

I tried to remember the layout of the place before darkness had fallen. I pulled him with me into the murk, towards where I had found the ladder. 'There might be room behind some of the boxes. If we're lucky they'll see the open window and think we've escaped.'

He just mumbled something incomprehensible.

In the darkness I tripped over the junk I had noticed earlier. I kicked it to the side and carried on, right to the wall. I groped my way forwards and felt a stack of wooden boxes to the left of us. I tried to insert my hand behind them. It was possible, but not for very far. I pressed a hand against them to check their weight and see if I could push them out further. No, it was hopeless. They were much too heavy.

Again I tried to picture what had been there. All I could remember was the same kind of box I had used to reach Hansen hanging from the hook. I searched around blindly. Could we build a wall and hide behind them?

At the same time I kept an ear open for sounds outside. Now I couldn't hear anything. All the engines had been switched off, but through the open window I heard voices and I thought I recognised Torfinn Vangen shouting orders to those around him.

At breakneck speed I managed to collect enough cardboard boxes and pile them up far enough from the wall for us to slip behind. Then I pulled Hansen in with me. He allowed himself to be led wherever, like a giant cuddly toy and about as talkative.

Now I could hear noises coming from the iron door, as though whatever was stopping it from budging was being removed, and then the sound of the heavy door opening. The light in the ceiling came on, presumably operated from outside. I looked up. It was a single neon tube without a cover. At first it gave off a weak glow, but it became stronger and stronger by the second. I blinked and looked at Hansen. He scrunched up his eyes as if the light was too strong for him. He stood there, his mouth agape, gasping for air like a fish on land.

'What the fuck!' I heard someone shout by the door.

Then came Torfinn Vangen's voice. 'Jesus Christ!'

'Look up there. The window.'

'Who tied them up?'

There was a silence.

A reedy voice said: 'You checked them both yourself, Torfinn.'

'Yeah, right, checked. I was relying on you, for Christ's sake – who was it? You, Anders? Bjørn?'

I could make out some evasive answers.

'It doesn't necessarily mean they've escaped yet,' said a voice I hadn't heard before. The brains in the gang maybe.

'No,' Torfinn Vangen said, and I could literally hear him hunting around. 'You're right.'

I squeezed up against Hansen and made myself as small as possible behind the narrow column of cardboard boxes. We heard the crunch of heavy boots moving through the room, closer and closer.

The boots stopped on the floor in front of us.

I held my breath.

There was an indefinable gurgle, like a semi-stifled gasp of laughter. I heard some low mumbles and then the sound of more boots joining the first pair. Now it was unmistakeable. They were laughing, a coarse masculine laugh, like when the first stripper comes into the room on a stag night for a forty-something reprising the bridegroom role.

'Well, what do you know! Have we got mice here?'

'Mice? More like rats, boys. Big, fat rats.'

'Squeak, squeak. Come on out, we've seen you.'

Robert Høie Hansen and I stood there like a pair of reject window dummies waiting to be transported to the refuse dump. I sent Hansen a sidelong glance. He had opened his eyes and was staring ahead with an expression of boundless fear. A strangulated squeak came from his mouth and two large, shiny tears ran down his cheeks.

'Hear that?' I heard from the other side of the boxes.

Then they made a move. One of them kicked the cardboard boxes away and we stood gawping at them like two despairing teenage girls stripped naked and defenceless in front of a mob of men.

They were the same five who had seen to us before, but not in quite such a wing formation now. Three of them were holding the same baseball bats as the last time we met, and they were already eagerly whistling through the air in front of us.

'My goodness me,' mocked Torfinn Vangen. 'The call of the wild, eh? But you didn't get far, did you.'

'Far enough,' I muttered.

'Think so, Grandpa? But you'll be going a great deal further by the time we've finished with you.' He half turned to his pals. 'Boys, do you know the song "Se der danser bestefar"? Shall we see how good Grandpa is at dancing?'

He stepped forwards quickly. I tried to anticipate what he was planning to do, but wasn't fast enough. He kicked out with one foot and hit me on the side of a leg, so hard that I lost balance and fell sideways onto the concrete.

'That wasn't very good, Grandpa. Get up and let's try again.'

I knelt in front of him and looked up. 'Unless you've got some better dancing partners I'm staying down here.'

'Oh, yes?'

This time he launched a brutal kick at my face, but I twisted my left shoulder up to take the impact. He wound himself up for another kick when Hansen groaned: 'Torfinn! Don't...'

Torfinn Vangen stopped in mid-swing, stamped his foot down hard on the floor and turned to the last speaker. 'What? Are there more takers for a dance?'

'Torfinn! I don't understand why you're doing this to me. I haven't said a word.'

Torfinn Vangen stretched out a hand. 'Give me a bat.'

One of the others quickly obeyed. Then he advanced on Hansen and rammed the bat into his stomach, as they had done to me earlier. 'No? But you could, couldn't you? Because you've always been the weakest link in the chain. The rotten apple in the basket. I've always known that at some point or other we'd have to ... get rid of you. Now the time has come. If it's any comfort, you won't be going on your own. Grandpa'll be joining you.'

Once again I felt the desperation grow in my body. I looked at the other bikers. 'Are you up for this, all of you? Do you realise what'll happen? You're going to be behind bars for years, all of you, when they find out.'

Torfinn Vangen turned to me again. 'Find out? There'll be nothing to find. We'll make sure of that. Boys, get ready to do as we planned.'

'Boys,' I continued. 'Have you got no spines? Do you just follow orders with no minds of your own? Surely some of you have families, don't you? Partners? That must...'

Torfinn Vangen swung the bat through the air and hit me at the junction between the neck and the shoulder, paralysing the whole of my neck. The next blow hit me directly on the skull and I lost control of my knees; they gave way and I lay spreadeagled across the floor like a slaughtered animal, face down on the concrete. I didn't lose consciousness, but made no attempt to get up either, hoping he would leave it at that.

'You shut your mouth,' he snarled above me. I didn't reply and he didn't hit me again, but scornfully kicked me in the ribs.

He turned back to the others. 'Unroll the plastic. When they're wrapped up properly, we'll take them down to the sea, add the rocks and … plop! Down to the bottom of Oster Fjord with both of them.'

Again the coarse laughter in unison.

'To the bottom of the fjord,' repeated one of them, a slightly higher voice than the others, possibly the youngest of them.

'They won't even be crab food. They'll stay down there like mummies for eternity.'

I heard the thick plastic being unfurled and broke into a cold sweat. Of all the tight spots I had been in, this was the worst. And all the signs suggested it would be the last. I felt my throat constrict. Images began to flutter through my head like a warning of doomsday. Flashes of my childhood from Nordnes, Ryfylke and Sunnfjord. My schooldays in Nordnes and afterwards at the Cathedral School. My mum and dad, if he was my dad. My first loves – Sylvelin, Reidun, Elisabeth and Rebecca. Going to sea, to Oslo, to Stavanger. Training to be a social worker in Stavanger. Beate and Thomas. Family life and working in outreach for the social services – a bad combination. Children I had searched for, children I had found. It all flickered past, memories of the many cases I had worked on, finding corpses, showdowns with the guilty, meetings with members of the police force. Dankert Muus, Vegard Vadheim, Jakob E. Hamre. And now Norma lying in an unnatural position on her kitchen floor, Emma whom I hadn't found, Veslemøy who wouldn't talk, then this dead end that looked as if it was going to live up to its name. I thought of little Helene, who had lost her father a few years ago, and Sølvi, who would once again experience losing someone close to her, but this time he would be gone physically, too. To the bottom of Oster Fjord, dark, cold and…

'OK, Torfinn.'

'Good. Get rid of this dead meat here. Bjørn, you come here and help me with the traitor.'

'No!'

'Hey, what the f—!'

I heard a dull thud above me. I slowly turned my head in the direction of the noise. Torfinn Vangen had staggered backwards. Robert Høie Hansen went after him swinging his fists.

'Gonna go for it, eh?'

Torfinn Vangen had both feet on the ground again. When Hansen was near enough he let fly with the bat and hit Hansen on the forehead, with a sickening, skull-cracking crunch. Hansen ploughed on regardless and hit Vangen with two further punches, one from the left and one from the right, then launched his whole body at him and both fell to the floor like two sacks of potatoes.

'Boys,' Torfinn yelled from under Hansen's dead weight, 'get him off me!'

The others charged over. With all four of them busy lifting Hansen off Torfinn, I got to my feet and ran to the door. But my knees were weak and I was slow off the mark.

Torfinn was the first to notice what was happening. He pointed to me. 'Boys, stop him! Kenneth – you and Tore!'

I shot forwards, grabbed a rusty-brown metal object, lifted it and threw it behind me. It hit one of the two on the shoulder, but he just let it glance off him and wasn't hurt.

I made for the doorway and had my nose almost level with it when one of them caught me up, grabbed my arm and twisted me round. He attempted a head butt, which I avoided with a twist of my body, then he and his pal knocked into me so hard I was thrown back against the doorframe with a bang. They grabbed me around the waist and threw me back into the room.

Slowly and laboriously I staggered to my feet in time to see the cavalry arrive, as if on cue for the last roll of a Western in the Eldorado Cinema, 1958. Armed with guns, the Police's Rapid Response Unit stormed the building.

Commands rang through the air: 'Police! Police! Down on the floor! Down! Now!'

One of them stared at me through the bulletproof plastic visor in front of his helmet. 'You too! Down!'

I felt tears welling, but attempted a smile.

'Down!' he ordered, pointing with his weapon.

Without a protest I slumped to the floor, spread myself flat and felt the sobs shaking my body. Strong hands bent my arms behind my back and I heard handcuffs click around my wrists. From other parts of the room I heard corresponding clicks, initial protests, oaths and curses from some, before everything quietened down, though it wasn't still and peaceful – more like a frozen shot taken by a war reporter of a bloody battlefield, where in the end only the victors were left standing.

I raised my head and looked around. Through the door came someone I thought I recognised. It was Moses Meland.

'We can make this a habit,' I said. 'You arriving at the last minute and saving my life.'

The undercover detective met my gaze and grinned. 'I'll give it some thought…'

Then my eyes shut and everything around me was gone. Inside my brain images still whirred, as though this was the last ever film of my life I was watching. In the darkness all the lights to the emergency exits were extinguished. I had my fingers crossed they would come back on when the performance was over.

35

When I awoke I was lying in a room with white walls and had a head-ache that was so bad it felt as though all the crows in the town were holding a meeting inside it and the loudspeakers were on full blast. I turned my head to find my bearings and the whole room went into a spin. I held onto the edge of the bed so that I wouldn't fall off. I didn't. But the nausea rising from my stomach was enough to make me close my eyes again and groan aloud while I was trying to remember where I had seen the face beside the bed; it looked like a wind-blown balloon floating up to the ceiling above us.

A cool hand was placed on my brow and a husky voice said my name: 'Varg?'

Without opening my eyes, I answered: 'Yes?'

'It's me. Sølvi.'

Ah, that was it, yes, Sølvi. I should have remembered, of course.

'How are you feeling?'

'As if my whole head were about to explode. Has it grown?'

'Your head? No.'

'Just feels like it then.'

'You have bad concussion and a large bump on your forehead, bruises and grazes over the rest of your body, but the docs say that oth-erwise you're in good shape.'

'And … the other guy?'

'Høie Hansen?'

'Yes … Robert.'

'News is not so good there.'

'Right. Is he … ?'

'He's in a coma.'

Bang on cue, I passed out too. The next thing I recalled was someone injecting me in the arm and a high-pitched voice saying: 'We'll give him something to put him to sleep. And a painkiller.'

'Alright.'

'You can go home now. Nothing more will happen this evening. If we're lucky he'll sleep all night.'

'OK, I have a little daughter who … But I'll be back tomorrow.'

'That's fine.'

Then came the night, and the darkness, and all the dreams. She was proved wrong, the lady with the high-pitched voice. I woke up at least once every hour, opened my eyes and received confirmation that the room was still in motion, but the waves weren't as high, perhaps we were moving into calmer waters.

The following day I was better. I could sit up in bed and eat breakfast from a tray handed to me from the side, even if I didn't manage to get much down. And the coffee tasted just as bitter as I had expected. But the boat had docked. There was only passport control to go through.

During the ward rounds a young male doctor with a shaven head and round glasses sat down on the chair beside me and explained in plain words and Latin mumbo jumbo what was going on in my head, even though all the crows had flown off and only the incessant rush of wind prevailed.

'You've got severe concussion, Varg. You've got a muscle rupture in your neck, here…' He pointed to where on himself. 'And lesions and swellings – most of them here…' He pointed to both sides of my upper arms. 'In the abdominal region there is severe bruising, but so far we haven't been able to locate any internal damage. However, we'd like to keep you under observation for at least another twenty-four hours before we draw any conclusions.' He sent me a reassuring smile. 'Considering your age, you've come out of this surprisingly well. Your basic constitution is good, no doubt about that. But you'll notice after-effects for quite a while to come, so we recommend a long period off work when you're discharged.' After a little pause he added: 'Anything you'd like to ask?'

I ruminated. 'How old am I?'

He examined my face with concern. Then he looked down at the card in his hand. 'Sixty-one according to our information.'

'Thank you.'

'Couldn't you remember?'

'Yes. It's just that I feel closer to a hundred.'

He nodded, but his face still wore the scrutinising-doctor expression. 'You'll feel younger by the day.'

'I hope so.'

'We'll see each other tomorrow.'

'I hope we do.'

He smiled. 'We need a bit of humour. Everything's so much better then.'

This time I just nodded. Even that hurt.

I asked one of the nurses if they had anything to read. She came back with the latest edition of the local paper – it required the least use of muscles to hold, but when I tried, the seasickness returned and I had to put it down. All I saw was the headline in capitals and a page reference to the news article: 'BIKER RAID IN LINDÅS'. I kept the paper for later.

Late that afternoon Sølvi came again. This time I recognised her and remembered her name and as a reward for that she leaned over and kissed me lightly on the cheek, then sat down and asked me how I felt.

'Today? You know those reports you see in the papers sometimes – where they empty people's dustbins and analyse the contents? I feel like what they find, and every bit of me is past its sell-by date.' She smiled, and I added: 'Still usable, mind you.'

'I'd better pick you up then.'

I caught sight of the newspaper on my bedside table. 'Do you feel like reading that article to me?'

She took the paper and nodded. 'There's not much. I've already read it. It's just about the raid. Five men were taken to the police station and put on remand, and more arrests are expected in the next few days.'

'Nothing else?'

'The police have had the biker club under surveillance for several years, but there's nothing about why they raided it just then.'

'OK.'

'But I'm very happy they did.'

'How...?' I searched for words.

'I rang them. When you didn't return from their so-called open day I was worried. I tried ringing you, but didn't get an answer. The phone said you were out of the coverage area. Then I became very worried, and fortunately the police took my call seriously. At ten in the evening an officer rang me to say you were safe, but on your way to Haukeland Hospital. That was all. I was only allowed to come and see you yesterday.'

'Yesterday? So what day is it today?'

'Tuesday.'

'Tuesday! But I've got ... a job to do.'

She smiled indulgently. 'First of all you've got a head to put on straight. You're off work until further notice.'

'I'm a freelancer.'

'And I'm your next of kin.'

That got me thinking. 'When did we agree that?'

'I agreed it.'

That got me thinking even more. 'Thomas! Has someone ... spoken to him?'

'I've spoken to him. He's coming over at the weekend to see you. I said it wasn't urgent. Otherwise he would be here now.'

'But Emma...'

'Who?'

'The young woman I was supposed to find. My job.'

She rolled her eyes and sent me a look of despair. 'That'll have to wait, Varg. Surely you realise that? You can hardly stand upright.'

'I haven't tried.'

'No. Exactly. Do you feel like trying now?'

'No, not really.'

'There you go. So I suggest we drop the topic. But...' She took out a small, slim phone with a pink lid. '…I came across this. It's an old model, but as yours has disappeared you can borrow it. I've already put in a prepaid SIM card, and here are a couple of spares if you need them.'

'Not sure I like the colour, but … I suppose they dispatched mine to mobile-phone eternity. After I've recovered I'll try and tap in the most important numbers.'

'Mine's there already.'

'And mine?'

'It's in the phone, too. Under V.'

After she had gone I started on it. They had most things at the hospital, even a telephone directory. Accompanied by a gradually worsening headache I worked bit by bit through the important contacts I could remember, vaguely peripheral acquaintances, people involved in the present case and other useful phone numbers. After I had finished I was exhausted. The rest of the evening I spent dozing and at night I was given something to help me sleep better.

The following day I received an unexpected visitor. I had been informed by the doctor that they would like to keep me in for another day, but all the test results looked encouraging. He had recommended that I get out of bed and onto the floor, and I had followed his advice. It didn't go too badly. I staggered from one wall to another and after a bit of training in my room I ventured out into the corridor, where I hauled myself between patients, passing staff and the odd visitor. Among the latter I happened upon Moses Meland.

'Hi, Veum! We've been informed we can speak to you today.'

'Informed by the top brass?'

'No, by the hospital.'

'I assume it's OK then. Shall we do it in my suite?'

'Preferably.'

He went with me to the room. I sat on the edge of the bed. After a short inspection he perched on the only chair.

Moses Meland was, as usual, casually dressed in what to my mind was the undercover uniform. He wore a dark-blue denim shirt and matching stone-washed jeans, a black leather jacket and a grey scarf knotted loosely around his neck. His hair was dark blond, thicker around his ears and neck, and he had the obligatory three-day stubble electric shavers were set to in his department.

'This isn't a formal interview, Veum. We'll do that at the next juncture. We only want to know, with regard to our further investigation, why you were in such a critical situation that we had to intervene.'

'Has he said anything?'

'Has who said anything?'

'Robert Høie Hansen.'

He leaned forwards and lowered his voice as though someone might hear us. 'Hansen's still in a coma, in another room up here. But, unlike you, he won't be going anywhere if he gets onto his feet again. Of course we're interested in why he fell out of favour. Were you doing some undercover stuff on them as well?'

'No. The thing is Hansen's daughter from an earlier life has gone missing and I was commissioned to find her. I was at the bikers' open day on Sunday primarily to talk to him. His chum took the view that he was grassing them up, but in fact he wasn't.'

'Right. But two days previously you were in a confrontation with them somewhere in Ryfylke and on the ferry home you spoke to Hansen.'

'You're well informed, I must say.'

He lowered his voice a notch, so low that I had difficulty hearing what he said. 'I can tell you this much, Veum, as it's already in the papers. We've been watching this gang for the last two or three years, and we have so much on them it was only a question of time before we raided them anyway. They're under suspicion of possession with intent to supply drugs between Østland and Vestland and down to Haugesund, among other places. Last Friday they trooped down all together, then scattered into so many small groups that we lost track of them. But Hansen and a couple of others supplied drugs to Haugesund, Kopervik and right down to Skudeneshavn, while some others went to Sauda and afterwards Buvik, where they have a central distributor.'

'Åsmund Vangen?'

'Right. And you were there, we heard.'

'Tell me, have you had me under surveillance as well?'

He grinned wryly. 'No, no. But your car registration number was noted, and then it wasn't so difficult to work out, you know.'

'Does that mean ... you've collared him as well?'

'The Vangen brothers plus another handful. The Haugesund police are taking care of the arrests down there. This is one of the biggest hauls we've had, Veum. And we feel we have a good case against them. Most of them will end up behind bars for quite a few years to come.'

'I suddenly feel a lot better.'

'I can understand that. You experienced them at their most brutal. If your girlfriend hadn't phoned us that afternoon there's a good chance we'd have been too late.'

'And Hansen and I wouldn't be here, but at the bottom of Oster Fjord.'

His expression became serious. 'Was that what they threatened to do with you?'

'Not just threatened. They were well on the way to pickling us and neither of us would've been a tasty morsel.'

'It was when we saw your car on the main road, parked between the trees, that we realised where you were. We knew about the warehouse in Lindås although we'd never been there. But that was when we decided to strike.'

'You came in the very nick of time.'

'By the way, we towed your car to your girlfriend's house in Åsane.'

'Thank you. Thank you for everything, I should say. But ... can I ask you one thing?'

He opened his palms as a sign that he was willing to listen at any rate.

'You said you had Hansen on your radar when he was in Haugesund.'

'Yes.'

'During that time was he in the vicinity of a street called Gange-Rolvs gate?'

'I don't have that kind of detail to hand, but I can try and find out. Why do you ask?'

'I had a sister who lived there. And she was found dead on Friday evening. The same day that I met him on the ferry.'

'Dead as in … killed?'

'Probably an accident, but … Inspector Liland can give you more information about that case if you need it.'

'All I remember from the report is that he'd been to a specific address after he'd delivered … all the goodies. Where his ex-wife lived apparently.'

'Ingeborg! Did he visit her?'

'According to our people down there she's just a customer, not a major figure on the scene.'

'So no one's spoken to her?'

'Not as far as I know. As I said, we'll have to go through all of this properly at a later date, Veum. You'll be summoned for an interview when you've been discharged.'

'Long before Torfinn and Åsmund are, I hope.'

'Definitely.' He got up. 'See you at the next crossroads.'

'I'll let you know when I need urgent assistance.'

'Not too often though, Veum.'

'No, about every eighteen months, isn't that right?'

He grinned and went on his way with a friendly wave of the hand. I sat hoping my words wouldn't come back to haunt me.

36

Later that day I was in the corridor doing distance-walking training from one end to the other. The pains in my head had turned into a constant ache along a glowing line from one ear to the other. I still had problems keeping my balance, but when I fixed my eyes on a point ahead of me and didn't look down, it was better. The doors I had to pass through I opened by pulling a string hanging from the ceiling, which made me feel like a king as I slowly moved from one end of the high-rise building to the other with a host of invisible servants around me.

I bumped into her as she came through one of these doors, but since she was in uniform I didn't recognise her at once.

She didn't waste any time. 'See what you've done now!'

I stopped so quickly I had to support myself against the wall, and when I turned to her I had trouble focusing.

'Yes, you might well have a bad conscience.'

'A bad con— What about?'

Behind her the door opened automatically again. She half turned and pointed in that direction. 'He's been in a coma for three days now. We don't know whether he'll wake up and what state he'll be in if he does.'

I recognised her now. 'It wasn't me who put him in that state, Liv.'

'Of course not, but it all started with you sticking your nose into … our lives.'

'Sticking my nose into your lives? I was given a job and I've tried to do it. I've suffered a painful loss during the course of the investigation. Life comes at a price. Robert dug his own grave many years ago, and the story he told you was a lie. The whole of your relationship is built on it.'

She paled visibly. 'Lie … What lie?'

'The one he told you about Veslemøy. He wasn't as innocent as he made out to you, you see. All three of them were involved: Åsmund, Torfinn and him.'

'I don't know of any Åsmund or Torfinn.'

'Maybe not. But they grew up together and still meet. Torfinn's the main reason he's in a coma now. He's the leader of the biker gang Robert was in.'

'Torfinn Vangen?'

'Yes, so don't you come talking to me about a bad conscience.'

She had tears in her eyes now. Her lips quivered and she had to swallow before she could speak. 'OK.'

'When he wakes up, ask him yourself. He told me everything.'

'*If* he wakes up.'

'Yes, *if* … And while you're at it ask him why he called on Ingeborg when he was in Haugesund last Friday.'

'What? Ingeborg?'

'And they hadn't spoken for almost twenty years.'

'But…'

'But now Emma's missing. So perhaps that was the reason they re-established contact. Or he did.'

'I know nothing about this!'

'No, I don't, either. Yet.'

With those words we parted company. I went back to my room and considered my training more than complete. I felt exhausted, as if it was after a marathon, and the finishing line had been taken down long before I arrived and only the very last officials were standing around impatiently waiting for me.

The following day I was discharged, with reservations. The doctor made it clear that I was to take time off, and Sølvi – my self-appointed next of kin – turned up in person to drive me home, which on this occasion meant Pensione Saudalskleivane with full board and lodging.

I remonstrated gently, but she insisted: 'I'll make sure that you get enough food and sleep, and don't you even think about doing anything until you're up to it. No work on cases that are to your detriment. And don't worry, I'm putting you in the guest room, so you'll have the whole night to yourself.'

'And Emma…?'

'Emma will have to wait. Either she's fine where she is or it's too late anyway.'

'At any rate, drive me home first so that I can take my laptop with me.'

She hesitated, then gave in. 'OK. If you absolutely have to.'

'In addition, I might have to go one day to Haugesund for the funeral.'

'In which case I'll go with you.'

I nodded silently and gave up. There was something about this situation that had crushed all my resistance. I went with the flow, wherever it led, and right now the waters were pretty choppy. There were big rocks in the river and my body was already bruised enough.

37

For the next few days I had a kind of home office in Saudalskleivane. It consisted of a table, a chair, a laptop and Sølvi's landline. The view from the sitting-room window was the biggest distraction. I felt as if I could see to Iceland if I just stretched my neck a bit.

The first person I contacted was Thomas. I explained to him what had happened and that he didn't need to worry about coming to Bergen this weekend. I would rather go to Oslo and visit them as soon as I was up to it.

'Sure?' he said.

'Yeah, yeah. Just relax.'

He wasn't entirely convinced, but we agreed I would keep him posted and after chatting about how Jakob, my little grandson, was doing, we rang off.

Next on the list was Annemette Bergesen at Police HQ in Bergen.

I reminded her of what we had spoken about when I went to see her at the beginning of the previous week, and I informed her that there was still no trace of Emma Hagland. This time she reacted as I'd hoped she would the first time round. 'We have to take this seriously, Varg. I can see that now. We'll set up the electronic-tracking system for her mobile phone, any bank cards she might have and, of course, activity on her email account. If we don't see anything over the last few weeks we'll go back in time and see if can find anything there. I logged all the important info the last time you were here, but unfortunately I haven't had the time to follow it up.' When I didn't comment, she added: 'I hear you've been embroiled in some drama since then, too. Was it connected with this?'

'Well, it was a lead in this case that took me to the bikers. I don't know if there's a direct link with the disappearance. The person who could tell me that is still in a coma at Haukeland Hospital.'

'That's … the father?'

'Yes.'

'Well, as I said, we'll take over the case now, Varg.'

'Take over? It's still my assignment.'

'Yes, of course. But our resources are of a different order than yours, so … Could you ask your client to contact us again?'

'She's dead.'

'What? Dead?'

'Yes.'

There was a silence. 'Now this case is really beginning to interest me. Could you give me a bit more background?'

Suddenly I felt tired. 'Well, I … A colleague of yours in Haugesund has the case: Inspector Liland. I suggest you call him.'

'OK, I'll do that.'

We hung up, and even though I wasn't at all in the mood, I decided I would steal a march on her. I dialled the number for Haugesund Police HQ and asked to speak to Inspector Liland.

He came on the line with remarkable speed. 'Liland speaking.'

'Veum here.'

'Are you alive then, Veum?'

'Just about.'

'OK. A colleague here told me you fell foul of the drugs gang the police have arrested down here and up in Bergen. You're back in the saddle, though, I take it?'

'Yes, but I'm ringing now as a private person. I was wondering, naturally enough, if you'd made any progress regarding my sister.'

'The autopsy didn't give us a clear answer. There are signs of a blow to the back of her head, which she might've received when she fell. But there was no evidence of either cerebral or myocardial infarction. She may have felt ill of course, but … We haven't shelved the case yet. One of the neighbours said she'd heard a furious row earlier in the day, but she wasn't sure whether that came from your sister's house or somewhere else nearby. The postman working in that street said he saw a woman leaving the gate as he passed, but there was no post for your sister that day, so he wasn't absolutely certain if it was her house or another.'

'A woman? Was he able to give a description?'

'Pretty vague. A middle-aged woman, normal clothing. Slightly ravaged face.'

'That could've been … If I were you I'd check out Ingeborg Hagland. She's part of the drugs scene in Haugesund. I paid her a visit with my sister when I was down there.'

'Really?'

'She's the mother of the young woman I'm still looking for, and according to the police in Bergen – that is, thanks to your colleagues in Haugesund – she's supposed to have received a visit from her ex-husband, Robert Høie Hansen, last Friday, the day after my sister and I called on her, and the same day I found Norma dead.'

I gave him the address in Haugevegen.

'Thank you for that, Veum. We'll contact her.'

Afterwards I rang, without success, three young women: Åsa in Berlin, and Kari and Helga in Møhlenpris. Not one of them picked up and I didn't leave any messages. I had to get back on my feet before I could continue my assignment.

I went to bed early and slept till late the following day. The house was empty, but a note on the kitchen worktop made it clear that I was to rest and not to leave the house. Sølvi would take care of all the shopping.

I started to think about something else, so as not to bang my head against the wall too hard. The business that had been churning away at the back of my brain ever since the meeting with my second cousin, Ruth Kjærstad, in Haugesund was forcing itself to the forefront, like an impatient speaker trying again and again to hijack the agreed agenda for a meeting. I still wasn't sure what I should do about it, but the least I could manage was to investigate further.

I searched the name 'Leif Pedersen' on the internet and got two hits: a funeral parlour and a chiropractor. When I added 'saxophone' there were no results. When I searched for 'Atle Eliassen' and combined it with 'jazz' there was in fact a link. It led me to an article about the pianist Tore Lude, in which there was reference to a concert in the early 1970s, and one of the musicians had been 'Atle Eliassen, on trumpet, a real veteran'.

In fact, I had met Tore Lude in connection with a case I had been investigating ten years previously. Later I had heard him play various times, in the Swing'n'Sweet jazz club and at Bergen's Natt Jazz festival. I found his telephone number, took a chance and dialled.

He sounded as if his mind was elsewhere when he answered: 'Yeah? Tore here.'

I said who I was and why I was calling.

'What? Atle Eliassen? But he's dead, isn't he?'

'Sadly, yes. But the person I'm really interested in is a saxophonist of about the same age – Leif Pedersen.'

'Leif Pedersen? Yep, I played with him a couple of times too, when I was very young. But…'

'Yes?'

'Varg, actually I've got a dental appointment and I'm on my way out of the door. But I'm playing at Swing'n'Sweet tomorrow afternoon. From two o'clock on the Den Stundesløse stage. Can you drop by then?'

I hesitated. 'I can try.'

'Great. See you there.'

I put down the phone and jotted the details into my notebook. Then I sat immersed in thought.

I had an idea. I went onto Google and searched for 'moribund'. There were several hits. Not far down the list was a webpage called www.moribund.uk.

I clicked onto it, but was met by a page requiring a username and a password before I could enter. Not having either, I stared at the screen.

The colour of the background was black. In the middle of the page was the word: *Moribund*. With the aid of an elegant graphics technique two shadows came off the capital M, two long shadows as if cast by a low sun, and there was an outline of two stylised, genderless persons, hand in hand on their way to an unknown future … Although perhaps it was more specific: they were walking towards death.

I felt myself go cold inside. Could this be what Emma had referred to when she spoke to Åsa earlier this autumn? Had she found this webpage and accessed it? And how could I enter it myself?

In another Google search I found a link to an article in a Norwegian newspaper, a few months later. It was a report about young people committing suicide together – often with people they didn't even know, but had just met online.

The main story was about two young Scots who had carried out a suicide pact like this. They had met up online and after a long exchange of emails they arranged to meet. When they did they walked out to some steep cliffs by the sea and threw themselves off. One was found six days later, the other was washed ashore after several weeks. After examining their computers, the police found the suicide pact they had made.

Corresponding events in Norway were cited. Two youths had thrown themselves off Pulpit Rock in Ryfylke a couple of years before. Others had committed suicide by gassing themselves on exhaust fumes inside a locked car. Another young couple swerved their car into the path of an oncoming juggernaut and were killed instantly. Even if it was never conclusively proved, there was a strong suspicion there was a similar motive behind this traffic accident.

A psychologist discussed the causes of such behaviour:

'Many of them have mental problems already. Eating disorders, depression, other illnesses. They make contact online with like-minded types, egg each other on and – in the worst-case scenario – make such pacts.'

Often a long time could pass before the dead bodies were found. Not all of them left a trail after them, online or anywhere else.

I called Annemette Bergesen once again.

'Varg? Aren't you off work?'

'Yes, but listen to this.' I told her about the article I had read, the webpage I had discovered and how Emma had mentioned this self-same word, moribund, in a conversation with her friend in Berlin. 'This isn't a word a young woman would normally be familiar with. The reason I'm calling you, however, is … that you have officers working on cybercrime. I remember that from my own bitter experience.'

'Yes. I remember as well.'

'Could you get one of them to try and enter the webpage. I'm sure someone who understands this stuff would know how to find a back way in.'

'And then?' she said, not entirely without a note of sarcasm. 'Ring you and tell you what we've found?'

'That would be nice.'

'Forget it. But fine. I've said I'll follow up this case, and I'll pass this on to my colleagues. I recommend you do some convalescing, otherwise it won't be long before you're moribund as well.'

'So you know what the word means then?'

'Don't even have to look it up, Varg.'

Afterwards I sat staring at the enticing webpage. I tried to get in using a random variety of usernames and passwords, including Emma and her date of birth, but without success. They wouldn't let me in, however hard I tried.

I had an idea where I could get some help, though, if what I suspected was really true.

38

All music reflects its own era. When the town's classical-music lovers went to the Grieg Hall every Thursday to listen to the Bergen Philharmonic Orchestra play, it was rarely their own era they heard. The music came from the Vienna, Berlin, Paris and London of long-since vanished times. When types like me went to jazz clubs like Swing'n'Sweet and listened to conventional jazz, we could just as well have gone to a cellar in New York or Copenhagen fifty years before.

Sølvi had eyed me with justified scepticism when I had said over breakfast that I was planning to go to Swing'n'Sweet at midday to listen to Tore Lude and have a chat with him. I said nothing about where I was going afterwards.

'A chat? Is this to do with the case?'

'No, no, no. This is what my half-sister started when we met in Haugesund.'

'Oh, yes?'

'The paternity question from more than sixty years ago. The saxophonist.'

'But are you up to this?'

'Absolutely! I'm feeling a lot better already,' I had said, even though my brain was whirring where I sat.

She had still looked sceptical. 'Well, I have to take Helene to the dance performance anyway, but I would feel a lot happier if you rested for a few more days.'

'I promise not to do anything hasty.'

'OK. Would you like a lift with us?'

'I think I'll take my own car so that I don't have to tramp around town.'

I could see it in her face – she wasn't convinced; but she said nothing.

Perhaps she realised it wouldn't have helped. I could be the most obstinate person in the world when I felt I was on the trail of something.

Den Stundesløse was in the cellar under what had once been the Ole Bull Cinema, but now it had become a bar of variable quality. The poster at the entrance announced that the Tore Lude Trio would be in action, with the boss himself on the piano, Reidar Rongved on bass and Terje Tornøe on trumpet.

Below ground, the atmosphere was perfect: a room with suitably cluttered sight lines, where there was invariably a discreet corner to take a lady, if that was what was on your agenda. You could still hear the music wherever you sat, even if you couldn't always see who was playing. There was a greyish-white mist of cigarette smoke above the tables, as though the clientele were inhaling as much as possible into their lungs before the brand-new antismoking law came into effect. According to the parliamentary statute it would be valid as of the following summer. Then all the mist would lift and the musicians would even have a chance of seeing what they had written on their sheet music.

I showed my membership card at the door and was given my entrance ticket at a reduced price. The three musicians were standing at the bar, wetting their whistles on half-litres of beer before they started. Tore Lude was over fifty and his silvery curls were thinner than they had been. Reidar Rongved was around forty with dark-blond hair and strikingly thick glasses. It struck me that that might have been why he had chosen the bass: the instrument was big enough for him to see. Terje Tornøe gave an anonymous, world-weary impression, but there was nothing staid about him when he breathed life into the trumpet.

They watched me expectantly as I walked over to them. 'Hi Lude … My name's Veum. Varg Veum.'

Lude nodded, Rongved peered at me and Terje Tornøe gave a wry smile. 'Yes, I remember you,' he said. 'Private investigator, aren't you? The Hagenes case in 1993, wasn't it?'

I nodded. 'You've got a good memory.'

'I remember that one,' Tore Lude said. 'I knew I'd heard your name before.'

I signalled to the waiter behind the bar that I wanted a beer. While he was filling the glass, Tore Lude said to his fellow-musicians: 'This time he's after Leif Pedersen.'

'Who?' Reidar Rongved said, looking bewildered.

Terje Tornøe nodded. 'Leif Pedersen, yes. He was one of the really old saxophonists. Played with Atle Eliassen and some others back in the interwar years.'

Tore Lude gestured towards the trumpeter. 'There you have our brains. Just ask him, Veum.'

Terje Tornøe sent me a professorial look. 'The Hurrycanes: Nils Petter Solberg, piano; Torfinn Gåsland, violin; Leif Pedersen, sax; Atle Eliassen, trumpet; and Terje Stockflet Nielsen, drums.'

I knew the type. You met them in all jazz clubs. They knew the names of the musicians in all the bands, from Louis Armstrong's Hot Five to the Miles Davis Quintet, knew exactly when they had cut which disc and in which studio and could, if asked, scat the rhythm of many of them.

'Did you ever meet Leif Pedersen?'

He looked at Tore Lude. 'Yes, didn't both you and I play with him several times, Tore?'

Lude nodded.

'But then we were just striplings and he was well into his sixties, if not his seventies. His horn-playing was a bit flabby, of course, but he cultivated a kind of Ben Webster style and so he didn't need so much energy.'

'Webster's my favourite, too,' I said.

'Oh, yes?'

'But what I want to find out … Did you get to know him? Did he talk about the old days?'

'Of course! All ageing jazzmen talk about the old days. How everything sounded better then. Before rock and fusion and so on.'

'And in private … Was he married or anything?'

'He was indeed. Married *and* anything, if I can put it like that. Eva Høiland – do you remember her, boys?'

Lude suddenly seemed a little coy. Then he nodded. Rongved shook his head from side to side.

'Came from Kristiansand and sang in The Golden Club and places like that. A beautiful, sexy blonde with a voice redolent of pipes and cigars. And Leif Pedersen was crazy about women. She was just his type. I think they were having an affair then. But she went to Stockholm and was there a while. When she came back with a little baby, a few more kilos all over and a voice that hadn't withstood the ravages of time, they got married. I remember occasionally meeting them in the street after he'd stopped playing. They lived somewhere in Landås.' He stood musing. Then he pointed to Lude. 'Do you remember the story he told once, Tore? About the boat trip from ... Haugesund, wasn't it?'

My ears pricked up.

'No-o.' Lude was hesitant.

'He'd been playing at some wedding down there. Yes, now I've got it. It was Atle Eliassen's. He got married to an Arab,' he said, looking at me. 'Someone from Haugesund, that is,' he added, thinking I knew the old story about why Haugesunders were called Arabs. 'On the boat back to Bergen he met a girl who gave him everything he wanted ... just like that.' He snapped his fingers. 'And that was that.'

'Now you mention it...' Lude said.

'The full works! And that was a long time before the term "a one-night stand" existed.'

'Must have been the heavy sea that moved something inside her.'

They looked at each other and chuckled.

'And?' I asked.

'Well, that was that, as I said. He never saw her again. That is, he may have said he'd seen her in the street a few times with a husband and a child. Bergen was no bigger then than it is now, you know. And he may have wondered ... For all he knew, the child whose hand she was holding as they walked could've been his!'

'And he said this ... in so many words?'

'We-ell.' Tornøe smiled his crooked smile again. 'That's the strange thing. When we jazz musicians sit through the night, after all the sets are over and most of the bottles empty … there comes a point when we either get into a brawl with each other or swap confidences.'

'This Eva Høiland – do you know if she's still alive?'

'I've heard nothing to the contrary. But she must be well into…' Again he shifted his gaze to Lude. 'Unless I'm much mistaken, Tore, didn't you and she have a little rumpy-pumpy when she was on her comeback with Lasse Tydal and his band in the late seventies?'

Tore Lude seemed ill at ease and was clearly relieved when we were interrupted. Someone from the management came over and asked if the guys were ready to go on stage. They were. Before leaving me, Terje Tornøe asked: 'Did you get what you were after, Veum?'

I just nodded. 'I reckon so,' I said to their backs when they were far enough away. 'More than I bargained for, actually.'

Afterwards I sat at a table on my own listening to the first set. They played 'Sophisticated Lady' and 'Lover Man' so well I could almost visualise them – my mother at thirty-four, and the charming ladies' man, Leif Pedersen, on the boat from Haugesund to Bergen one winter's day in 1942. And I pondered whether there was any way I could find out more about this story, supposing, of course, that was how it had been.

But I had a much more pressing mystery to solve as well. The next item on the agenda – the way I saw the case progressing – was a 'chimney' house in Møhlenpris. I headed there before the first set was over, spurred on by no other good wishes than my own, and they had rarely proven to be effective.

39

When I arrived in Konsul Børs gate a silver Volvo V70 estate was standing by the front entrance with the rear door open. Knut Moberg was leaning over and pushing a big red suitcase into the boot. He was wearing casual clothes: faded jeans, a blue-and-white checked shirt and white trainers. He stroked back his dark fringe as he straightened up and caught sight of me.

'Veum?' he said with a rather disgruntled expression.

'On the move, Moberg?'

He pinched his lips and went red. 'Not me. The young ladies.'

'Helga and Kari?'

He gave a quick nod.

'Yes, last time I was here the joint was rocking.' He didn't answer, and I added: 'It was them … or your wife, wasn't it?'

His eyes flashed. 'None of your bloody business!'

'But you're helping them?'

He nodded. Then he turned and walked towards the open door. Realising that I was following him, he spun round. 'And where do you think you're going?'

'Actually I came to talk to the two of them – Helga and Kari. So if you wouldn't mind …' I gestured that I wanted to go round him.

He came up close to me. 'I do bloody mind, Veum!'

I closed my eyes. I felt a strange form of dizziness, as though I was losing feeling throughout my body, from my head to my knees. When I opened them again, he was on his way into the building.

I followed him quickly and managed to put my foot in the door before he closed it.

'I can ring the police, Veum.'

'Yes, that was what your wife did the last time I was here. But it wasn't because of me.'

He turned so fast I barely had a second to react. But he didn't throw a punch. 'I'm warning you. Any more trouble from you and—'

I held up both hands in defence. 'I'm not going to make any trouble. I just have a couple of questions for the young ladies … regarding Emma Hagland. Do you remember her?'

The muscles in his face swelled, from his jaw to his temple. However, he managed to retain control. He opened and closed his mouth. Then he turned and strode quickly up the stairs. I followed him at a slightly more unhurried tempo.

On the second floor, the door to Helga and Kari's flat was open. He walked straight in and this time he didn't try to close it on me. I went into the hallway, which was empty, and from there into the living room I recognised from earlier.

There weren't many changes to be seen, except that the bookshelves were empty. The TV was where it had been, the furniture clearly belonged to the house, the pictures on the wall were the same, and even the empty wine bottle with the Cheval Blanc Saint-Émilion label and a burned-down candle were on the coffee table as before.

The two young women were sitting at the table, surrounded by suitcases, bags and a total of three laptops. Helga had a desperate expression on her face and glanced sadly in my direction when I entered and stood beside Moberg. Kari held her head high and sent him a defiant look, as though waiting for him to say something that could improve the whole situation.

He sighed loudly beside me. 'This cuckoo insisted on coming up with me.'

'I've come about Emma. I need to have a word with you both and I can see I've arrived in the nick of time. You're moving out?'

'We've been thrown out,' Helga said in a low voice.

Kari shifted her gaze quickly from me back to Moberg. 'Fru Moberg insisted,' she said acidly.

'Yes, erm, my wife … I don't know what got into her.'

'No?' I said, unwilling to risk a further explosion from that quarter. 'But if you carry on moving the baggage, I can ask my questions here in the meantime.'

'I'm not taking bloody ord—' Red-faced, he broke off. 'Oh, alright then.' He grabbed hold of two suitcases, lifted them and went out of the door, as though he was doing piecework.

I stared at what remained on the floor. 'Three laptops?'

Helga looked up guiltily. 'Yes, two of them are mine.'

Kari sent her a malignant glare. 'Don't tell lies! One of them is Emma's. I recognise it.'

Helga looked down without answering.

'You've had it in your room all the time. Ever since she went missing.'

'Right,' I said. 'Helga … is that true?'

She nodded defiantly, but without looking up.

'Why didn't you say so before?'

She didn't answer.

'You have to understand that means … she hasn't moved anywhere.'

'One of the suitcases is hers, too,' Kari said.

Now I focused my attention on her. 'One of the suitcases? And it contains what?'

She shrugged. 'No idea. Clothes. Books. I've never seen inside. Helga had it.'

'And you've never even been suspicious about that?'

Kari met my gaze, but her defiance was weakened by the uncertainty she suddenly revealed. 'No. Why would I?'

'Have either of you any idea how her family are feeling? You must understand—'

'What are you talking about?' Knut Moberg interrupted from the doorway.

I turned a little too fast and had to take a step to the side not to lose my balance. I was dizzy and concentrated hard to focus on his face. 'We're talking about Emma leaving all her possessions here when she moved.'

'Really?'

'Are you pretending you didn't know?'

He looked at the two young women. 'Of course I knew she'd moved out, but not that she hadn't taken her things with her.'

I turned back to Helga and Kari. 'Tell me – which suitcase is hers? Has it already been taken down?'

'That one,' Kari said, pointing to a large dark-blue suitcase of the solid variety, the only one left on the floor with the laptops.

'And what had you been planning to do with it? Take it with you?'

'No, we…' She glanced at Moberg again. 'We'd planned to leave it here.'

I noticed Helga was staring up at him from where she was sitting.

'Here? What the hell were you two thinking?' he barked.

'This is news to you?' I asked.

'All I know is that she moved out.'

'I still haven't heard you deny you made advances on her.'

'What!' exclaimed Moberg.

'On Emma?' Kari asked.

Helga was glaring at him now.

'But perhaps you do that with all your female tenants?'

'Knut!' said Kari. 'Is that true?'

'True? The silly mare misunderstood. I … I didn't make any advances. I … just stroked her back … to cheer her up, the way you pat a child.'

'And how did she react?' I asked.

'Furiously. She jumped with surprise, spun round, swore at me and…' He held his cheek like a rejected young girl. 'She slapped me here.'

'And you put up with that?'

'Yes, I…' He gesticulated. 'It wasn't worth fighting over. We agreed it was a misunderstanding and we would forget it. But afterwards her eyes followed me wherever I went until I was out of the door.'

'Maybe some past trauma at play?'

He shrugged. 'I have no idea.'

'And you didn't have any more confrontations?'

'No. I barely saw her after that, and never alone. *She…*' He stared at Helga. 'She was always close by. Like a … cat.'

Yes, I could see what he meant. Sitting there, she did remind you of a cat – half crouching, watching us warily while listening to what we were saying, no reaction apart from the measured distance she had shown us from the first moment.

'Now you've got a problem, Moberg. A suitcase and a laptop belonging to a young woman who vanished without trace over three weeks ago. Perhaps we should phone the police?'

Kari reacted first. 'The police? I'm not taking responsibility for this. She was the one who said we shouldn't say anything.'

All three of us looked at Helga. She met my gaze.

'Why not, Helga?' I asked.

'This is driving me crazy,' Moberg burst out. 'Women! The next time I'll let the flat to male Bible school students.'

'Sounds like a good idea,' I said, without taking my eyes off Helga. 'What do you have to say, Helga? What do you know that you haven't told us?'

'Come on!' Kari said. 'Everything's going to come out now.'

Helga looked remarkably unmoved, as though nothing that had been said was any concern of hers. As though she was in the room alone, far removed from us.

I took out my pink phone. 'I'll ring the police. They'll have to examine the suitcase and go through her laptop.'

'No,' Helga said. 'Don't … just wait.'

Kari looked at Moberg and me. 'There was a webpage Helga and Emma were fascinated by.'

A chill went down my spine. 'A webpage?'

'Yes … what was the name again, Helga?'

Helga glared at her.

'Ah, in fact that's why I've come here,' I said. 'To ask you about exactly that. The name's www.moribund.uk, isn't it?'

'Yes, it is. And that's where they met these other depressive people with only one thing on their minds. To die. To get away. To disappear off the face of the earth.'

'You visited the page as well, did you?'

'Never. Not when I heard how these two were behaving. But ask her.' She pointed at Helga. 'Just hand her over to the police. She knows everything about what happened.'

Moberg took a decision. 'That's the only thing to do. I'll go and ring.'

'Ask for Inspector Annemette Bergesen. Say hello from me.'

'I'll go with you,' Kari shouted.

He half turned to her and looked her straight in the eyes. 'You're staying here.'

'Very well.'

He left. Kari glanced from me to Helga and back again. 'I'm going to the loo.' She went to the hallway, and I heard a door slam and a key twist in the lock.

'You can tell me now, Helga. There's only you and me here.'

Her eyes filled up with tears. Her lips quivered. She whispered: 'I let them down.'

'You let who down?'

'This webpage … It's just a forum where people who have experienced dreadful things can … talk, exchange experiences … console one another.'

'But moribund means … doomed to die, dying, something like that.'

She looked down. 'Yes.'

'Only yesterday I read an article about young people, with the kind of background that you mentioned, giving up and making a pact. A suicide pact. To become … *moribund*, as it were.' It was still difficult to get her to react. 'Was that what happened to you, too? Did Emma meet someone online, someone she made a pact with?'

Her eyes widened. Then she nodded softly. 'How… ?'

'I have a lot of experience of young people, Helga. I can read between the lines. I suspected it when I read the article. But why didn't you say so before? This might explain the whole case.'

She blushed. 'I was so ashamed.'

'About what?'

'About not going with her. About failing her. On that day.'

'The day Emma disappeared?'

'Yes.'

'And what was the agreement?'

'We were supposed to meet Freeman and go where Amos told us.'

'Freeman, Amos? Who are they?'

'They're the people we met online.'

'Usernames?'

'Yes.'

'And you didn't find out who they really were?'

She hesitated. '... No.'

'Helga ... I can see you know something.'

'But I was so terribly frightened that ... I pulled out. I didn't want ... I couldn't...'

'Anyone could understand that. But Emma went?'

'Yes.'

'Where?'

'I don't know. Freeman was supposed to get ... a map.'

'A map. Who from?'

'Amos.'

'And they would go through with the pact there – Emma and this Freeman?'

'Yes!'

'And who was Amos?'

'I don't know!'

'Freeman though?'

She looked away.

'Helga.'

She whispered: 'Emma twigged. There was something he wrote.'

'I see.'

She swallowed hard. Her eyes flitted around. For a moment I was worried she would faint. 'It was him – her brother.'

'Andreas?'

'Yes.'

There was a noise in the hallway and Knut Moberg came through the door. 'They're on their way. The police.' He looked around. 'Where's Kari?'

'In the toilet,' I said without letting Helga's eyes go. 'So you, Emma and Andreas – it was you who had made the pact?'

'Yes.'

'Which you didn't keep.'

'Yes!' At once she burst into tears; long, hysterical sobs. She leaned over and hid her face in her hands as her whole body shook.

From the hallway I heard Moberg banging on a door. 'Kari, are you in there? Are you alright?'

From behind the door came Kari's tearful voice. 'Just go away! I don't want to see you any more. Go away!'

I let them cry and bang as much as they wanted. I was dead tired. Maybe not moribund, but not far off it, either. In all of our separate ways we were waiting for the police to come and take over. Not completely though. I wanted a little chat with Freeman on my own first.

40

Mount Sandvik towered over me, one of the steepest mountainsides, and so close to the town. With my eyes I followed the green, forest-clad gap where the Stoltzekeiven climb was. At the top I saw the Sandvik arrow that had indicated the direction of the wind since 1835. The present one was a second-generation weather vane, as the original one had literally gone with the wind. It wouldn't have surprised me if Liv Høie Hansen was on her way up or down this same mountain today as well, because no one opened the door when I rang.

But I didn't give up. I kept my finger on the bell until he could stand it no more. Andreas wrenched open the door and snarled at me: 'Whaddya want?'

'To talk to you.'

'About what?'

'About the pact you made with your half-sister Emma, and what happened when you two left her to carry it out on her own.'

Something happened to him. It was as though his whole face flattened out, as if I had pressed a heavy weight onto it, while the colour drained away. He couldn't raise his eyes any higher than my neck, but he slowly retreated back into the hallway and left the door open – a signal that I could follow him. In a kind of trance and with his head bowed he walked in front of me through the hall to his open bedroom door. There he stopped, still with his back to me, and faced the illuminated computer screen as if it was his house god, to whom he turned for advice about what to do next.

I stopped directly behind him. He was sixteen years old, barely over the age of criminal responsibility, and I had to be careful how I expressed myself. On the other hand, he was older than his father had been when he raped Veslemøy.

'Isn't your mother at home?'

He mumbled something I didn't catch.

'What was that?'

He turned round quickly and we were so close to each other that now it was me who felt the need to retreat. 'She's at work.'

I nodded. 'Right.'

He looked up, but only as far as my chest.

'What happened to your father was terrible.'

He didn't answer.

'Did you know I was held captive with him?'

For an instant he glanced up. He confirmed that there were still visible marks on my face, pursed his lips and looked down again. He nodded so gently it was hardly perceptible.

'Had it not been for the police, both of us would be dead now.'

No reaction.

'Have you been up to visit him?'

Minimal shake of the head.

'But this isn't what I came to talk to you about today.' I paused. Then I continued: 'We talked about it the last time I was here. At first you acted as if you'd never had any contact with her, not before she appeared here in September, nor after. But then you lied.'

He tossed his head, his lips still a thin, taut line in his face.

'But she found out about you several years ago. She and Åsa came to Bergen in 2000 to meet you. But they had to return home with nothing for their pains. What did you think of your father's behaviour on that occasion?'

He looked up. Deep inside his green-speckled eyes there was a flash. 'My dad's an asshole.'

'And you both agreed on that?'

He nodded defiantly.

'You and Emma?'

'Yes,' he mumbled.

'You told me you'd only met her once, in the autumn. At Dromedar Kafé in the pedestrian precinct. But you were in contact with her both before and after.'

He said nothing. He was a hard nut to crack.

A screensaver came up on his computer: heavenly bodies moving above a black, starry sky. For a moment my attention was caught by the movement. I pointed in that direction. 'Did you have contact online?'

Another almost imperceptible nod.

'When was that?'

He just waggled his head.

'Before she came to Bergen?'

He bit his lower lip and nodded.

'A great deal earlier than you told me when we last chatted about this, in other words. It might've been because of you that she decided to come to Bergen and not Berlin, like her friend?'

This time his nod was more definite.

'You established contact on the net – her in Haugesund, you here. But when she came to Bergen you were able to meet physically?'

Again the vague waggle of his head.

'Surely you did meet?'

He shook his head. 'Only on the one occasion I told you about. At Dromedar.'

'Why only then?'

'Well, because … my father might've found out.'

'Your father, yes. Neither you nor Emma liked him much, did you.'

'We loathed him.'

'Why—?'

He cut me off. 'For being the bastard he was! For what he'd done to make Emma's mum throw him out. For the way he treated me. We just … hated him.'

'And what were you going to do about it?'

Now his tongue was loosening. 'Do! What could we do? He would beat me to pulp, and she …' He shrugged.

'Did he hit you? When you were smaller?'

He nodded. 'Often.'

'And …?'

'Nowadays as well.' The dam was about to burst. 'Because I was never the son he wanted. I wasn't interested in motorbikes, didn't want to go to football matches, didn't want to go fishing with him. None of ... the man things. All I wanted to do was sit here and ... first of all read, then later...' His eyes moved towards the computer.

'But your mother...'

'Mum – what could she do? Why do you think she's out running every day when she's not at work? To get away, of course.'

It occurred to me that the picture I now had of the Høie family was quite different from the one I had earlier.

'All Emma and I wanted was to get away.'

'To get away, yes, but how far?'

'We didn't talk about that until we ... met somewhere else.'

'At Moribund.'

He looked at me in amazement. 'Yes.'

'What led you there?'

He paused. 'I was surfing the net, as I often do. Somehow I got to chatting with someone about this webpage. Then I was given a recommendation and a password and ... that was that.'

'And you met Emma there?'

'Yes, but not immediately. There was something I wrote in one of my blogs that made her email my normal account. She asked: "Are you Freeman?"'

'And you confirmed you were?'

'Yes.'

'But this webpage – what goes on there, the thoughts you exchange – it's pretty morbid stuff, isn't it?'

'Morbid?'

'Yes, erm, sort of having an unusual interest in death.'

Again a short nod.

'Young people coming to the conclusion that it's best to leave ... everything. That was why I asked how far you wanted to get away.'

He stared into the middle distance, unmoved. 'Yes.'

'So you were Freeman. What did she call herself?'

'Seagull.'

'The English word for *måke*?'

'It had to have something to do with Haugesund.'

'Yes, that's right. It's on the town's coat of arms. Three seagulls.' Something else struck me. 'So there were three of you in the pact. Freeman, Seagull and ... ?'

'Sleeping Beauty.'

So that was how she saw herself. Helga. A princess who had fallen into a deep sleep behind the hedge, and why did a handsome prince never go to her, only to Kari? Anyway, in principle, he was much too old.

'But she pulled out?'

He nodded.

'But you and Emma, you were agreed. You would go through with it. That's what Sleeping Beauty told me, anyway.'

'OK.'

'But what about Amos?'

Again his eyes widened. 'Amos?' As I didn't respond at once, he added: 'He was ...'

'Yes, what was he?'

'Our mentor.'

A chill went through me. 'A mentor? A kind of guide?'

'Yes. He told us ... Gave us different options ... for how to do it.'

'Do it? Go through with the pact?' After a pause I added: 'Commit suicide?'

'Yes,' he said sulkily. 'And where.'

'How and where?' I could feel a dull fury building up inside me. 'And who was this Amos who had such wisdom?'

For the first time he looked me straight in the eye and held my gaze. 'I don't know.'

'You don't know? You ... took advice from a total stranger behind an anonymous username – advice that would help you to kill yourself?'

'But ...'

'Yes? What do you mean?'

'Amos. He ... It was as though he knew us inside out. Not only me but Emma, too. As though ... as though he knew everything about us.'

'I see. A school friend maybe? Someone in the family?'

He shrugged. 'I have no idea. But everything he said … In a way it was so clever. Saying that what he suggested was the only way out for us.'

'Andreas, I've worked with children and teenagers in many contexts. I've met many whose lives were so difficult I'm sure they wanted to take their own lives – out of despair, out of fear for their futures. But I have to admit I've never experienced anything like this: two healthy young people – yes, that's how I see you – simply sitting down and agreeing that you're going to commit suicide together.'

He swallowed. His eyes sought the laptop screen, which was black now. He whispered: 'When you have nothing left to live for.'

'Nothing left to live for! You two were … you *are* young. You've got the whole of your life ahead of you. In a few years you'll move away from here. If you don't want to, you don't need to have anything to do with either your mother or your father for the rest of your life. You can't just give up on all that's waiting for you. You're only sixteen!'

'Of course not. But I didn't do it.'

'No.' I had to give him that. 'You changed your mind, in other words?'

'Mhm.'

'But Emma … ?'

He closed his eyes and moved his head, as though searching for an answer inside himself. 'She … went in.'

'Went in … what, where?'

'In the boat shed.'

'In which boat shed?'

'The one Amos had told us about.'

'Let's take this bit by bit now, Andreas.'

'There's no bit by bit. You have to listen to what I'm telling you. She went into the boat shed and she never came out again. I went up to the main road and caught the bus back to town.'

'And when was this?'

'It was the day we'd agreed. The 29th of October. It was a Wednesday. Amos said that was the right day of the week. Odin's day.'

'Uhuh. And this Amos told you where to go, did he?'

'Yes. He knew a place, he said.'

'And it was … where?'

'On Radøy. Quite a long way. We caught the bus, past where the cowboy church is.'

'Sletta.'

'Yes. He drew us a map and wrote where we should get off and how to get down to the sea. It was thick forest. All overgrown, and down in a bay there were three old boat sheds. No one would go there, he said. We could do what we'd planned without anyone getting in the way.'

'And what you'd planned, that was … ?'

Suddenly he turned round. He walked further into his room, over to the desk, and crouched down. He pulled out one of the drawers and removed a long piece of sturdy rope. When he straightened up and faced me again, he was holding the rope in his hand. 'We each had our own – one like this.'

'I see.'

My head was spinning. I felt exhausted, as I had done after the conversation with Helga and Kari. I wasn't sure I was going to be able to do what I had come here for. But I couldn't give up now. I had to finish the marathon.

Looking at Andreas again, my eyes flickered, as though my whole vision had broken into small, pulsating sections, and my focus blurred. I had never experienced anything like this before and I felt a sudden fear grip me: What was going on? Was I losing my sight? Or was this too an after-effect of what I'd been through less than a week ago?

I took a series of deep breaths. He watched me, not reacting to this, either. He was on his way back into the same laconic mood he had been in when I came here.

'This is more than three weeks ago, Andreas.'

'Yes.'

'And you never considered reporting this after you returned home?'

'Why would I? It was a pact we'd made.'

'Which you broke!'

'I did. But she may not know that.'

'Know?'

'Yes.'

'But when I came to the door searching for her, when you heard she was missing, didn't you consider telling me what you knew even then?'

A faint blush spread across his cheeks. I hoped it was of shame. 'Then of course I would've had to admit ...' He searched for the words.

'That you'd been on the point of doing the same yourself?'

'Yes.'

I eyed him heavily. I swayed to and fro. Did I have the strength for this? Or should I let it go? Leave the rest to the appropriate authorities?

But I had a form of honour, too. My half-sister Norma had commissioned me to do this job. Now she was gone, but I had sworn that I would complete the assignment whatever the cost. No one would thank me. No one would pay me. All I would be left with was a final crumb of self-respect. *You didn't give up, Varg. You finished the marathon.*

'Let's you and I go for a drive, Andreas.'

'What?'

'You show me where on Radøy this is, and you show me the way to the boat shed. And we're going right now, this evening.'

He looked at me aghast. 'But ...' He glanced at the window. 'It's dark. We won't be able to see anything out there!'

'I've got a powerful torch in the car.'

'But ...'

'No ifs, no buts. You owe her this. Emma, your own sister.'

'OK then,' he mumbled. He walked past me into the hallway, snatched at the same blue-and-green all-weather jacket he had been wearing when I met him after school ten or so days before, took the *HALF-LIFE* cap from one of the pockets, put it on his head and made for the door with the bearing of a noble on the way to the guillotine in Revolutionary Paris. All hope was gone. Destiny called.

I followed hard on his heels to make sure he didn't try to do a runner.

41

Andreas was right. It was pitch-black outside, but there was a faint glow of light in the sky above Lindås, where the oil flame in Mongstad burned like a beacon in the east.

He struggled to find the bus shelter where they had got off and it wasn't easy to find the path through the forest either, but at last he pointed to a large rock at the side of the path, on which a cross had been engraved a long time ago. 'There … That was the sign Amos told us about. The path goes down to the left.' He gave me a sceptical look. Clearly he wasn't very keen to continue.

I shone the beam of the heavy-duty torch on the vegetation beside the rock. It was a dense, black spruce forest, probably planted some time in the 1950s or 1960s and subsequently forgotten by both God and the plantation owners. 'Is it far to walk?'

'You have to go right down to the sea. Must be a couple of kilometres.'

'Well, so long as we can see the path it shouldn't be a problem. I'll walk in front and shine the torch and you bring up the rear. Shout if you think we're going the wrong way.'

He appeared to be viewing the venture with even greater reluctance. 'Can't we … another day?'

'Some people have waited for long enough as it is, Andreas. Since you chose not to go into the boat shed three weeks ago, you and I will have to do it instead.'

He didn't answer, just looked at me, sullen and unsmiling.

I set off. After a few metres I turned towards him. He was still standing at the side of the path. 'Of course we could do this differently. I can ring the local chief of police and ask him to send out some officers. I'm not sure that would be any nicer. What's certain is that you'll have to go down and show us – or me – where the boat shed is this evening.'

He pursed his lips. 'Alright then,' he snapped. At once he started walking. I waited until he was directly behind me before I continued through the trees.

It was not easy. The path was barely visible. It was obvious that it wasn't used much any more. In a couple of places I had to stop and ask him: 'Left here, or what?'

With a long face, he looked where I shone the torch. Then he shrugged. 'Could be.'

Gradually the ground began to slope downwards. Now I could smell the sea and between the trees I glimpsed what I assumed was Lure Fjord. The dense forest continued down to the water's edge, but now the path with the rock underfoot was clearer and walking was easier.

Once again I had to stop and wait for Andreas, who was dragging his feet behind me.

'Are we getting close?'

He didn't answer, just gave a slight nod.

From the fjord we heard the *chug chug* of a little cargo boat on its way north. There was no one else on the sea this Saturday evening in November. There had been some heavy downpours earlier in the day, but the clouds were breaking up now and in the gaps we caught sight of scattered stars, like a slight rash on the dark celestial complexion. I could make out what looked like three ramshackle sheds down by the water's edge. Involuntarily I slowed my pace; I wasn't looking forward to what in all probability was awaiting us there.

I heard Andrea take a deep breath behind me. He was looking past me and down to the boat sheds. His voice was tremulous. 'This is as far as I'm going.'

I eyed him.

'No! I won't! I refuse! You can ring whoever you like. I've shown you the way. I'm not going a step further.'

I sighed and nodded. I could understand. 'That's fine, Andreas. Just tell me which shed she went into.'

He pointed. 'The one in the middle.'

'You wait here then, and I'll go down and … investigate.'

He nodded, almost grateful.

I shone the torch around, found the remnants of the path and covered the last few metres that fell away to the sea

The three boat sheds were equally overgrown with moss. They reminded me of a line of neglected teeth. Two of them had cracked roof tiles. The third had corrugated iron on top. There were big gaps between the grey boards in the cladding. In all three sheds, the doors were hanging off their hinges. The shed in the middle had double doors with an opening big enough for me to pass through. According to Andreas, that was where I should go.

I strolled over a beach littered with pebbles, washed-up tree trunks, great clusters of seaweed and various bits of debris that had drifted ashore from the fjord. I tried shining the torch through the door opening, but I saw nothing until I was directly outside.

The opening was narrow; I made an attempt to lift the door and open it further, but the wood gave such a loud crack that I was afraid the door would come crashing down on top of me if I carried on. Instead I squeezed through and stopped inside.

An unpleasant stench of decomposition met me. Hesitantly, I shone the torch along the stamped-earth floor of the shed. In the middle the torchlight found two wooden stools. One was still upright. The other was on its side.

I shone above it, and there she was, more or less as I had feared.

The rope was fastened to a beam in the roof and she hung from one end, like a rag doll.

There was no doubt that she was dead. Her arms hung limply down beside her body and there was an unnatural kink in her neck. The skin on her face was dark green, almost black, and a swarm of flies buzzed around her head. Her mouth was open and between her front teeth I saw the tip of her tongue. When I shone the torch on her eyes, they stared back at me vacantly.

I moved the torch down. I had seen a few corpses in my life, but every single time it was painful. Only a few weeks ago the body hanging from the rope had been a young person with the majority of her life in front of her. Now she was hanging here, a wasted life, driven by a longing for something she didn't understand, for something she hoped would give her more, something better than her existence on earth had been able to provide her with. Now the flies were buzzing her requiem and the journey was over. I was the only person to hear it.

I didn't go any closer. She had been hanging here for three weeks and no one could do anything to change that. Besides, the shed had become a crime scene, which others would have to investigate as thoroughly as they deemed necessary.

I had practically solved the case. All that was left to do now was make a couple of unpleasant phone calls. I had done this before. In this area too, I had acquired a certain kind of expertise.

But no expertise could help with deaths of this nature. Emma had been much too young to take such a serious step. And she hadn't done it alone. Someone had been here and prepared the scene. Someone had put the two stools in place. Someone had invited the young people – three initially, then two – to come here and do what ultimately only one person had seen through. But why? Was there more to this? Or was it all just the consequence of a sick mind – someone who derived pleasure from egging others on to do what he or she would never dare?

And if so, who? Someone still had questions to answer. One person in particular. The man or woman calling themselves Amos.

42

I called the police station on Radøy. There was only an answer machine on duty this Saturday evening, but I was automatically transferred to the duty officer in Lindås. When I explained the situation to the person taking the call I was asked to give precise details of my location. That wasn't easy. In the end we were asked to go back to the main road and meet the patrol car there.

I had told Andreas what I had found in the boat shed. He stared at me in silence as I spoke, unable to stop his tears falling, and on our way through the forest I heard a mixture of stifled sobs and loud sniffles behind me. I made no attempt to console him. I had more than enough to do dealing with my own thoughts. We stood waiting on the main road, stiff and silent like two zombies in the darkness.

When the car came there were two uniformed officers inside. They introduced themselves with local surnames, Kviste and Myking. Both appeared to be reliable policemen: Kviste was strong and thoughtful; Myking had a thinner face and more to say for himself. When they asked us to show them the way to the boat shed Andreas dug in his heels. He refused point-blank to go back down and to Myking's question regarding his age, he said: 'Sixteen.'

'OK, can we ring your parents?'

As he didn't answer, I said: 'You can ring his mother. I've got her number here.' I held up my phone and Myking wrote it down.

After talking to Liv Høie Hansen, Myking decided he would accompany me back down to the sea while Kviste would stay with Andreas on the main road waiting for a local taxi to take him home. Myking had his own powerful torch, which meant we were a lot quicker than Andreas and I had been.

On the way I explained the background to him and what had led us there. He answered in monosyllables, registering that he understood the majority of what I told him. When we arrived by the sea he nodded in recognition. 'I know these from the sea. They've been crumbling for decades. They belong to some farms further up the island; the heirs have never agreed on what to do with them.'

'She's in the middle one. But I don't think we should go in.'

He shot me a quick but patronising glance, then went over, peered through the opening in the door and stood still. Slowly he shook his head. I watched him shining the light around the room, from one side to the other, up under the roof and back down to the ground. Then he pulled away and turned to me with a glum expression on his face. 'This has to be cordoned off. We'll have to post a watch here until tomorrow. I don't think there's much point in SOC officers starting their work until it's light.' He flicked his head towards the boat shed. 'We've come too late for her anyway.'

'There's an inspector in Bergen who knows the case. Annemette Bergesen.'

He nodded. From the little rucksack he'd been carrying on his back he took a roll of tape. He fastened one end to the adjacent boat shed and then walked round all three boat sheds to cordon off the whole area as a crime scene.

'I need to have a provisional statement from you, Veum, but we can do that when we're on the main road.'

That was accomplished in no time. The taxi had been to collect Andreas and the two officers discussed the next steps in the procedure. For my part, I called Sølvi and asked if there was still a room at the inn.

'Varg! Where have you been?'

'Sorry. I texted you, didn't I?'

'Ye-es, but all it said was that you would be home a little later than planned.'

'Ah, I can explain.'

'I've been worried, don't you understand that? Only a few days ago you were on your back staring at the ceiling in Haukeland Hospital.'

'You have no idea what nice ceilings they have.'

'Very droll. Ha ha. Are you coming now?'

'If the police let me, yes.'

'What? The police?'

'Yeah, yeah. There's no reason for any concern. I'll tell you every-thing when I'm back.'

Myking looked at me, not without a sort of irony in his eyes. 'Missus on good form?'

. If only he knew how good her form could be when she was in the mood, but I just nodded in the direction of my car. 'Can I go now?'

'That's fine, Veum. You'll be hearing from us, if we need anything.'

*

But for the first day they obviously didn't.

Despite my fears of the opposite, Sølvi was full of forgiveness when I arrived at Saudalskleivane at around eleven that evening, so full that, for the first time since my stay at the hospital, we went to bed together, made love with great care and afterwards slept as tightly coiled around each other as Russian Vine – or Architect's Consolation, as we called it in Norwegian. In which case, I was the failed façade. But she got up and went downstairs before Helene woke and we sat around the breakfast table talking about anything but what you could find in a tumbledown boat shed on Radøy if you started to look.

After breakfast I asked Sølvi if I could borrow the little room she used as her office. From there I made the two phone calls I couldn't say I had been looking forward to making.

The first was to Ingeborg Hagland. Initially she didn't answer. When I tried again after a few minutes, she picked up and spoke in such a croaky voice it sounded as if I had woken her from a deep sleep.

After saying who I was I heard her tone change character but, without being able to see her, I couldn't determine whether it was to one of vigilance or anxiety. 'Yes? Have you … found out anything?'

'I'm afraid I have some bad news for you, Ingeborg.'

'Oh?'

'We … found her late last night. She had … It happened three weeks ago, but … I'm afraid she's dead.'

'Oh, no!' There was a sharp intake of breath, then she began to sob.

I sat with the phone in my hand. A couple of times I tried to speak, but she was crying uncontrollably. I raised my voice: 'Ingeborg! Have you got someone who can help you?'

She was sobbing. 'No. No one. Not now that Aunty Norma's gone, too.'

'The council must have a service. Would you like me to ring them for you?'

'No! They'll only … They just talk. I have to … manage this on my own.' After a pause she added: 'Does Robert know?'

I wavered. 'No, but his wife's been told.'

'But…'

'Robert's in a coma at Haukeland Hopsital. He was … had an accident. I can give you the details when we meet.'

Another painful sob. 'Alright. Are you coming down for the funeral?'

'Funeral? Do you mean Norma's?'

'Yes, it's tomorrow in Skåre Church. At two o'clock.'

Once again a sense of unarticulated grief washed through me. Norma … Obviously I would travel down. 'Yes, I'll try to make it. Let's talk then.'

'Just tell me … what happened to her?'

'To Emma? It was … self-inflicted.'

She sobbed. 'She killed herself?'

'It seems so.'

'B-b-but how?'

'Let's talk about it tomorrow, Ingeborg. After the funeral. Are you sure I shouldn't ring for someone?'

'Yes, I told you. Ohh!'

With that she hung up. I wondered whether I should phone someone down there anyway, but concluded it wouldn't make much difference. She sounded as if she had enough strength to survive this as well, on top of everything else she'd had to endure in her life.

The next person I rang was Åsa. She answered after two rings.

'Veum here.'

'A new phone number?'

'Yes, it...'

'Is there any news?'

'Sadly, there is.'

'Oh, no! Is she...?'

'We've found her, and it was as feared. She's dead, Åsa. And from what we can see, by her own hand.'

'What! Are you saying ... she committed suicide?'

'Yes, I'm afraid so. Everything points to that. The word you gave me, moribund, led me to a webpage where young people chat and make ... suicide pacts.'

She burst into tears. 'Oh, my God! Yes, I've heard about it. But ... was that what she did? Who was she with?'

'It was just her. Actually three of them had made a pact.'

'Three!'

'One withdrew early on, the second when they were approaching the place.'

Without mentioning that the latter was Andreas, I briefly told her what I had found out.

In a strangulated voice she said: 'So she ... hanged herself?'

'Yes.'

'Oh, poor, poor Emma!'

There wasn't a lot more to say for now. I told her I would call her once I had found out when the funeral was, in case she wanted to come home for that, and she thanked me and we rang off.

I went back in to Sølvi. Helene wasn't there; she was probably in her room. She looked at me and said: 'Hard?'

'Yes. Being the bearer of bad news is never a nice job.'

'No.' She smiled sadly.

'There's another conversation I have to have, and I can't do it over the phone. I have to do it face to face.'

43

Vognstølbakken is a long, steep road ending in what is a cross between a turnaround and a car park. Vetle Valaker lived in one of the higher blocks on the lower side of the road. As I reached the entrance the door was opened from inside by a young woman trying to manoeuvre a buggy with a little child out of the building. I hurried forwards and held the door open for her. She smiled gratefully and didn't react when I continued into the hallway after she had left.

Valaker lived on the ground floor to the right. I looked at my watch. It was ten minutes to twelve on Sunday morning. If he was at church I had made a serious misjudgement. But I had a feeling he was so far beyond the state church that he preferred an evening meeting in a more fundamentalist circle than Landås parish.

I was right. He opened the door with an inquisitive expression. Then he recognised me. 'Veum? What brings you here on a Sunday morning?'

'Hi, Amos,' I said.

He paled. 'What do you mean? My name's not—'

'No, I know what your name is. Is there somewhere we can sit?'

'Why? We have nothing to discuss. We said all we had to say over a week ago.'

'Yes, but quite a lot's happened since then.' I nodded towards the centre of the flat. 'Shall we have a quick word, so that we can get this cleared up?'

He nodded. Then he turned and went back in without inviting me to follow him. I didn't regard this as a rejection; I walked behind him through the hall and into what was, if not a sitting room, then at least a kind of day room.

It was furnished in a Spartan fashion. There was an old-fashioned sideboard along one wall. Above it hung a selection of framed family photographs, so small that it was difficult to see the detail from where I was standing. In the corner nearest the door there was a suite of furniture, which, from its appearance, had been bought in Fretex, the Salvation Army shop. It was worn at the edges and greyish-green in colour. On the wall above there was one single picture, a classic picture of Jesus in which the Redeemer was looking gently upwards, dressed in red and blue and with a halo around his hippy hair. In the middle of the coffee table was a laptop with the lid up, the very latest model. Vetle walked over and closed it, then turned back to me with a guilty expression on his face. On this occasion, too, he was dressed in a way that made him look older than he was – an old-fashioned grey tank top, cream shirt, brown slacks and tartan slippers.

'What are you looking at while people are in church, Amos? Porn?'

'My name's not Amos, I keep telling you.'

'No, but you're a Bible-basher, aren't you. Quoting liberally, left, right and centre. And Amos is one of the judgement prophets, isn't he?'

'"For judgement *is* God's". Moses five: one to seventeen.'

'Yes, but occasionally he needs a helping hand, doesn't he?'

He sent me a curmudgeonly look. 'I don't know what you're talking about.'

'You don't?'

'No.'

'Then I'll tell you.' Again I felt an unpleasant dizziness. 'Can we … sit down?'

He appeared to consider my proposition. Then he shrugged and slumped onto the sofa while placing one hand on the closed laptop, as though afraid I might confiscate it.

I sat down in the chair facing him. My head was spinning and I had to clench my teeth to focus my gaze on him. He stared at me blankly while opening and closing his mouth with a barely audible smack of his lips, like a gorged toad. I would have to watch out for his tongue in case he became hungry.

When I started speaking again I seemed to hear the echo of my own voice in my head. This was unpleasant, too. But I brushed aside my discomfort and did everything in my power to repress it. 'I think we should move towards the right answers, Vetle.'

He gave a brief nod. 'Vetle's my name, yes.'

'But … Amos was a suitable username for someone with your background. Was that why you chose it?'

'I still don't understand what you're talking about.'

'And this Amos I'm talking about was astonishingly well informed about Andreas and his half-sister, Emma.'

'Who are they? These names are utterly new to me.'

'Oh, yes? They're both the children of Robert Høie Hansen, and you definitely know who he is.'

He glared at me without saying a word.

'You're a computer man. You know your way around machines like that one.' I pointed to his laptop. 'And the websites they can access. I'm fairly sure you know all the possible shortcuts and ways to mask your identity, and whatever else is needed to operate relatively unhindered on such websites. I was targeted by something similar a while ago.'

'Something similar?'

'You found a website called *Moribund*. You met some people there you knew – unless it was the other way around and you invited them in. It's the classic question: which came first? The chicken or the egg? But you know the answer to that, of course.'

'What?'

'Who came first?' When he didn't answer, I added: 'With your philosophy of life I suppose it must've been God. God created the chicken and the egg, so to Him it didn't really matter which came first. And in this metaphor it's you who is God, if you follow my thinking.'

His eyes were dull now, as though I were boring him. He was sitting with conspicuously bad posture on the old sofa, hunched up in front of the laptop and the wireless mouse, although neither was being used for the moment.

'Twenty-eight years ago something terrible happened to your big sister. Later, when you'd grown up, you loyally visited her as often as you were able. I have no doubt that your fury and despair were reinforced every time you went there. I don't know at what point you decided to give God the help I referred to before and to take matters into your own hands. Perhaps it was only when you came to Bergen, did your training and found yourself holding a lethal weapon in your hand, providing you knew how to use it.' Again I pointed to the laptop in front of him.

He pursed his lips, but his eyes were more alert now. He was following what I was saying.

'It was natural to search out the person everyone considered to be the guilty party.'

'He *was*—'

'Yes, we can agree on that for the time being. He was guilty. And he wasn't a particularly nice person. He used to beat his son until he was well into his teens, and we know nothing about what he might've done to his little daughter before she was two. Perhaps we never will.'

'A bastard,' he mumbled.

'Yes, lots of people have called him that. But now he's in—' This time I interrupted myself.

But I had whetted his curiosity. 'He's where?'

'We can come back to that. Let's stick to what we were doing. You discovered where he lived, who he was living with, what his son's name was: Andreas. And then – perhaps by chance, perhaps through skill – you got into his, Andreas's, email account.'

He looked at me without showing the slightest emotion.

'Andreas told me yesterday that this Amos knew an incredible amount about him and his half-sister, Emma. As the two of them mainly communicated by email it was likely that the person sitting on this knowledge had access to at least one email account. I asked myself the question: Have I met anyone during this investigation who might've had reason to hack into their accounts?'

Still he didn't react, but there seemed to be a veil of weary resignation over his eyes. He was absorbing every word I said.

'The answer was yes – one Vetle Valaker. He was an IT teacher. He had done supply work in all the upper-secondary schools in town. You told me that yourself. Was one of these schools maybe Bjørgvin? Did you have Andreas as a pupil there? Was that how you hacked into his emails and from there gradually implemented what was an extremely base act of revenge?'

He pursed his lips. His mouth was like a scar – red at the edges as if it hadn't healed properly.

'I don't care if you don't admit this. Tomorrow I can make a couple of calls and test if my theory is correct or not. The police will put their experts on the case.'

'The police?'

'Surely you don't think you'll get away with this? A very serious case is beginning to develop against you, Vetle.'

His jaw muscles tautened, as though there were words inside that wanted to get out. But he was successfully holding them back.

As he didn't say anything, I carried on. 'We can take the story further. That's no problem. When you got into Andreas's email account you probably found more than you'd hoped for. He'd contacted his half-sister in Haugesund and they were corresponding. They told each other confidences, about their father among other things. For Emma this came as another confirmation of what a terrible man he was, and the two young people created in each other a kind of common – what should I call it? – depression, psychosis … a hatred for their father, which they turned in on themselves, the way children often do. Was it their fault? Did Emma scream at night when she was small, keeping her father awake? Was Andreas unable to live up to his father's expectations of how he should behave? Did you realise that this was a way into both of their lives and the worst way of punishing Robert Høie? Because, even if he'd never expressed any form of love for either of his children, from your point of view, it would've still been a terrible blow for him to discover that both of them were missing and later found dead by their own hands. Wouldn't that be revenge worthy of Amos, the judgement prophet?'

Now he couldn't maintain the mask any longer. His eyes flitted to and fro with every word I uttered. His mouth opened and closed, much faster than before, and he gasped for breath.

'You contacted them via *Moribund*. And then you went into action. You manipulated them. For a while there was a third person involved, someone Emma opened up to and who had a similarly difficult background. She called herself Sleeping Beauty. But she withdrew and ultimately Andreas was unable to carry on, either. It was only Emma who executed your instructions and performed the final step.' I fixed my gaze on him. 'We found her yesterday, Vetle. She'd been hanging there for more than three weeks. She didn't look good, I can tell you. But someone had prepared the scene for them. Set up the stools. Shown them the way.'

He shrank physically in front of my eyes. His eyes were glued to his laptop as if what he would most like to do was creep inside and hide – in the virtual world that was situated there somewhere.

'How did you find the boat sheds, Vetle? They belonged to some disused farms. Anyone you knew?'

He didn't answer.

'The police are going to find out as well.'

Like an echo from before, he repeated: 'The police?'

'They'll find evidence of your presence. Fingerprints. DNA. For all I know, you were there to put the noose around her neck.'

He looked fearful and slowly shook his head, as if disclaiming responsibility for everything I was saying.

'In which case we're talking about an assisted suicide, perhaps even premeditated murder. No court in Norway will regard giving the Lord a helping hand as a mitigating circumstance.'

The air was beginning to go out of him right in front of me. One side of him was sagging, as though his whole skeletal structure was disintegrating. 'How…?'

I felt no sympathy for him. 'You saw the state your sister was in. You watched the way your parents wasted away after the assault. You knew how your own life had been shaped as a result. How could you do something like this to innocent young people? Because you didn't strike at Robert Høie, however guilty he was.'

He raised his head. 'He *was* guilty!'

'Yes, he was, Vetle. But he wasn't the only one. The Vangen brothers were the main villains of the piece. It was they who, if they didn't force him, were the main protagonists in what happened.'

He straightened up. 'The Vangen boys?'

'Perhaps it was them you should've targeted rather than Robert and his children.'

Now he began to slump back as if a gradually increasing sense of guilt had finally started to weigh him down.

'But they've got their come-uppance now anyway,' I said.

His eyes quizzed me.

'They're both in prison and Robert's in a coma. I lost my own half-sister a week ago. In Bergen there's a mother whose son is so psychologically damaged he'll never be well again. In Haugesund there's a mother who's lost her daughter.' I pointed to the Jesus on the wall. 'Do you think Jesus would've applauded what you've done?'

'What?'

'"Suffer little children to come to me",' I said. 'But not before their time, Vetle. Not before their time.'

'Jesus conquered death.'

'Some believe that, I know. But it won't happen in your case. There are no winners here, Vetle, and that includes you.' I raised my voice. 'Do you understand what I'm telling you? Or... ?'

I felt sick and dizzy, as though I might keel over at any second. I had to get out. God knows what he might do if I lost control of myself.

I forced myself to my feet, as weak in the knees as if I were standing on the edge of a steep cliff. He gave a start and curled up, afraid I would attack him.

When I didn't, he glanced up at me. 'You'll never be able to prove it!'

'Prove what? That *you* were behind all of this?'

He looked down, struck by his own words – his acknowledgement that everything I had said was true.

Inside, I felt a silent triumph, but, as so often before, it wasn't the kind of triumph where you jumped for joy and did somersaults, more a sorrowful verification that I had found the right way into another person's darkest secrets.

'I know I'm right, Vetle. Over the years I've met a lot of people. People like you, with a thirst for justice given them by a God fewer and fewer of us believe in. When the name Amos appeared as a username on the website and the link was IT skills, I put two and two together and came up with an unpleasant answer.'

He mumbled something I couldn't decipher.

I leaned forwards. 'What did you say? I didn't hear.'

'Andreas will regret his actions. She went to a better place than this. Life isn't much to shout about.'

I felt an unease in my body. With one hand I took out my phone and called Annemette Bergesen on her number.

'Hello. Annemette here.'

'It's Varg.'

'OK. I've been told. She's at pathology now. But this is actually my day off.'

'Sorry, but I'm here in Vognstølbakken with a man you ought to interview regarding this case. And...' I lowered my voice. '...I don't think I'd leave him here on his own.'

'Right, are you saying he's ... suicidal, too?'

'There's a chance he is.'

'And what role does he play in this case?'

'He's been instrumental to everything that's happened. It's up to you in the force to find out to what degree.'

She sighed. 'Varg, I'm walking up to the Brushytten cabins. But fine, I'll call Atle and ask him to send some officers. Can you give me the precise address?'

I did. Vetle Valaker and I didn't exchange more than a few words before they came for him.

I went back home to Sølvi without any sense of joy. It was as it had always been. No one thanked me for my help. No one gave me a medal. No one even paid my fee.

44

And I ended up going to Haugesund on my own.

Skåre Church was in Haugevegen, only a stone's throw from where Norma had lived, in Gange-Rolvs gate. It was a white timber church. According to a plaque by the entrance it had been built in 1858, the third church on the site. I arrived at the last moment and the mourners had already filled a large number of the rows of pews. Daylight streamed into the church through the high windows. The interior was very beautiful with natural-coloured woodwork, green-painted beams that supported an airy vault and the tasteful application of falu red on the pews and side doors. At the very front of the nave, facing the altar, hung a three-masted sailing ship – a visible symbol of Haugesund's maritime connections. From here Norma would also set out on her final journey across an ocean whose limits no one knew.

I guessed there were somewhere between a hundred and a hundred and fifty people present, many of them Norma's age, some younger. From the small service sheet pressed into my hand I discovered that the funeral would be conducted by Pastor Knut Kjærstad, who, I supposed, was my second cousin's husband. I saw her, Ruth, ahead of me in the assembly. On the front pew I saw the backs of the heads of those I assumed were closest family – three women near the central aisle.

I stood inside the door scanning the congregation. I found Ingeborg Hagland in one of the rows at the back. I went over, greeted her and she budged up to let me in. She was wearing a short winter jacket in various greys, and black trousers. Around her neck she wore a dark-green shawl with a long fringe. I passed on my condolences concerning Emma and said we should talk afterwards. She nodded, but paid me no more than a fleeting glance. After we had sat down she stared ahead. The organ was already busy with the prelude, a melody I recognised but the name of which escaped me. I looked down at the sheet. It was 'Adagio' by Ole Bull and was subtitled 'A Mother's Prayer'.

The first song was 'Alltid freidig', a hymn that reminded me of my childhood in Nordnes, when every single day started with the whole class reciting the Lord's Prayer more or less in unison and afterwards singing a popular hymn, very often this one. I joined in after a fashion. I heard nothing from Ingeborg.

Knut Kjærstad gave a warm, personal description of Norma's life without mentioning any specific details about her relationship with her biological mother. He only confirmed that she was born in the Spring-Spawning Herring Tariff Foundation Hospital on 3rd July 1927 and grew up with kind, caring foster parents. He spent quite a lot of time talking about her husband, Nils Bakkevik, and the secure home environment she and Nils had created for their two children, Petter and Ellen. He went on to describe the tragedy that had befallen the family when Petter was among the dead following the Alexander Kielland disaster on 27th March 1980. In the ensuing years Norma and Nils dedicated themselves to looking after their grandchild, Karen, for which their daughter-in-law, Elisabeth, was eternally grateful. After Nils died in the summer of 1998, Norma lived a quiet, withdrawn life in their comfortable home in Gange-Rolvs gate, although she still did charity work and showed the kind of commitment that revealed a generous heart. No one could have predicted that this heart would stop beating after a tragic accident at home. All the signs were that she had many years ahead of her, and it was with great sorrow that the family paid their last respects this Monday at the end of November. He didn't refer to her biological mother or half-brother in Bergen, although I imagined Ruth had told him about our meeting ten days previously.

While he talked I sent sidelong glances at the woman next to me. She was following what was being said. On one occasion a little sob escaped her. That was when the pastor came on to how she died, and towards the end of the speech tears were running from her eyes and she did nothing to wipe them away until the pastor had finished.

Before the ceremony of throwing soil onto the coffin, the congregation sang 'Abide With Me', and the service finished with 'Kjærlighet fra Gud'. As a postlude the organist played Grieg's 'To Spring'. It was a traditional selection of hymns and music that Norma would definitely have applauded, unless she had chosen them herself in advance.

We stood as the coffin was carried to the waiting car. Ruth met my eyes as she passed with the closest kith and kin behind the coffin. She nodded and smiled, and signalled that we should meet outside.

When Ingeborg Hagland and I left the church I leaned over to her. 'I just need to have a few words with the family. Will you wait?'

She nodded without saying a word and was then lost in the crowd of mourners queueing to offer their condolences to the family. I arced around them to where Ruth was waiting for me.

She hesitated initially, then she stood on her tiptoes and gave me a quick hug. Her cheeks glistened with tears, her eyes were red-rimmed and her smile was sad. 'How terrible that something like this should happen so soon after you'd met, don't you think?'

'Absolutely.'

'I told Knut about it and I know he was wondering if he should include it in his speech. But he decided not to. No one in Haugesund knows that side of Norma's life. For them she was no more than a very ordinary woman who had lived her life without any drama, apart from what happened to Petter in 1980. But you have to come to the wake afterwards. Ellen and Karen would both love to see you.'

I looked over to where the closest family were receiving condolences. They were the three women I had seen from the back of the church, two in their early fifties and one a little over twenty, all dressed in black. I assumed they were Ellen, Elisabeth – the widowed daughter-in-law – and her daughter, Karen. 'I don't want to impose.'

Ruth placed a hand on my arm. 'You won't, Varg. I can promise you that.'

I looked around. I couldn't see Ingeborg anywhere. 'Actually I'm meeting someone.'

She regarded me with a serious expression on her face. 'This is the time to honour your own sister, Varg. What could be more important than that?'

'Yes, you're right. I can do it later.'

It was a strange afternoon. I went with Ruth and her children in her tiny Golf. Knut was in another car. We didn't have to go far – straight past the park by the Odd Fellows house in Sørhauggata, a beige brick building with the triple-link symbol and the year 1937 above the front door.

In the reception rooms close family and friends were gathered over sandwiches, coffee, tea and mineral water. Ellen and Elisabeth both gave speeches in honour of Norma. One of her very oldest friends, going right back to their first school – an elegant woman by the name of Gudrun Vaage – did the same, and she and I had a long chat later. She introduced herself as Norma's confidante for many years, and she told me she knew 'everything' about me and my mother from when Norma herself had found out, many years ago.

'Everything?' I queried.

'Well, not everything of course. But Norma told me what she had heard about this itinerant preacher who had been her father, and that her mother had moved to Bergen and several years later had … you.'

'And who my father was?'

'Yes, but that … that was the tram conductor from Sunnfjord, wasn't it?'

'Yes, I suppose it was,' I said, without entering into that side of the matter.

I spoke to Ellen, Elisabeth and Karen, and we agreed we would contact each other again once we had gained some distance from this. 'We obviously have a lot to talk about,' Ellen said with a crooked little smile that reminded me of her mother.

Before we parted, both Ellen and Ruth asked if I was planning to go back to Bergen the same day. I answered in the affirmative, and we left after more hugs. In many ways it had been a heart-warming experience. Suddenly having a new family that I had previously no more than guessed at meant that the tragic death of my half-sister appeared in a more redeeming light. Even if she was still like a stranger in my life, in the course of the day she seemed to have come closer to me, as a result of the pastor's speech and meeting what was left of her family.

I found my car where I had parked it and drove straight to Haugeve-gen. I went up one floor and rang Ingeborg's bell. When she opened the door I breathed a sigh of relief. So I hadn't come in vain after all.

45

She had on the same black trousers she had been wearing in church, plus a white blouse and green velvet jacket I seemed to remember from the last time I had been there with Norma. I followed her into the shabby sitting room, which had not become any more appealing in the interim. The only visible change was that she had placed a cut rose in front of the photograph of Emma on the bookcase that held no books. The big round ashtray on the coffee table was full of cigarette ends, along with some apple cores, curiously enough. The TV set in the corner was on. The images on the screen were of a soap opera in a country with a lot more sunshine than Haugesund. The people were attractive, but spoke with dramatic gesticulations and despairing facial expressions, not that any of it reached our ears. She had muted the volume.

'I'm sorry it took a bit of time,' I said. 'But I didn't see you afterwards.'

She didn't look me in the eye; she spoke to an imaginary microphone somewhere at chest height. 'I noticed that you were busy with … family.'

'Yes, and they invited me to the wake.'

She nodded. 'Would you like a cup of coffee?'

'Yes, please.'

She disappeared into the kitchen and obviously she'd had some coffee on the go because she was back with a cup in her hand after thirty seconds. She motioned me to a chair by the coffee table. She took a seat on the sofa and grabbed the half-full cup there. In a way she seemed calm and resigned, as though she had come to terms with what had happened to her daughter.

'I suppose you'd like to know where I found her – Emma?'

'Yes … please.'

I spared her as much detail as I could. I didn't mention anything about *Moribund*, but said Emma had clearly decided to end her life and she had found somewhere so far off the beaten track that no one had found her until I finally got on her trail.

'How did you find her?'

'With the help of her half-brother, Andreas.'

'Oh?' With a trembling hand she shook a cigarette from her packet, poked it into her mouth and lit it with a black lighter emblazoned with the Statoil logo. 'How did he know about the place?'

'Via a friend.'

She inhaled the smoke so deeply it must have gone to the very bottom of her lungs. Not that much came back through her mouth. 'I can't understand how she could've been so desperate. Her father was a bastard, that's true enough, but he never did anything to her.'

'Didn't he?'

'It was much worse for her friend, Åsa. She was continually raped by her own father all through her childhood.'

'But Andreas has told me Robert could be pretty brutal. He said he'd been beaten until he was well into his teens. Did Robert never do anything like that to you two?'

'Not to Emma anyway. But she was so small. As for me...' She shrugged. 'He became quite violent when I confronted him after the business with that ... Veslemøy. But it was a showdown after all.'

'You threw him out.'

'Yes, but he walked out of the door himself.' She took another deep drag of the cigarette and stared into the distance with the same glum expression.

'And you never saw him again?'

She pressed her lips together. Her eyes narrowed. 'No. Never. He disappeared from my life for ever, and I wish he had from Emma's, too. Then perhaps things wouldn't have happened as they did.'

'You didn't see him later, either?'

She blinked. The cigarette had such an intense glow it was as though she had inhaled half of it already. 'Never.'

'Why don't you admit it? He was here ten days ago. The day after Norma and I were here.'

For the first time she looked me straight in the eye, but she soon lowered her gaze again. 'Who said that?'

'The police did. They had him under surveillance. Haven't they been here to talk to you?'

She shook her head slowly. 'N-no. No one's been here.'

'Well … what did he want from you?'

The glow was so near her fingertip she must have felt the heat from it. She stubbed it out with brutal force in the ashtray, took another from her scrunched-up packet, put it in her mouth and lit it.

'Pretty dramatic, him calling on you, don't you think? First time he's been to Haugesund since I came round asking about Emma. Was that why he came?'

She pushed her lower jaw out and back several times as though she was working hard not to say anything. There was a stony, irreconcilable look about her eyes that hadn't been there before. 'H-he threatened me.'

'Threatened you?'

'He said … what you just said. You'd been round here asking after Emma. She'd gone missing and perhaps you'd investigate what happened back then too – to Veslemøy. He said if I breathed a word about … I told him I hadn't said anything. But he carried on and said if you got back to him one more time and he realised I'd … blabbed, he would have a word with some people he knew down here and I'd never get any more of … what I needed.' She spoke in halting, breathless snatches, as if she were walking up a steep hill.

'Yes, I know he had contacts in the drugs scene here. That was why he was in town that Friday. To offload a consignment. So of course he could've done that.'

'Yes…'

'And what did you answer?'

'I just said what I've already told you. That I hadn't said a word about Veslemøy, but … that Aunty had.'

I tried to catch her eye. 'Are you saying you told him about … Norma?'

She nodded. 'But ... I said he wasn't to go to hers. If he did, she wouldn't stay quiet. She'd report him to the police.'

'What? For Christ's sake, woman!'

She bobbed her head up and down. 'And he didn't go to hers. I said ... I'd speak to her myself.'

'You'd ... So you got in touch with her?'

'I went to her house that same evening and told her what had happened. I said she had to tell you to drop the case, to stop the investigation.'

'Stop the investigation! This was about your daughter! Emma!'

'That's exactly what she said. That it was impossible to do anything now. You had to carry on doing what you'd started. But...' She whimpered. 'I couldn't cope without ... the pills. I couldn't get any more from the doctor. I just had to have them! I was so frightened ... I couldn't live without ... And she insisted. She just kept repeating the same and the same. She grabbed me, said I had to pull myself together, we had to think about Emma. I said Emma ... was bound to turn up. But she just went on and on until in the end I pulled myself free and ... pushed her ... and she fell.'

As she had been speaking, I'd suddenly realised what was coming, and now I had it from her lips, with such clarity it was impossible to misunderstand. I spoke slowly, word by word, to keep a tight rein on my own feelings. 'You pushed her. She fell and hit her head on the worktop. She lost consciousness?'

When she didn't answer I repeated what I had said. 'Did she? Did she lose consciousness? Didn't you see you'd injured her and she was bleeding?'

Her whole upper body was trembling now. Her hand was moving so much she could barely put the cigarette between her lips. 'I saw nothing. I just left. I thought she ... that she'd be alright. It was only a few days later that I heard ... And then there was a column in the paper and her ... obituary.' Once again she looked up and straight at me. There were tears in her eyes now. 'I didn't mean to! It was an accident. I can't be made responsible for it.'

I got up. 'That's for others to decide, not me, Ingeborg. If you haven't had any police round yet, you will have now.'

She shrugged. 'I'll deny everything. I have nothing to lose. Everything is over anyway.'

I looked at her. For the second time in twenty-four hours I was standing in front of someone who had caused the death of another person. But this time I didn't hang around for the police. I rang the station and asked for Liland, but he wasn't on duty. I explained the situation to the duty officer. He listened, then said they would send a patrol car.

'She has to be taken in today,' I said.

'We'll handle this from here, Veum. I've written down what you said. Liland or another officer will contact you later. Just go home.'

I did as instructed. I didn't have the strength to refuse. But the sight of Norma lying on the kitchen floor and the thought that she could have been saved tormented me all the way home. And I was sure the thought of losing a sister I had only just got to know would torment me for as long as I lived.

46

The following day I called Annemette Bergesen and asked how the interview with Vetle Valaker had gone. She told me he had admitted almost everything and on Monday morning the judges had decided he would remain in custody, provisionally for a week.

'A week?'

'Yes. This is a fairly unusual case and the police lawyer is looking into the charges that could be brought against him. Most probably it will be as an accessory to suicide, but sentencing in this area is very unclear. There's hardly any precedence. I'm afraid he's not going to serve a long sentence, if any at all.'

I heaved a sigh. 'Right. Did you find out how he knew about the boat sheds?'

'Yes, through a colleague at work. Apparently he was related to the owners. They'd been fishing there once.'

'In other words, he might've left clues there before.'

'Yes.'

'Do you believe what he says? Do you think he seems credible?'

'That's always a judgement, Varg. So far he hasn't said anything that doesn't tally with what we've found at the crime scene. From a purely moral point of view what he has done is downright reprehensible. But in principle not illegal, so long as what we're talking about is an exchange of views between adults.'

'Well ... she was nineteen and he's forty.'

'Yes, I hear what you say. Don't misunderstand me; I'm not defending what he did. I can't even explain it.'

'Of course not. We're dealing with a personality that needs psychiatric treatment, as far as I can see. Someone traumatised by what happened to his sister. But … what about Emma? Do you know any more about … how she died?'

'That's probably clear from how she was found, but she's still at pathology. We're expecting a report from them soon. This is our responsibility now, Varg. You can file the case in your archive and send an invoice to the relevant party. Think about something else. Go on holiday. Doubtless you need one.'

Send an invoice to the relevant party? Yes, right. C/o Pearly Gates, I suppose.

We rang off. I sat staring into middle distance. Think about something else? Go on holiday?

Well … I did have another trail to follow, not in this case, but in connection with something Norma and Ruth had put me onto. I took out my notepad and flicked back to the notes I had made when I met the old jazzers at Swing'n'Sweet. Eva Høiland. I switched on my computer and ran a search on her. In fact I did find an Eva Høiland Pedersen living in Erleveien, Landås.

I rang her, introduced myself and asked if she was the Eva who was married to a saxophonist by the name of Leif Pedersen. She replied that she had been, and when I asked if I could go to her home for a little chat, she seemed to be happy to have a visitor.

I arranged to be there for one o'clock.

*

At five to I parked at the back of Landåstorget and strolled over to the four-storey block built in the 1950s, when Landås was Bergen's first satellite town. I walked up to the second floor, where I found a plate bearing the name Pedersen.

The woman who opened up was, at a guess, in her mid-seventies. She had big glasses with thick lenses and a dark-blue rim. Her hair was neat and completely white. She was wearing a red dress that was tight against her stocky, buxom body, a string of pearls around her neck and a small brooch to the left of her chest. Her make-up was tasteful – her lipstick a dark burgundy and the mascara around her eyes discreet. I picked up a strong fragrance of lily of the valley, and when she asked me in, there was a smile that promised a great deal more than I had come for. She spoke with a charming, refined dialect that revealed her origins, and when I asked she confirmed my prediction. 'From Kristiansand. It's a long time now though. A very long time.'

I followed her into the living room, which was furnished in a 1960s style with a large radiogram cabinet along one wall and a TV set of the bulky variety, although I doubted it was black and white. A classic dining area – a table with six chairs – and a Stressless armchair completed the scene. The pictures on the wall were sixties' or seventies' graphics, except for a large, dramatic photograph of a saxophonist with the light casting a shadow onto the wall behind him.

'That's Leif,' she said. 'Taken in the Star Studio in the sixties. I had it enlarged after he died.' She gave a wry smile. 'He was past his best, if I can say so, but could still play the horn like a slightly breathless Ben Webster.'

'You sang, I've been told.'

'Yes. Who have you been talking to?'

'Terje Tornøe was the most informative.'

'We called him Teddy. He used to smoke ten cigarettes an hour of that brand when he could. But he was a good trumpeter. You know, Bergen in the fifties was pretty good for jazz. The Golden Club in Industrihuset, Møhlenpris. Big band concerts in Konsertpaleet and Ole Bull. And Leif had been there since the twenties. A proper grand old man on the jazz scene.' She tilted her head and looked at me. Then she touched the inside of my elbow. 'You know, you remind me of him.'

That fell like a sinker into my life and I bought it hook and line and all. 'What do you mean?'

'Mm, it struck me as soon as I saw you. And now. The way you move and…' She held a hand in front of her face. 'There's something here … from the nose upwards.' Then she turned. 'But you'd like a cup of coffee, wouldn't you?'

'Yes, please.'

'With something stronger perhaps?' she said with a seductive glint in her eye.

'Thank you very much, but I'm driving.'

'Oh.' She looked disappointed. Then she lit up. 'But I'll have a dram anyway.'

'Enjoy.'

She went into the kitchen. I went closer to the large photograph of Leif Pedersen. He was standing in a classic sax pose, leaning back, so that the whole instrument was shown to its full advantage and created the shadow on the back wall that the photographer had been after. He had a classic profile; hair combed back with a side parting, dark with streaks of grey by his temples and above his ears. I was unable to see anything of myself there; however, I was hardly the right person to judge.

She returned with a tray of coffee cups and a plain-black Thermos. After placing it on the coffee table, she went to a corner cabinet, opened a door at the front and took out a liqueur glass and a bottle of St. Hallvard. She glanced in my direction and held up the bottle. 'Sure?'

'Well…' I allowed myself to be tempted after all. 'I think I could manage just a tiny one.'

She beamed with pleasure, took another glass and poured.

After we were settled back on either side of the table, she raised her glass and we said *skål*.

'You said on the phone you were a … private investigator.'

'Yes, but in this context the emphasis is on private.'

'Oh, yes?' She was curious. 'And you were interested in Leif?' Almost flirtingly she added: 'Not me?'

In many ways she was the most attractive seventy-something I had ever met, but I had to confess it was Leif Pedersen I had come to hear more about. 'Can you tell me anything about him? *Con amore*, sort of.'

A veil of sadness crossed her face. 'Hm … When I met him he was in his late forties. We met on the music scene and soon became a couple, before I went to Sweden for a few years.'

'Uhuh?'

She gazed through the window. 'The jazz scene was even more excit-ing there. International big-band jazz. So I tried my luck, but … Well, I had a baby there, even though the father was from Bergen.'

'Leif Pedersen?'

'No, someone else. He was married,' she said with a serious little smile. 'But when I came back to Bergen, I met Leif again. We got married and he treated Dag as if he was his own son.'

'He … he didn't have any other children?'

'No. We didn't have any of our own, but, as I said, he was a good father to Dag.'

I took a sip of the tasty herbal liqueur. 'Listen, fru Pedersen…'

'Please call me Eva.'

'Eva … The reason I've come to see you today is that via quite a strange, circuitous route I find myself on the trail of … It could well be that Leif Pedersen is my father.'

Her eyes widened. 'That wouldn't surprise me. As I said, you have some features that remind me of him.'

'Did he ever say anything about … anything that might point in that direction?'

'I don't think he had a clue about you. If he had done, he would've told me. We … yes, you're old enough to know. We had a rich life together and we told each other … everything. I told him who Dag's father was, and he told me about his great passion – a woman who became a Nazi during the war, but whom he met again some time later. In Oslo during the years when I was in Sweden.'

'I see. Did he ever mention an episode with a woman he met at a wedding in Haugesund in 1942?'

She pondered. 'Haugesund? I can't remember that. He admitted he'd had some – what do they call them nowadays? – one-night stands. For a musician there were always such opportunities. They didn't call them groupies either, but it came to the same thing. But of course I can't remember everything. If I'm being honest, that's not what a woman wants to hear when she's in the arms of the person who ultimately became the man of her life.'

'No, of course not. As far as I know, they never met again. My official father is and has always been … another man. The one my mother
married.'

She smiled wryly. 'Exactly. By and large it's only we women who can
be sure of who fathers the children we have, isn't that true? At any rate
if we've lived a moderately ordered life.'

'Tell me though, what was he like?'

'You know, very few people could make ends meet playing jazz
at that time. Leif worked as a salesman in a gentlemen's outfitter's in
Strandgaten for large parts of his professional life. But he was a great
saxophonist, for as long as he had the breath. Towards the end of his life
his health declined. He drank too much, lost his hearing and finally …
well … he was more and more absent, and when he died it was actually
a relief for us all. But…' She held her forehead. 'Inside here I've kept
the memories of how he was at his best, as a musician and father and
… yes, in all ways.'

I stroked my hair. 'I wish I'd met him.'

'Yes, I can understand that well enough, my boy.'

That was the first time in more years than I cared to count that
anyone had called me a boy. I looked around the room. 'You know, Eva,
it is actually possible now to determine whether someone is related or
not, even after death.'

'You're thinking about DNA and suchlike, are you?'

'Yes. When did Leif die?'

'November 1989, just a few days after the Berlin Wall fell. He was
eighty-three years old.'

'I suppose it's unlikely you have anything of his that might still have
his DNA on?'

'Mm.' She gazed into the air thoughtfully. Then she got up. 'Wait a
minute. I'll have a look…' She went into the hallway and I could hear
her open another door. Again I stared at the photograph of Leif Pedersen on the wall. I couldn't seem to keep my eyes away from it. Perhaps
it was no coincidence that I'd always had a special affinity with saxo-
phones. Not that I had ever tried to play one, but I had always liked the

sound of it, and again and again I played CDs of the old masters of the art: Coleman Hawkins, Lester Young, Ben Webster and Stan Getz. Was it simply in my genes?

She returned with a faded woollen hat, blue with a greyish-white stripe around the turned-up edge. 'God knows why I haven't thrown out these things. There were some old mittens, a couple of scarves and this woolly hat in a plastic bag in one of the cabinets. The kind of thing he used to wear in the winter, but we packed them away in the summer. Inside the hat I can see a few strands of hair and no one else but Leif wore it, so … perhaps.'

I held out my hand. 'This might actually do the trick, Eva.'

She gave me the hat.

'I'll give it back to you of course.'

'Don't worry. But I'd like to hear if this leads to anything.' She smiled. 'The best news would be if we were almost related.'

She sat back down on the sofa and poured herself another glass. She glanced at mine, which still wasn't empty. 'Can I tempt you with a drop more?'

'I'm afraid not.'

We sat chatting for a little while longer. I was very comfortable in her company. She told me more about Leif Pedersen, about his old band from the interwar years, the Hurrycanes, and mentioned the names of a few musicians he had played with later. When she came to talk about Tore Lude, she fell into a reverie, and I remembered Terje Tornøe suggesting she'd had an affair with him, even though she had long been married to Leif. She was ageing now, but she still radiated a form of well-preserved sensuality that gave me the sense she had known how to partake of life's pleasures for as long as she had access to them.

She seemed to be able to read my thoughts. 'I'll be honest with you, my boy. Leif and I had an on-and-off relationship. As I said before, when I went to Sweden in the fifties I was expecting a child by someone else and I never thought I would see Leif again. But when I came back to Norway it was because of him I settled in Bergen – and not in Kristiansand, for example. Our relationship blossomed and we got married. We were a good fit – in all ways – and we enjoyed ourselves, if you know what I mean.'

I nodded and smiled. 'I think I know what you're referring to.'

'When you're young you think life stops at fifty, sixty or seventy. But those of us old enough know that's not how it is.' For some reason two roses had appeared in her cheeks. 'In fact, I do have a gentleman friend nowadays as well. Someone of my own age, the perfect gentleman, who takes me for drives and takes me abroad. It's like life's dessert, isn't it?'

'That's good to hear.'

'So what you were telling me – about your mother having secrets; you shouldn't blame her for that. I mean, how much do we really know about our parents?'

'No, you're right.'

Again I glanced up at Leif Pedersen. I tried to imagine a younger version of him in my mind's eye, dancing with my mother at a party after the wedding in Haugesund. But I only had a slightly stiff, posed wedding photo of my parents from 1933, and I had never really been able to associate my mother with this, not from my memory. The way people are at the end of their lives overshadows the pictures we have of them in earlier phases. The very last conversation I had with my mother was clearer to me than any other memories I had of childhood and growing up. I had a clearer image of my father on his way down Haugeveien in his tram conductor's uniform or at home engrossed in a book or on the boat trip to Sunnfjord, which he and I made in 1950. And now perhaps I had to stop thinking about him as 'my father' and more as 'the tram conductor', 'the Sunnfjorder' or just as Anders Veum. I had lost my mother many years ago and my half-sister ten days ago. Now I was on the way to losing my father, whichever one he was, and that made me feel even lonelier and more abandoned than I had been for many, many years.

'Perhaps you shouldn't have the DNA test done,' said Eva Høiland Pedersen, sending me a look that, in the circumstances, was somehow maternal.

'I'll give it some thought. I'll take this with me anyway,' I said, holding up the old woollen hat.

A little later we said our goodbyes. She gave me a hug as I left, as though she had already determined that she was going to be a sort of stepmother to me, if I needed one.

Before I had reached Landåstorget my phone rang. I grabbed it and checked the name on the display. It was Annemette Bergesen. I answered at once.

'Hi, Annemette. Any news?'

'Yes, Varg. We've just received a provisional report from pathology. And it was quite a surprise.'

'Uhuh?'

'It looks like the case you're investigating isn't quite over yet after all.'

'Really? I'm not with you ...'

'It wasn't Emma Hagland you found in the boat shed.'

'What!'

'Her dental records don't match.'

'So who was it then?'

'We don't know yet. It was a woman of about the same age, but it definitely wasn't Emma Hagland.'

47

Two days later I met her in Berlin. Even though she had concealed herself under a large, ribbed-knit hat, I recognised her at once as she came through the door to the cosy café not far from the train station in Frie-drichstrasse, where she had suggested we should meet. Had the weather been warmer we could have sat outside under the summery awnings and watched the Spree glide slowly past at a calm, leisurely pace through the central areas of the old Prussian capital. But it was cold outside and I had retreated indoors to wait for her. Through the window I could still see the famous TV tower hovering like an anchored UFO over the town, giving you the sense that you were being watched wherever you went.

When she came in from the street I stood up and waved. She came over to me, smiled tentatively and said: 'Veum?'

'That's me.'

We shook hands, and she said: 'Åsa.' She cast a glance at the table and noted the half-full glass of Schwarzbier I had in front of me. 'I'll go and get a cup of hot chocolate.'

I watched her as she went to the counter. She was wearing a beige duffel coat, tight, stone-washed jeans and high, dark-brown boots with a light-coloured sheepskin cuff at the top. While she was waiting for the hot chocolate she peeped several times in my direction. I nodded each time to reassure her I wasn't planning to do a bunk.

She returned, put down the cup and took a seat in the chair opposite me. 'So kind of you to travel all the way to Berlin to tell me what you've found out about Emma.'

'If you're lucky, a return Bergen-Berlin ticket costs no more than a better meal at a standard restaurant, so that part wasn't so hard. But ... we don't need to play hide and seek any more.'

She looked at me in confusion and blushed. 'What do you mean?'

From my pocket I took the photograph I had of Emma. I placed it on the table between us. 'I have no problem recognising you even if you have hidden your hair under the hat.'

She gazed down at the photograph and seemed to submit it to a thorough examination before lifting her gaze again. 'I…' She rolled her shoulders as if to suggest she didn't know what to say.

'I know what you've been doing. Some people will be happy when they hear. Others … hm. All I'd like to know is … why?'

'Why what?'

'Why did you and Åsa change identity, Emma?'

She looked at me with a serious face. Then she seemed to realise there was no point pretending any more. She started slowly and hesitantly: 'I'll try to explain. I'm not sure if you'll be able to put yourself in our shoes … and understand how we felt, but I'll try.'

She swallowed hard and her eyes flitted around before focusing on me again. 'We were so sick of our lives, her and me. We wanted to escape. Start afresh. With a *tabula rasa*. She went to Bergen, I came to Berlin. I think I've told you this before. On the phone.'

'Yes, up to a point. But vice versa, if you know what I mean.'

She sighed and gazed past me. An elderly couple sat at the table next to us, her big and buxom, him rather meek with a little Hitler moustache his sole characteristic feature. They were slurping away at a bowl of potato soup with the help of some hunks of local rustic bread. At another table four youths, each nursing a beer, were deep into a loud conversation, interrupted only by gales of laughter. Through the panoramic windows we saw a black-and-white barge glide past towards Museum Island and the eastern districts of the city.

'But that must've required quite a bit of work.'

'It did … but it wasn't as difficult as it sounds. After all, we looked very similar. People have always said that. We were often mistaken for each other. And hardly anyone looks like their passport photo. Besides, no one else has asked for any ID apart from the admin department here at the UdK. Generally you can travel from one end of Europe to the other without having to show your passport. At any rate, I didn't need to on the plane from Stavanger to Copenhagen or on the train to Berlin.'

'But why?'

'I've already told you. At least some of it. Åsa was a damaged soul. She'd been grossly abused by her father all through her childhood. She'd already talked years ago about ending it. She had nothing to live for. I persuaded her not to, though.'

'But…'

'Not only that, there was a criminal case that ended in her getting a conditional sentence. Isn't that what you call it?'

'A conditional sentence? What for?'

'She had a summer job working in a pharmacy, and she'd snaffled quite a few pills. Mostly Valium. She needed more than the doctor was giving her, she said. They caught her at it and the case was reported. Because she was so young and the pills had been for her own use, they let her off with a conditional sentence.'

She was more eager to talk now, as if it had some meaning for her to be able to explain what had driven them to this very unusual move. 'The only thing Åsa wanted to do was go into nursing, but she was afraid the conditional sentence would create problems for her getting a job later and perhaps also being accepted as a student. Besides, to be quite frank, her grades were a great deal worse than mine.'

'That must've created problems for you, too, then?'

'Yes, it did, but I was also better at drawing. We'd played as fashion designers all the way through school, and to get on the course I liked in Berlin your grades weren't necessarily what counted. They were more interested in your samples – showing what you were able to … create.'

'I see.'

'And so we struck a deal. I said: What about if we turn over a new leaf? I go to Berlin to study there. And you…? I asked her where she wanted to go, and she said Bergen.'

'Why Bergen?'

'That was far enough away for her. She didn't want to live in Haugesund any more. Stavanger was too close. Bergen was perfect.'

'But she had family there. That is, you did.'

'Yes, but neither of them had seen me in many years. I'd just seen my half-brother once, and that had been from a distance.'

'You were in contact with him later, though, via email.'

She started in surprise. 'You know?'

'Yes. In the end, he had to admit it.'

She nodded slowly. 'But that was all. Email. Never face to face.'

'Nevertheless ... Weren't you frightened when she said she'd visited them – your father, his new wife and Andreas?'

'Yes, we talked about it, but she said ... She'd never had any proper family. Perhaps this was her only chance. She'd followed my email conversations with Andreas for several years already anyway.'

'Really? So you did that together, too?'

'Yes, we ... we sat together in the evenings emailing him and various others. It was our way of getting away from the sadness of everyday life. It was the same for me. I also wanted to put everything behind me. The family, everything! But I can see now that Åsa was much more damaged than I've ever been. Well, in the end she took her own life.'

'She was helped.'

'Helped?' Her jaw dropped. 'By whom?'

'In truth this is a very complicated story, Emma, and the roots go way back, to what your father did to a young girl where he grew up...'

'Please! I know the story. Mum never talked about anything else. Not in any detail, but as the main reason she'd never allow him to have anything to do with me.'

'There was someone who lost his elder sister as a result. And who thought he had a crime to avenge.' I told her about Vetle Valaker, the contact he had established with Helga, Andreas and, in fact, Åsa, and how Åsa had been the only one desperate – or whatever – enough to carry out what he planned.

She listened and her mouth opened wider and wider as her chin fell. In the end she burst out: 'He should be punished!'

'I hope he will be. But you never know. If he gets the right defence counsel...'

'But this is my fault too! If we hadn't swapped identities … I'd never have fallen for anything like that!'

'No?'

'No!'

'But … what did you think when she was reported missing?'

'I was scared, naturally. And I thought about what she'd said earlier. About killing herself. But … I hoped for the best, prayed to God it wouldn't happen. Should I say that? Is that why you've come all this way to talk to me?'

'Perhaps you should. But that's not why I came here. Two days ago – when I found out that the deceased we thought was you, wasn't – I quickly put two and two together. I already knew, especially after the phone calls to you, that you were both winged birds, if I can put it like that. Neither you nor Åsa were at fault for what happened. It's the generation before you that should carry the burden. You shouldn't be blamed for finding a creative way out of the problem … directly. But you had to know it couldn't have lasted, and what then? And you … Didn't my half-sister, Norma Bakkevik, ring you to ask after … you?'

She nodded vigorously. 'Yes, she did, and I almost gave myself away. But then I made my voice gruff and said I had a cold, and she didn't seem to realise. At any rate, I didn't hear any more until you rang some time later – and you weren't a danger.'

'No, I was fooled, as indeed was everyone who met Åsa in Bergen. Your father hadn't seen you since you were two, and when you and Åsa went to Bergen to visit him in 2000 he didn't even come to the door to say hello. The same applied to Andreas. He didn't have a clue it wasn't you at the house in September.'

Outside the window we heard an ear-piercing whistle. On the quay a man came running past with something under his arm. Twenty metres behind him was a police officer with a whistle hanging from a cord around his neck. 'Schnell! Schnell!' shouted one of the youths at the table away from us, and the others all laughed, while the couple close to us turned towards them in annoyance. 'Really!' the woman said disapprovingly.

Emma smiled a little despondently. 'So ... what happens now?'

'I need a written statement from you. I can take it with me to Bergen Police HQ. If you're lucky, nothing will happen, except that you'll have to resume your own identity, especially with respect to the university here. To tell the truth, I have no idea what repercussions this – what should I call it? – deception will have. It'll be another legal problem for the appropriate authorities. But ... you should ring your mother and tell her. If not, I'll have to do it.'

'And ... fru Bakkevik?'

'Fru Bakkevik's dead,' I said, and as I said it, it struck me that it wouldn't be so easy to ring her mother after all. For all I knew, she was already in custody awaiting further investigation into the case.

'What! She's dead, too?'

'Yes, and then someone will have to contact Åsa's family and give them the sad news.'

Emma's expression was fierce. 'Åsa's mother committed suicide ten years ago. But I'm sure her father's out of prison now. It'll serve him right to hear this. It'll rub his face in it!'

I could see it now, the desperation that had made them do what they did – the uncontrollable desire to start anew, without any baggage, without any bad memories.

It was only now she took off her big hat. She shook her blonde hair free and ran her hands through it. Like a wounded lioness, she sat there with tears in her eyes and a fury she still hadn't managed to assuage. But I could read from her expression that she wanted to say something, and not only to me, but to all those I represented, to men in general and all the power they exercised over people weaker than themselves. And the weakest of them all: their own children.

She gave me a signed statement before she left. Then I was alone at the table. The smell of the potato soup from the neighbouring table had been too tempting, and I reckoned I could manage a second *schwarz-bier*. Later I took a taxi to Tegel and caught the last plane home.

In the duty-free shop I bought my quota. On the journey home I drank nothing but mineral water. I had some champagne with me, but

I didn't touch it. Whether that made me a better person, I very much doubted. Only a little more sober when I arrived home.

But then I had nothing to celebrate. The journey to Berlin and back felt like one of the longest I had ever undertaken, and when I did arrive home, an as yet unanswered question awaited me. To do the DNA test or not? That was the question. That was all there was to say on the subject. Most had already been said. And you would have to be pretty simple-minded if you thought the rest was silence. You could hope, of course. Hope hadn't killed anyone yet. Or had it? I hadn't found the answer to that particular question anywhere, and I got off the plane as wise as before, just richer by one tragic experience.

And the champagne? I saved that for a later occasion.